"I can't believe I'm actually proposing to commit a felony in order to prove I'm not a prince."

"It does sound weird," Serena admitted.

"It's the stuff of comic opera. Ordinary man on the street is suddenly informed he's a prince. He quite naturally denies it. Then his mother informs him she has been kidnapped, and a dubious figure from the local consulate of the country involved confirms it. Ordinary-man-slash-prince knows better. Neither is he a prince, nor has his conniving mother really been kidnapped. But in order to save this flyspeck of a country buried in the Pyrenees, said ordinary man must now break in to a museum to discover who the real prince is."

"If I were an editor, I'm not sure I'd buy the book." Serena was laughing silently, her eyes dancing.

Darius laughed with her, aloud. "This is sheer insanity."

"I know it is. But I love insanity."

The
PRINCE
Next Door

Sue Civil-Brown

HQN™

ISBN 0-373-77076-6

THE PRINCE NEXT DOOR

Copyright © 2005 by Susan Civil-Brown

This edition published by arrangement with Harlequin Books S.A.

® and TM are trademarks of the publisher. Trademarks indicated with
® are registered in the United States Patent and Trademark Office, the
Canadian Trade Marks Office and in other countries.

www.HQNBooks.com

Printed in U.S.A.

PROLOGUE

MARIA TERESA MAXWELL believed in God. That He existed was beyond question. Still, it would be nice if He would listen when she told Him what to do. Instead, like her late husband and her son, God insisted on making up His own mind. *Men,* she thought with a huff of impatience.

Worse, her late husband, her son and God all seemed to have something else in common. They had absolutely no sense of humor or adventure. Okay, God *must* have a sense of humor, but He certainly kept it well hidden. And as for young Darius, well, if he ever blew the universe a raspberry, she hadn't seen it.

That simply had to change. The boy was entirely too stable and solid. Stable and solid were good to a point, but a man was never going to attract a good woman, the kind of woman who would melt his butter for life, without at least a little bit of the wild side. His father had had one, after all; and bless his dear departed soul if he had hidden it too often, but when he had let it out, oh my, her world had rocked!

She smiled at the memory. The elder Darius had lit up her life for forty-one years. And while God had taken him far too soon, she had come to accept that he was now safely among the celestial beings, which made him fair game.

"So, Darius, it's time to get your sainted butt in gear and talk to His Omnipotence. It would be nice if you and He could get little Darius off his bubble. Soon. I've never prayed for patience, and I don't especially want to learn it. So *now* would be nice."

But she didn't really expect Him or him to do anything. After all, what influence did a poor shepherd's daughter have with beings on high, anyway?

Plenty, she decided. Especially if she set the ball rolling and the celestial beings had no choice but to catch it and play the game.

So she would, naturally, start the ball rolling. She always had. Darius, Sr., had gotten used to it over the years, and even sometimes admitted that the most exhilarating times of his life had come when she had done something naughty beyond belief and he'd had to rescue her.

He had actually swashbuckled fairly well, once pushed to it.

But Darius, Jr.—or Darius I as he would soon become, like it or not—was as immovable and as solid as the Rock of Gibraltar.

Now what, she asked the beings above, could be more boring than *that?*

Of course she received no answer. She rarely did. But the silence didn't make her feel as if they weren't listening. Right now she would bet her diamonds at Monte Carlo that her late husband was standing right there beside her, covering his angelic eyes and begging her *not* to be outrageous.

She sniffed again. Whatever had possessed her to marry a Swiss banker? She couldn't imagine anything stodgier. On the other hand, she had been quite certain she'd seen a twinkle in his beautiful green eyes on more than one occasion. It was that twinkle that had won her heart.

But that did nothing to solve her problem with Darius the son. *Her* son. Sometimes she wondered if they could possibly share the same gene pool.

But the gene pool was exactly the issue right now, and she was going to give that boy a run for his money that he would never forget.

She looked heavenward and said stoutly, "Kidnapping is a crime, but not always a sin."

She could almost hear the groans from above.

Then she called those funny little men from the Masolimian Consulate, the ones who had given her the fantastic news.

The news that would push Darius off his bubble for good.

CHAPTER ONE

THE MAN IN THE CONDO next door was up to no good.

Serena Gregory, M.D., dermatologist-on-vacation, peered through the fish-eye lens in her door and watched a distinctly criminal-looking weasel pass by. Then she heard the door of the condo next to hers open and close.

No good at all. Putting her hands on her hips, she cocked her blond head to one side, her blue eyes narrowing with thought.

The balcony, she decided. Maybe she could hear something from the balcony.

Stepping out through the sliding glass door, she paused as the persistent breeze caught her hair and whipped it across her face. With impatient fingers she combed it out of the way and looked out across the sparkling expanse of the late-afternoon Gulf of Mexico. Eleven stories up, she was well above the tourists below.

This view, and the privacy afforded by this eagle's eye height, had been her primary reason for purchasing this condo.

Now that man had moved in next door, probably bringing the underworld with him.

Her eyes narrowed again, and she moved toward the concrete wall that separated her balcony from his. Maybe she would hear something.

After all, what else did she have to do? It was her vacation. Her job was usually boringly humdrum, removing minor imperfections from bodies and faces so that everyone could look luminously plasticized, punctuated by serious cases like melanoma. Vacations were her time to cut loose.

Unfortunately, the Federal Government had interfered with her two-week, clothing-and-common-sense-optional cruise. They had impounded the ship, claiming that the owners hadn't paid taxes. She knew better, of course. The Feds were just afraid that someone might have a good time out there on the Caribbean.

But the man who had moved in next door only three weeks ago had caught her attention. He looked entirely too urbane and suave for the local island culture, even in expensive condos like these. As far as she could tell, he had no visible means of support, he came and went at all hours, and he never so much as socialized with anyone else at the complex. A cool nod, a faint smile.

He might as well have introduced himself as Bond, James Bond. The thought made her snicker quietly to herself. The man actually wore ascots with his blue blazers and khaki slacks. Ascots! Too much for Florida.

And now that weasely looking man had come by twice today. If he didn't look like the underworld on the hoof, then Serena didn't know what the underworld looked like.

Which was entirely possible, she admitted, as she realized she'd forgotten to put sun block on her overly sensitive skin. Sighing, she went back inside and got a tube of SPF 50. No basal cell carcinomas for her. No melanoma. No early aging.

Just gobs and gobs of SPF 50, until no matter how she rubbed, she felt sticky over every exposed inch.

As a result, she was a very young-looking thirty-five, albeit a sticky one.

That's when she realized that with the wind blowing like this, she wouldn't be able to hear anything from next door unless it turned into a major argument.

Drat.

What she needed was an excuse to be outside her front door. Like most structures in Florida, there was no enclosed hallway, only a covered balcony running along the street side of the building, and exterior elevator shafts. Hence, her condo window ledges held flower boxes full of geraniums.

Excellent excuse to be outside and thus observe the squirrelly crook when he reappeared.

Almost—just almost—she stopped herself. She was being silly and overimaginative. She knew it. But this was her vacation, darn it, and she was going nuts for lack of adventure, all because some IRS agents had chosen *this* week to seize the cruise ship. What alternative did that leave her? Another trip to Orlando to stand in lines forty-five-minutes long to take rides she'd already taken? Sitting on the beach below where she could sun and bathe at *any* time of year?

That wasn't a vacation.

A vacation was a time to cut loose and get into trouble of some kind.

But she did pause. Maybe she should just get a flight to Aruba and go play Texas Hold 'Em. She could get into some serious trouble doing that. Trouble of the financial kind. No matter how often she played—and if she never saw Tunica again, it would be too soon—she was still the sucker at the table.

What harm could it do to tend her geraniums, though? None. Absolutely none.

So she got out her gardening gloves, her shears and a bottle of premixed fertilizer. She'd fertilized the plants last week. At this rate she was going to have geraniums taking over the world. She'd need to call the army to put them back in their place.

The thought made her giggle, easing some of her irritation at the IRS, who were already robbing her blind, so why had they stolen her cruise, as well?

And why was she letting irritation ruin her vacation?

Implements in hand, she stepped outside and surveyed her window boxes. No sound came from the condo next door. Pity. But maybe that would change.

The plants were actually doing quite well. She wondered how long she could legitimately spend out here snipping off three yellowed leaves and six dying flower heads. Fifteen minutes?

She was just reaching out to trim the first leaf when the elevator door twenty feet away slid open, and her nemesis neighbor stepped out, dressed as always for London rather than Florida. She glanced at him, received the usual cool nod and gave him one in return.

He did go a little farther this time, though. His gaze raked over her in a way that left her feeling naked, rather than clad in a tank top and shorts. Typical man.

Feeling her cheeks heat, she looked away…and snipped a perfectly good leaf off her plant. She almost winced, imagining the cry of outrage from the geranium.

Looking out the corner of her eye, she watched her neighbor walk up to his door and pull his keys out of his pocket. She felt a twinge of nasty pleasure as she realized he was looking a little wilted. So he wasn't impervious to the climate.

Then, for reasons she would never know, she blurted, "There's someone in your unit. I hope you were expecting him."

He paused and turned to look at her. "There is?"

"Yes."

A frown creased his handsome face. "How…odd."

"You weren't expecting someone?" She straightened, facing him, thinking that now here was an adventure at last. "Should I call the police?"

He didn't even hesitate. "I'll look into it first. Thank

you for the warning." Then he unlocked the door and disappeared inside.

So he *was* a criminal! Anyone else would have wanted the police. No one else would have gone in there alone. Drug dealer? No, too urbane looking. Cat burglar?

Oooh, she liked that idea. Like David Niven in *The Pink Panther,* or Cary Grant in *It Takes a Thief.* Smooth. Cultured. Daring. Dangerous. *Yummy.*

She was standing there, debating just what kind of crook she might have next door when a familiar voice caught her attention from behind.

"Hi, Serena."

She whirled around, startled, and saw another neighbor, a young woman, barely grown up, named Ariel. "Shh," she said, holding her gloved finger to her lips.

Oops. Making *ptooey* sounds, she tried to spit dirt from her sunscreen-sticky lips. It didn't work. She tried to rub the dirt off with her forearm, only to notice—one moment too late—that her forearm had also been sporting a dappling of semiadhered potting soil. Which had now made its way to her face. An attempt with the other forearm had the same effect, with the result that she was sure her appearance now resembled Sylvester Stallone in *First Blood.*

Ariel proceeded to tiptoe toward her. "What's up?" she asked in a stage whisper.

Ariel had the clearest, greenest eyes Serena had ever seen. They held depths of mystery in them that no woman so young, no girl-woman, ought to have. And yet they could still be as clear as dewdrops. She also had two servings of imp in her personality, which is why they got along so great together.

"I'll tell you later. Right now I want to listen."

Ariel nodded, as always ready to fall in with the scheme. For the next few minutes, they edged closer to the door, Ariel all the while trying to wipe flecks of soil from Serena's face. Sidestep. Wipe. Sidestep. Wipe. Marcel Marceau would have wept.

A few minutes later the door of the neighbor's unit opened up, and the weaselly man stepped out, bumping Ariel's elbow in midwipe, causing her hand to skid across Serena's face like an ice skater after an all-night bender.

Turning, he said through the open door, "Just remember. We have your mother!"

Then he stomped away toward the elevator in what Serena could only think was a perfect imitation of high dudgeon.

Serena stared after him for a moment, then caught Ariel's glance. Her eyes slid to the still-open door. Of course.

"You've a bit of dirt on your face," James-David-Cary-Bond-Niven-Grant said, as smoothly as if he were commenting on an expected afternoon thunderstorm.

Then he stepped back into his unit and closed the door, leaving both Serena and Ariel agape. Ariel paused for a moment, pursed her lips like Spassky pondering a chess move, and finally spoke.

"Ice cream?"

THIS REQUIRED A PLAN. And plans required ice cream. Conveniently, there was a quart of Godiva in the freezer, whispering her name. Serena scrubbed off potting soil and sunscreen—*how* had it gotten *there?* she wondered—while Ariel ladled out obscenely large bowls of frozen chocolate sweetness and fat. She also added chocolate syrup, in case the ice cream wasn't sinful enough on its own.

Serena liked that idea—serious plans called for serious calories—and rooted around for whipped cream and a jar of maraschino cherries. And the shaker of chocolate sprinkles. And the ground cashews. In for a penny, in for ten pounds.

Five minutes later the two of them were sitting crosslegged on the living room's plushly carpeted floor, one on each side of the coffee table. The first mouthful of ice cream carried enough chocolate that Serena figured she wouldn't have PMS for the next year.

When the mouthful had melted into a frigid memory, Serena spoke. "Okay. Let's talk about the creep next door."

Ariel lifted both of her eyebrows. "About Mr. Maxwell?"

Serena felt her jaw drop. "You know him?"

"Well, not exactly." Ariel scooped some more ice cream into her mouth and closed her eyes as she savored it.

"What do you mean, not exactly?" Serena could barely wait for the girl to swallow.

"Well," said Ariel, fully a minute later, "I introduced myself to him one day. In the elevator."

Now Serena was fully agog. It was one thing for a grown woman to take risks, but a girl Ariel's age? "You spoke to a strange man in the elevator?"

Ariel shrugged. "Not exactly a stranger when he lives in our building."

"Jeffrey Dahmer lived in someone's building!"

Ariel looked at her as if to say, you poor frightened person. "He looks rather respectable, don't you think?"

"No I don't think. Nobody dresses like that around here. In London he would look respectable. Maybe even in France. But not here. Here he looks like a man who lives a pretense."

Ariel frowned. "Do you really think so? He seemed perfectly nice to me."

Ice cream forgotten—if only for a moment—Serena tapped her finger on the marble top of the coffee table. "Don't you listen to the news, Ariel? What do they always say about the killer or the drug dealer? 'He was quiet, kept to himself, never caused any trouble.'"

"Oh." Ariel shrugged and took some more ice cream. "Well, he didn't bother me. I said hi, told him my name, he told me his, and I welcomed him to Gull's Rest. That was it."

"You don't know how lucky you are."

"I don't?"

Serena had the distinctly uncomfortable feeling that

those green eyes were laughing at her, but Ariel's face merely looked interested.

She took another tack when she spoke again, hoping this fey young woman wasn't speaking to every stranger she met in elevators. "Didn't you hear what that weaselly man said when he left?"

"That he had Mr. Maxwell's mother?" Ariel nodded and dabbed the corner of her mouth with a paper napkin, erasing the evidence of chocolate syrup. "That *was* odd."

"It was more than odd. It sounded like a threat."

"True." The young woman sat up straighter. "But it still doesn't mean that Mr. Maxwell is up to any wrong. He might be a *victim*."

"Hah. When I told him there was a man in his apartment and offered to call the police, he refused. Said he would handle it himself."

"Hmm." Ariel once again frowned. "That's a strange response."

"I think he's a rogue. A dangerous rogue."

Ariel nodded. "Probably a pirate. He looks like he's fresh off the boat from Marseilles, doesn't he? What with the peg leg and the eye patch and all…."

Trust youth to make an older person feel stupid, simply by pointing out the absurdity of the obvious. "Okay, maybe he's not *that* dangerous. But something's not right about him. You mark my words."

Ariel, once again attacking her sundae with a gusto that would have shamed wolves, paused to speak. "Well heaven forfend that there should be anything not right about someone. Those perfect people are *so* hard to come by."

"Okay, you win. He's probably a perfectly ordinary, dime-a-dozen junior executive."

"Anything but, I hope! God, how boring would *that* be?" The girl took another heaping spoonful of ice cream, laden with nuts, syrup and sprinkles. "But there's a lot of room between boringly ordinary and dangerous rogue."

Serena gave the girl her most serious look. "I," she said, her voice weighted with significance, "am on *vacation*."

Ariel looked up, chocolate staining one corner of her mouth, her unusual eyes suddenly looking very puckish. "And you can't go on that naked cruise."

"Clothing *optional*," Serena corrected her.

Ariel shrugged. "Same thing." She ate another huge spoonful of ice cream. Serena wouldn't have guessed Godiva could go down quite so fast.

"It's vacation," Serena said again, ominously.

Ariel nodded. "And you need to get into trouble."

"Right."

"Okay." That charming smile speared again. "A little trouble."

"Certainly not enough to get me arrested."

"Well, you didn't get arrested last winter when I suggested you take that job playing Mrs. Santa Claus at the mall."

"Only because I didn't commit murder."

Ariel laughed. "You sure raised a ruckus, though."

In spite of herself, Serena had to smile.

"And," Ariel added, "I'm sure there are quite a few parents who now take child-rearing more seriously."

"I hope so, for the sake of civilization. But that won't do this time, Ariel."

"No, of course it won't. It's the wrong time of year." Ariel put down her empty bowl. "I suppose you want to spy on Mr. Maxwell." Her eyes danced. "He does have a job, you know."

Serena felt her stomach sink. She didn't want the man to have a job. That would ruin all her fun. How boring it would be if he were a loan officer. "How did you find that out?"

"I asked him," Ariel replied complacently. Her eyes started dancing. "He's an international art dealer."

Serena's eyes widened with joyous anticipation. Her heart leaped. "Do you have any idea how many illicit activities that could cover?"

Ariel laughed. "I was afraid you were going to say that."

"Afraid? Why?"

"I didn't really mean afraid. Just that I guessed you were going to say that."

"Oh." Serena settled back, satisfied. "Well, you know I don't want to get *you* into any trouble."

Something passed over Ariel's face, at once amused and wise. "I won't get in any trouble. Have I gotten into any trouble yet?"

"Not that I'm aware of, but there's always a first time."

Ariel rolled her fey eyes. "This won't be it," she said, as if the future were as clear to her as writing on the wall. "I know how to take care of myself. You might get into trouble, though."

"That's the point."

Ariel leaned forward gleefully. "But it might be *more* trouble than you're looking for."

"Pish-tosh," Serena said with a wave of her hand. "I can take care of myself, too."

"So how are you going to start?" Ariel asked. "Wire-tapping? Spy cameras?"

Serena frowned. "That *would* be illegal. No, I'm just going to follow him. And so are you."

"But that's *boring.*"

Serena had to agree. Especially in this heat. "Well then, what do you suggest?"

Ariel's eyes danced. "You have to *meet* him."

All of a sudden Serena had an inkling that she might be in for real trouble, and not of her own making.

"I've already met him," she said, remembering the encounter just a few minutes before.

"No, I mean meet him when you don't look like a condo commando."

"Was it that bad?" Serena asked, having spared herself the indignity of a mirror before she washed up.

"Arnold Schwarzenegger would have quailed," Ariel replied. "'More flies with honey than vinegar' and all that. So, you have to meet him."

"If I must." Unfortunately, Serena could think of no

other plan that didn't involve wandering all over town in the heat trying to stay out of sight, an activity she suspected she would not be very adept at.

"Don't worry," said Ariel. "I'll take care of it."

Serena wasn't at all comfortable with that notion.

CHAPTER TWO

PABLO MENOS RETURNED to the consular office from his meeting with Darius Maxwell hot and seething. Hot from the climate, seething from the encounter.

His position as deputy for administration to the consul-in-residence for the country of Masolimia had its perks, but living in Florida was not one of them. Even this late in the year he still longed for the cool mountain country of his home, a flyspeck in the Pyrenees between Spain and France.

In keeping with the size of Masolimia, the consular offices were a storefront in a run-down strip mall entirely too close to the Port of Tampa. In short, not the best neighborhood. Train tracks ran right behind them, and on a far too regular basis all conversation was drowned by the deep thrumming of locomotives practically driving through the offices.

Not that the consul cared. He was rarely around.

The glass door swung closed behind him, its little bell ringing a note of alert, and modestly air-conditioned air washed over him. In a half hour or so, he might actually cool off.

Juan Mas, his underdeputy, was sitting at his battered desk reading a comic book. He barely looked up. *"¿Qué pasó?"* he enquired, bored.

"It was terrible!"

That got Juan's attention. A small man with a beard that defied the sharpest razor, giving him a perpetual five-o'clock shadow, he finally *really* looked up from his comic book. "Huh?"

"Exactly," Menos said, going to stand under the nearest air-conditioning vent, hoping to dry out the Hawaiian shirt that was sticking to him everywhere. How did people ever manage to live in this horrid, humid swamp?

"He called the police?" Mas sat up straight and looked wildly about as if afraid the local SWAT team was about to burst in on them.

"Worse," Menos said flatly. *Ay, Dios,* the air was barely lukewarm, emerging as a trickle. "He doesn't care."

"Huh?" That was one American expression Mas had learned well.

"He doesn't care," Menos repeated in a snarl.

"But we kidnapped his mother! What kind of son is he?"

"What kind of prince is he going to be if he doesn't care about his own mother?" Menos corrected darkly.

"I can't believe it."

Neither could Menos. He'd been there, he'd seen the reaction, heard the words, and his jaw was still dragging on the ground, metaphorically speaking.

"That's inhuman," Mas said. "Maybe he doesn't really believe us."

"Oh, he believed me," Menos said, plucking rayon away from his chest. "He said, 'I pity you. You don't know what you're in for.'"

Mas's eyes widened, then a snicker escaped him. "He's right."

Menos, whose world view was rather dour to begin with, silently agreed. Why, oh why, had he ever allowed that woman to talk him into this?

But then he squared his shoulders and reminded himself his country's future was at stake, and it was riding on his shoulders while the consul-in-residence chased bikini-clad bimbos down in Key West.

"We will call her," he announced. "She must call her son and convince him she's in danger."

Mas nodded, only too eager to agree to anything that would allow him to get back to his comics. "Good idea."

MARIA TERESA STOOD on the stool while her dressmaker jabbed industriously at the waist of the green watered-silk gown she was having made for her son's coronation.

The call from Menos in Florida hadn't pleased her at all. Imagine Darius not being upset that she'd been kidnapped! Even Menos, squirrelly as he was, had sounded appalled by the utter lack of concern Darius had displayed.

What was it Menos had quoted Darius as saying? "Enjoy your time with my mother."

Humph.

Rolling her eyes heavenward, Maria Teresa demanded to know why His Lordliness had given her such an unfeeling son. Why, in fact, the stolid Swiss side had predominated to such an extent.

Was the boy not of her flesh, as well? Where was his passion and fire? Why wouldn't he take up his lance and tilt at windmills for the sake of his mother?

Why didn't he believe it?

And how could he laugh at being told he was the prince of Masolimia, a not-inconsiderable flyspeck of a principality in the Pyrenees? It was, after all, bigger than Monaco. It was his birthright. And hers, for that matter. To return as the dowager princess, rather than as the daughter of a despised shepherd family…well, what more could justice demand?

She sniffed and looked down at the dark hair of her dressmaker as the woman worked to pin a fold in at the waistline.

"I'm not sure I like this silk at all," Maria Teresa announced.

The dressmaker's hands froze. Without looking up, the woman said, "But it becomes you so well, madam."

Maria Teresa glanced sideways at the mirrored wall, taking in all the expensive, basted fabric that covered her. Fabric her own mother could only have dreamed about. It *did* flatter the olive tone of her skin, she decided.

"But blue," she said, anyway.

The dressmaker, now on solid ground, looked up. "Madam doesn't want to look as if she has a liver disease."

Maria Teresa sighed theatrically. It was true, blues made her look sallow.

"Oh, very well," she said irritably, hating to be reminded that there was anything she couldn't do. "Perhaps yellow…"

The dressmaker, Adele, straightened, stepped back and put her hands on her hips. "Madam," she said sternly, "we tried every color of the rainbow and agreed this flattered you best. Moreover, it will not be so green once we add the pearls."

Of course it wouldn't. She needed to remember that. She was just being difficult because of Darius. Speaking of whom…

"You're right, Adele. Keep working. After you bring me a telephone."

"Yes, madam."

Help just wasn't what it used to be, Maria Teresa thought. But Adele was one of the best dressmakers around, unless you were interested in the ridiculous fashion ideas that were called haute couture in Paris these days, and Maria Teresa definitely was not.

When Adele passed her the phone, Maria Teresa didn't need to look up the number, even though Darius had only moved into his new residence three weeks ago. She had memorized the number instantly, just the way a bloodhound memorizes the scent it wants to follow.

Or a predator.

But such unflattering descriptions of herself were not on her mind as she tapped her toe and waited for her son to answer. It seemed to take a long time, but when she absolutely needed to, she could be patient. Barely.

"Maxwell."

"Darius," she said, making her tone as pathetic as she could. *"Estoy secuestrada."* I am kidnapped.

"Sí, so I've heard. How much are you paying them?"

She puffed up with indignation and heard the faint tearing as pins ripped through silk. Adele cast her a disapproving glance, but Maria Theresa ignored it. She would deal with this woman's impudence later. First, though, she had to deal with her son.

"Darius!" she snapped, in a tone that every mother knows and at which every child quails. "I'm not paying anyone anything. You have to help me!"

"Just how am I supposed to do that? I have no idea where you are."

She frowned, tapping her toe. This was certainly not the treatment she had expected from him, and certainly not when she employed the *voz de la madre,* the stern voice of a mother. Looking heavenward, she blasted a handful of saints and her poor departed spouse for having cursed her with such a child.

"Ma mère?"

In this family, a plethora of languages were spoken, and Maria Teresa had always insisted her son address her by the French rather than the Spanish for "my mother." Sometimes he liked to irritate her by calling her *mamacita.*

Regardless, she didn't hear nearly enough concern in his voice. Feeling frustrated, she twisted just a bit, and one of the seamstress's pins jabbed her side. She cried out.

Which had the desired effect, she realized instantly.

"Ma mère?"

"They're torturing me," she cried with great relish.

Adele jumped back, her face paling. Maria Teresa waved her concern away. "You have to *save* me at once!"

"Where are you?"

"I don't know!" Which was a lie. The Riviera was a little hot this year, but otherwise comfortable.

"Mother." This time Darius spoke in English. "Has it occurred to you that kidnapping is a very dangerous thing to do?"

"Only if the police catch them before I am killed," she wailed.

"That isn't what I meant."

She hesitated. This wasn't going as expected. "What do you mean?"

"Just that if they're doing this to make me accept that I'm prince of Masolimia, they're making a big mistake. Because if I accept the throne, I can have these kidnappers beheaded."

"My dear son, beheadings are so déclassé." The wheels were truly spinning in her brain now. This was a kink she definitely hadn't expected, and she was glad that neither Menos nor Mas was able to hear this conversation. They were *loco* enough without fearing they'd lose their heads.

"Then I'll have them shot."

"That's better," she approved. She feigned every ounce of pathos she could muster. "But you *will* rescue me?"

"Which hotel are you at?"

She almost slipped. The answer rose naturally to her lips, but she bit it back just in time. "Believe me, this is not a hotel! It's a hovel!"

Now Adele was looking seriously annoyed, but Maria Teresa hardly cared for that. A generous tip would bring the smile back.

"Really." Darius sighed. "If you want the truth, Mother…"

"But of course!"

"If you really have been kidnapped, I feel sorry for your abductors."

"Darius!"

"Tell you what, Mother. I'll save you."

Her eyes lit up, and she sent paeans of praise winging heavenward to the lately slandered saints. "You will?"

"Of course."

Now he would swashbuckle. At last. Her son was going to play Errol Flynn, John Wayne, Sean Connery….

"How soon?"

"I'm not sure. First I have to prove I'm not the prince."

He disconnected, leaving Maria Teresa to feel as if she had been struck by a truck.

Prove he *wasn't* the prince? *¡Dios no lo quiera!*

SERENA WAS SUNBATHING, dermatologist-style. She was lying beside the condo swimming pool, clad in a maillot, coverup, wide-brimmed sun hat and half a tube of sunscreen. And just to be sure, she'd chosen a chaise beneath an umbrella. Immediately to her right on the pool deck sat a tall bottle of spring water and a kitchen timer which she had set to twenty minutes.

To her left was a patient-to-be, Marco Paloni. She considered him a patient-to-be because he wore only a Speedo—which left little to the imagination and much that would haunt her dreams—and a thin sheen of olive oil, which he had applied with the same loving care a chef might use to baste a leg of lamb. He had then proceeded to spend the next fifteen minutes regaling her with tales of his days on the Grand Prix circuit.

"And then there was Monza," he said. "The Italian Grand Prix. My home country. My home course."

"Of course," Serena said, doing her best to appear polite, just in case he ended up in her office.

"I was driving for Ferrari, of course. A beautiful car, the 312T2, with a transverse mounted gearbox. What a wonderful machine."

To judge by the tone of his voice, he might have been describing a fondly remembered lover.

"Emerson Fittipaldi was the favorite, as always. But this was the course I'd been weaned on, watching Fanglia as a boy. It was the first course I'd ever driven. I knew it like…how do you say…the back of my hand."

"And you won?" Serena asked, glancing at the timer. Three more minutes. Just three more minutes.

"Did I win?" Marco asked. *"Did I win?"*

"Yes. Did you win?"

"No."

"No?"

"No."

"How sad," she said.

Two minutes, forty-five seconds.

"Sad? No!"

"No?" she asked.

"No!"

Two minutes, forty seconds.

"It was *better* than winning. I came to the chicayne on the last lap, dead even. I took a page from Lauria's book. Fittipaldi downshifted. I didn't. Two hundred fifty kilometers per hour."

"That's fast," Serena said.

"Sì! Prestissimo!"

Two minutes, thirty seconds.

"I passed Fittipaldi. Took the first half of the chicayne, no problem. Tapped the brakes. Just the tiniest tap. Turned the wheel."

"And?"

"Guess!" he said.

"Guess?"

"Guess!"

Two minutes, fifteen seconds.

"Ummm…"

"I flew!" he exclaimed. "Flew! Over the tires. Over the retaining wall."

"You crashed?"

"Right into the net! That beautiful machine hung right there in the net. The right-front tire had come off, and the car hung by the axle. The ambulance, it comes."

"Were you hurt?" Serena asked, now concerned. She didn't care for auto racing, for that very reason. Too many drivers got hurt.

"Hurt? No!"

"No?"

"No!"

Two minutes.

"I climbed out of the cockpit. And fell...*right* into the arms of my Isadora."

"Isadora?"

"Isadora!"

Serena turned off the timer. "And?"

"The woman of my dreams. Strong. Gentle. Kind." He reached into his Speedo. "The paparazzi were there. They captured the moment. The moment I met my Isadora."

His hand emerged, holding a laminated snapshot out to her. He *had* cut a dashing figure back then. And there was no mistaking the smile on his face in the photo, his eyes fixed on the raven-haired medic into whose arms he had fallen as if by an act of God. Her face was radiant.

"She's beautiful."

"*Sì. Bella. Splendida.*" His eyes darkened. "She became...my life."

"She's...?"

"Yes," he said. "Four years ago."

"I'm sorry."

"No," he said, simply.

"No?"

"No. I would have been sorry if I had not taken that chicayne at 250 kilometers per hour. I would have been sorry if I had not tapped the brakes and turned the wheel at exactly the wrong instant. I would have been sorry if my beautiful automobile had not gone airborne and flown into that net. I would have been sorry if I had not fallen into her arms. For all of that, I would have been sorry."

He paused a moment, deep-brown eyes fixing on her. "No. I am not sorry. If I see only how she died... Doctor Serena, if we see it that way, life has no happy endings. For any of us. No, God gave me twenty-five years with her. Twenty-five glorious years and four beautiful children. Those years, those memories, my children...they are my happy ending."

She passed the photo back to him, certain that she'd exceeded her allotted twenty minutes, and equally certain she did not care.

"That's beautiful, Marco."

His fingers lingered on hers for a moment. "Dr. Serena, don't be afraid to fly into the net."

She nodded and withdrew her hand. "I need to get out of the sun, Marco."

"And I need to wax my car."

"Let me guess," she said. "Ferrari?"

He winked. "Always."

"EXPLAIN SOMETHING to me?" Ariel asked as she licked an ice-cream cone—chocolate with sprinkles.

Serena had run into her in the elevator on her way up from her sunbath. "Yes?"

"How could you go on a clothing-optional cruise when you barely let the sun touch your skin?"

Serena looked at her young friend and found green eyes innocently looking back at her. She didn't for one second believe that innocence. "Sunblock," she said, "can be put anywhere."

"Were you going to hide inside the ship all the time? What's the point of going to the Caribbean, then?"

"I wasn't going to stay inside all the time."

"Just most of it."

Serena scowled at her. "Are you making fun of me?"

"Moi?" But now there was a definite twinkle in her eyes. "I thought you'd like to know. Mr. Maxwell drives a Ferrari."

The elevator lurched to a halt at the eleventh floor. The door hissed open. Serena didn't move. Two seconds later she punched the *G* button for the garage level.

"What are you doing?" Ariel asked.

"I just had a brainstorm."

CHAPTER THREE

MARCO, STILL CLAD in his obscene Speedo, was indeed in the parking area beneath the condos. On the coast like this, buildings were elevated on stilts to avoid flooding during severe storms, and the area beneath was quite handily used for parking.

He was busy applying a thick coat of something milky to the lovingly preserved red paint of his Ferrari. He smiled when he saw Serena. "This is so important to preserve the finish in this climate," he explained.

Thinking of the condition of the paint on her four-year-old car, Serena was inclined to agree. Between salt and sun, a car didn't stand a chance. "Have you met our new neighbor?" she asked Marco.

He paused and straightened. "No, I don't think so."

"He lives next door to me. He drives a Ferrari."

Ariel snickered quietly, and Serena shot her a warning glance.

"He does?" Marco's face, usually quite happy, brightened even more. "He appreciates fine workmanship and speed, no?"

"Actually," Serena said, "I don't know what he appreciates. All I know is…Marco, I think he may be up to no good."

Marco's expression sobered. "Why you say that?"

Ariel beat Serena to the punch, in her usual, tactless and straightforward way. "Serena thinks he might be a drug dealer."

Marco's face darkened. His chest swelled with ire and he spouted something in Italian that definitely sounded threatening.

"Now wait," Serena said hastily. "I don't know anything for a fact." Then she shot a glare at Ariel. "Don't make mountains out of molehills."

"I thought that was your job," Ariel agreed sweetly.

Marco, meanwhile, had let his chest sag once more. "Why do you think this?"

"Because…because he dresses oddly and claims to be an international art dealer. I mean…" She was starting to feel foolish, but Marco saved her.

He nodded. "International art dealer? Here? Hah!" He made a gesture that Serena had never asked the meaning of and suspected she really didn't want to know. "So what do we do?" he asked.

"Well…" She didn't feel quite so foolish anymore, now that Marco, a man familiar with a more cosmopolitan world than this part of Florida, found it absurd that an international art dealer would choose to live here of all places. Oh, there were some fine-art museums in the Tampa Bay area, and even the famed Dali Museum in

St. Petersburg. But enough business to keep a major art dealer busy? Not likely.

"Yes?" Marco prompted.

"I thought…perhaps….well. Since you both have Ferraris, I thought you might be able to strike up a conversation and learn more about him."

"*Sì.*" Marco nodded once, then vanished into his own Italianate thought. After a few minutes, during which time Serena hardly breathed, he nodded again. "Yes," he said. "I will be a spy. I have grandchildren visit here. No drug deals in my building!"

For an awful instant Serena wondered if she was being too hasty. Then she remembered the weaselly visitor, and the threatening words he had spoken, "We have your mother." Surely that was a sign of some illicit deal gone bad.

"But," she said, having a final twinge of conscience, "we don't know for sure anything's wrong with him. We just need to find out."

"I'll find out." Marco beamed. "No one can resist my personality."

"No?"

"No."

Serena had her doubts, considering how she had been clock-watching—or rather timer watching—just a little while ago. "Just don't go overboard, Marco."

He smiled. "Trust me. We will become bosom buddies."

ARIEL LICKED the last bit of stickiness from her fingers as she and Serena rode the elevator back up to the eleventh floor.

"I wish," Serena said, "that you wouldn't be so…"

"Brutally honest?" Ariel asked. "It's just the way I am. Besides, you wanted Marco to help, didn't you? So why beat around the bush and waste time?"

Serena didn't have an answer for that.

"Anyway," Ariel continued blithely, "I hope you realize you may just have totally slandered an innocent man."

Serena's heart thumped. "I didn't say he was a drug dealer. *You* did."

"But it was your idea." Smiling, Ariel got off the elevator ahead of her. "I hope you have a good lawyer." Then she skipped down the balcony toward her own unit like a gleeful child.

Serena stared after her, thinking that while Ariel might be an adult by law, she was awfully immature in some ways. Sometimes it didn't seem to Serena that the young woman ought to be living on her own.

But then, she thought with painful honesty, she could probably say the same about herself.

What had she just done?

SERENA'S SINUSES HURT. Guaranteed there was a storm coming. Her sinuses were a better predictor than the weather service. Certainly better than that dweeb on TV, who one day had stood talking about clear skies while it was raining everywhere, including on his own building.

Sighing, she pulled back the drapes, stretching out the morning stiffness and looked through her glass doors. Her sinuses were right. They were pounding like a tympani because the sky was leaden, the gulf was gray and white-capped, and the only thing missing was the rumble of thunder.

No morning run. She'd lived her entire life in the lightning capital of the world, and she knew better than to get down there on the beach and trot along the water's edge when there were clouds visible, even at a distance.

As if in answer to her thoughts, a purple-blue-red bolt suddenly shot out of the heavens and appeared to hit the water near shore. It was followed by an eerie green halo that seemed to hang in the air like a huge ball of plasma…which it probably was.

Curious, she stepped out on her balcony—not the wisest thing but she wasn't always the wisest person, as everyone acquainted with her knew—and glanced down.

"Oh my God!" The words escaped her as she saw what appeared to be two men dragging a third person out of the water. Idiot tourists. Someone else was running toward the beach bar at a mad dash. Probably to call 911.

Serena was a dermatologist, but she was also a medical doctor. Grabbing a blanket and the CPR kit she was never without, she dashed out of her condo. The elevator would be too slow, so she ran down eleven flights of stairs, bursting out onto the beach and churning up gouts of sand behind her.

People were crowded around the person lying on the sand. "I'm a doctor," got her right through until she could look down on the body.

"What happened?" she demanded as she dropped to her knees.

"Lightning," said a man.

Serena bent forward, putting her ear to the man's mouth to listen for breath as she also felt his carotid artery for a pulse.

Neither.

She tipped the man's head back and used her fingers to ensure his air passage was clear. Then, holding his tongue with her thumb so it wouldn't fall back in his throat, she applied the breathing bag.

"Can someone use this bag?" she asked. "Like this? While I try to resuscitate his heart."

"I will."

She suddenly found herself looking in the brown eyes of her mysterious neighbor, who knelt across from her. She didn't have time now to think of that, though. "Like this," she said. "Every time I tell you."

"Got it."

She began compressions, timing them, leaning fully into them with all the weight in her body, while her mysterious neighbor pumped air into his lungs as ordered. Every five compressions, she paused to listen.

Then she heard it, the thud of a heartbeat. Then a weak lub-dub.

"Stop for a second," she said, and put her ear to the

man's mouth. A shaky breath. Another, deeper. Feeling the carotid, she found a pulse. A little irregular, but recurring.

"Thanks," she said to her neighbor.

He nodded, his dark eyes grave. "It's the least I could do."

But the danger wasn't past. In the distance she could hear the wail of approaching sirens. She looked along the length of the man's body and realized his swim trunks were shredded, and a zig-zaggy burn, almost like a lightning bolt itself, marked his left side and left thigh.

She grabbed the blanket and spread it over him. "Elevate his feet with my bag," she said to one of the people in the crowd.

Then she returned her attention to her patient's face. His color was improving, he was still breathing. Thank God. She touched his cheek, shaking his head gently. "Can you hear me?"

A moan escaped him.

"Does anyone know his name?" she asked.

"It's Jack," said a woman.

"Jack. Jack! Can you hear me? Open your eyes!" Much to her relief, his eyelids fluttered. His eyes were unfocused, but they were open. "Stay with us, Jack. Stay awake. Help is coming."

He moaned again, but his eyes stayed open.

"I told him," said the woman. "I told him not to go in the water! But no, he's a tough macho idiot…" Her voice trailed away in sobs.

"Nobody ought to be on this beach," Serena said firmly. "Nobody."

"But it's our vacation," some man argued. "Damn it, I paid a fortune…"

"You'll pay even more in hospital bills," Serena said shortly, trying to pick out the speaker from the crowd. "This place isn't known as the lightning capital of the world for nothing."

As if to back her up, another bolt sizzled and crackled downward, farther out in the water.

As if on cue, the curious began to hurry away.

Then, other than the woman who was Jack's companion, Serena and the mysterious neighbor were alone with the patient. She couldn't avoid his eyes then.

"Thank you," she said again.

"You saved his life," he said, and smiled.

God, it was a devastating smile. Things inside her went all fluttery and soft, and she wanted to kick her own butt. She cleared her throat and shrugged. "I'm a doctor."

"I heard." He extended his hand. "Darius Maxwell. Art dealer."

"Hi." She had to drag her gaze away from him and return her attention to Jack, who was beginning to actually focus his eyes. They found her and he said thickly, "You're an angel. Oh, God, I'm dead."

"No you're not," the sobbing woman said, "but you damn well oughta be."

Jack actually smiled.

Serena was saved by the arrival of the paramedics. She gave them a crisp, professional report and let them take over responsibility. Her specialty didn't involve caring for lightning victims...until they wanted scars removed. "Take care," she said to Jack and his wife.

Then she gathered up her things and headed back toward the building while another crackle of lightning sizzled behind her.

"Excuse me!" Darius Maxwell caught up with her.

Who was following whom? "Yes?" She didn't want to look at him. Absolutely not. He was too...too...attractive.

"Listen, since we're neighbors...can I buy you dinner?"

Her instinct was to refuse. After all, what did she know about this man? On the other hand, getting to know him would be a wonderful way to find out what he was up to.

Uh-uh. Moth, flame, singed and all that. "I don't think so. But thank you."

"I understand." They had reached the shelter of the parking garage, safer from the lightning, which was now forking across the sky like Thor's own fireworks show. "You don't know a thing about me."

She darted a glance at him, hoping he was about to spill the beans. He disappointed her.

"Tell you what," he said. "I'll order takeout and we can eat at my place or yours."

Serena didn't know if that was much safer. She hesitated before the elevator door. On the one hand, here was a sterling opportunity to learn something about this man and his evil doings. On the other, she'd be about as safe as a lamb in a cage with a tiger. Or so she wanted to believe.

"Compromise," she said finally.

"Yes?"

God, his smile was just too inviting. "I'll ask Ariel to join us. You know Ariel?"

"Of course. The lovely young woman who lives at the other end of the wing. That would be delightful." His dark eyes creased at the corner.

Damn, he was oozing warmth. She wondered if she was going to get a sunburn standing here.

"One more condition," she said.

"Yes?"

"We eat inside if it's still storming."

He laughed. "Of course. Say seven?"

The elevator door opened, and she didn't know whether to be grateful or disappointed when he didn't join her.

"I've got an errand to run," he said pleasantly. "See you tonight."

The door closed. Errand? He probably needed to deliver some dope, she thought sourly.

That's when she realized that she was looking forward to the evening with entirely too much excitement.

Idiot.

"WHAT DO YOU need me for?" Ariel wanted to know. "I'm too young to chaperone someone your age."

Serena tried not to grit her teeth. "I don't know anything about him! I don't want to be alone with him."

"I thought that would be exactly what you'd want. So you could tie him to a chair and threaten to beat him with a kitchen appliance until he tells you the truth."

Serena rolled her eyes. "Traitor."

Ariel frowned. "No, he might like that."

Serena gasped. "What do you know about such things?"

Ariel only laughed and winked. "A bullwhip would be better. You know, some leather, handcuffs—"

"Stop it!" Serena's cheeks were so hot she felt she could illuminate the darkest night. All too often, Ariel seemed to read Serena's mind.

Ariel just laughed. "Okay, I'll be good…"

"Good!" Serena replied.

"…and you can be good at it!"

With that, the young woman dashed out of reach and into the kitchen, leaving Serena to consider what she would wear for this soiree. Shorts and a halter top were out of the question. Her eyes flicked over the leather corset she kept folded and hidden in a corner of the closet shelf, and her cheeks reddened again. *Damn you, Ariel!*

Finally she settled on her favorite sundress: light yellow, cotton, sleeveless. It was comfortable, casually attractive without going overboard. Most of all, she felt confident wearing it. And she had a feeling she would need all the confidence she could muster.

When she emerged from the bedroom, Ariel had already set the table, complete with rose linen napkins and a set of burgundy candles that Serena had forgotten she had.

"Do you like digging through my cupboards?" Serena asked.

"Of course!" Ariel replied, as if poking around in someone else's kitchen were the most natural thing in the world. "You'd have used paper plates and napkins. And that would *not* do…not for an international art dealer. So I decided to give you some class."

"Ummm, thanks. I think."

"You're welcome," Ariel said, her eyes suddenly deep as the Marianas Trench. "You're very welcome."

What did that girl know?

CHAPTER FOUR

HE WAS LATE.

Not fashionably late, ten or fifteen minutes. Not even a half hour.

No, it was ten minutes to eight. Serena's stomach growled as she tapped her nails on the glass tabletop. She had rearranged the place settings three times. She had chilled the sauvignon blanc, and decanted the merlot, just in case. She had even deigned to endure that most hated of feminine habits and put on makeup. Not much. A light brushing of blush on her cheeks, mascara and a shimmery pink lip gloss. Just enough.

And he was late.

The grandfather clock in her living room had swung and ticked its way to 7:58 when the doorbell rang.

"I shouldn't even answer," Serena said.

"Of course you should," Ariel replied.

"He's late."

"So?"

"It's disrespectful."

The doorbell rang again.

"Perhaps. Or perhaps he was unavoidably detained."

"Making a drug deal?"

"Maybe," Ariel said. "Or maybe he was caught in traffic. Or maybe he had to close a million-dollar deal on a painting. There's only one way to find out."

The doorbell rang again.

"And that's it," Ariel said, pointing to the door.

With a heavy sigh—wondering yet again why this young girl intimidated her so—Serena walked to the door and opened it.

Damn him.

"Hi," Darius said, holding out a bouquet of yellow carnations. "Sorry I'm late."

The flowers even matched her dress.

"No problem," Serena heard herself say, without so much as thinking about it. Then, as if another brain had taken charge of her vocal chords, she added, "I was late getting ready myself."

What was she doing?

"It worked out well, then," he said. He lifted the large plastic bag in his other hand. "I hope you like Italian."

"Sounds yummy!" Ariel said, reaching out to take the bag. "Come on in."

"Yes, do come in," Serena added.

"Thank you," Darius said, stepping into the small, tiled foyer. He paused a moment to look around. "You have a lovely home. That's a Robert Franklin, isn't it?"

"I guess so," Serena said, looking at the painting above her sofa as if for the first time. It was a pastel watercolor, a man and a woman caressing each other's cheeks. "I just picked it because I liked it. I really don't know anything about art."

Darius offered a disarming smile. "Not to worry. You've chosen well. It fits the room."

She hoped he'd turn that smile off soon. Before her brain made yet another detour into complete abandon. She fell back upon safe territory. "Well, let's eat!"

In the kitchen, as she and Ariel transferred the steaming food from the containers into serving dishes, Ariel whispered, "Well, he recognized who did the painting in your living room. One point for art dealer."

Serena, shocked back to reality for a second, was about to admit she may have been wrong, when a thought struck her. "The painting is signed."

Ariel gave her one of those long, deep looks, then nodded. "That's true."

But Serena was beginning to wonder if her need for excitement hadn't pushed her right over the edge. Then she remembered the weaselly man saying, "We have your mother." Darius Maxwell was not acting like a man who was in any way worried about his mother. The weasel's words had certainly sounded like a threat, not a reassurance.

Hmmm.

Food in serving dishes—scampi, pasta primavera, ravioli stuffed with Portobello mushrooms, and garlic bread, she and Ariel paraded into the dining area with the offerings.

"I hope," said Darius, standing near the table, "that the selections please you."

"Oh, definitely," Serena said, managing a bright smile. At least he'd turned off that thousand-watt smile of his. It had settled into a pleasant curve of his very pleasant mouth.

After the women had finished placing the dishes on the table, Darius held their chairs out for them, Serena's first. That was an old-world courtesy, so old that Serena had actually forgotten men could do such things.

Ariel's gaze seemed to say, *And you think this guy is a drug dealer?*

Serena felt herself blushing, faintly, she hoped. Damn her fair complexion. Maybe she should bake in the sun, set herself up for melanoma, and make sure the world could never again see her cheeks pinken.

When they were all seated, Darius apologized again. "I really was unforgivably late. But like an idiot, I decided to go to this small mom-and-pop restaurant where they have the most wonderful Italian cuisine, and I totally forgot about rush hour across the drawbridges."

Serena smiled politely. "It's all forgiven. The food smells wonderful. Don't you have to deal with rush hour?"

A clue, she thought. *She* had to deal with rush hour, as did every other upstanding American, except perhaps the president.

"Well, not usually," he admitted as he passed the scampi. "My job has rather irregular hours."

"Oh?" She lifted her brows at him, then scooped a

small portion onto her plate before passing the dish to Ariel.

"I'm an art dealer, as I said," Darius explained smoothly. Maybe too smoothly. "I'm working on a project in St. Petersburg right now. A new gallery is opening, centered on the works of Mateus Davilla."

Ariel perked up. "Like the Dali Museum?"

"Yes, like that." He smiled at her. "The gallery is very well funded by a collector, and I've been scouting for some additional paintings for them. Some of Davilla's works have been missing since World War II. I've managed to find a few of them, along with a truly priceless collection of his charcoal sketches. But there are some provenance issues I need to work on while I continue to scout. At present, I have reason to believe a number of Davilla's works are here in the U.S."

"So you're based here for a while?" Ariel asked.

"Yes, until my project is finished."

So he was a drifter, Serena thought, stuffing her mouth. Then the flavor hit her and astonishment filled her. "My goodness, that's the best scampi I've ever had!"

Darius grinned at her. "So maybe getting stuck at the drawbridge was worth it."

Much as she wanted to, she couldn't resist that smile. As the scampi warmed her stomach, that smile warmed every inch of her, including the cockles of her heart.

"It sounds like an exciting job," Ariel said.

"It is," Darius agreed, turning to her and releasing Serena from his thrall. "Well, to be fair, most of the time it's terribly routine. I breathe a lot of dust in old archives chasing clues. But occasionally…well, there have been a few times when it's been rather dangerous. One doesn't always know who one is dealing with, and some of these paintings are stolen, so…" He shrugged, a very European gesture. "I've met a few thugs in my day."

Like the one outside his door, Serena thought. She wished she had the nerve to ask him about it. Then it struck her that she did. "I was concerned about that man who let himself into your apartment yesterday. I'm glad it was all right."

Darius shook his head. "As it happens, it was merely a nuisance."

"But…you say you've met thugs. Why didn't you let me call the police?"

There, it was out, the question that had been plaguing her.

He tilted his head, studying her, as if reading her mind. "Sometimes unsavory characters merely want to sell me a painting. Other times…well, I know how to deal with them."

"Oh!" Ariel exclaimed, looking as thrilled as any teen faced with her idol. "Do you carry a gun?"

For an instant he looked shocked. "Never!" he said firmly. "Not ever. I realize you Americans depend on them, but I was raised in a different culture. I tend to believe that guns only elicit greater violence."

Serena heartily agreed with him on that point, and

felt herself thinking she might actually be able to like this man. How unfortunate, when he was probably just feeding her a pack of lies. Very good lies, but lies, nonetheless. Lies that could provide an excuse for all the unsavory characters that might come to his door.

Hmmm.

The evening light that poured through the sliding glass doors began to grow golden. The glow it cast through the living-dining areas was almost surreal, as if the room were under a spell.

"I wish," Darius said unexpectedly, "that I had an ounce of artistic talent."

"Why's that?" Ariel asked.

"I'd love to be able to capture this light."

"Did you want to be an artist when you were little?"

He nodded. "I most certainly did. I grew up surrounded by fine art, and was given every opportunity and a lot of very expensive lessons. Nothing helped. I can identify masterworks, but I'll never paint one." Then he laughed. "Oh, well. At least I spend my life looking at the things I love most. Not many can say that."

Serena was beginning to believe him. She didn't want to believe him. It would ruin her entire vacation, not to have a criminal living next door. Nonetheless, her suspicions were falling away like dead leaves. If this man wasn't exactly what he said he was, then he deserved every acting award in the universe.

But still nagging at her was that threatening statement: *We have your mother.*

AFTER DINNER they moved out onto her balcony to watch the sun set over the water. Serena served Tia Maria in liqueur glasses along with Blue Mountain coffee. Between that, the wine they'd had with dinner, and the soothing glow of the sunset, Serena felt…delightfully buzzed.

The evening breeze was just warm enough to be delightful. The passing of the storm had left the air surprisingly dry, creating the kind of evening that made Serena want to close her eyes, let her head fall back and feel her hair toss gently.

"I love the wind," she said impulsively. "Gentle or fierce, it always gives me such a feeling of freedom."

"I love it, too," Ariel said. "It makes me feel as if I could fly."

Darius said nothing. Curious, Serena turned to him. He appeared lost in thought, not necessarily of the happiest kind. Maybe he wasn't completely indifferent to that threat made earlier.

"Do you have any family in the area?" she asked, hoping to pry some information loose.

"No. My family, such as it is, is in Europe."

"Such as it is?"

"My mother is the only close relative I have left." His mouth twisted wryly. "She is, however, the world's biggest schemer, highly manipulative, and highly volatile. And I love her dearly."

Serena didn't know how to reply to that. In fact, she

was beginning to wonder if she had utterly misheard that weasel's words. "Do you…see her often?"

"Whenever I'm in Europe, which is quite often. It can be something of a trial, though. She's forever plotting to find a way to turn me into something I'm not."

"Which is?"

"Well, it used to be James Bond. Right now it's something else." He waved a hand, as if to brush away the thoughts. "What about you ladies? Your families?"

"Well," said Ariel, "I have none."

That was a question Serena had never asked her, and now, hearing the answer, she felt her throat tighten. "I'm so sorry, honey."

"Oh, it's okay," Ariel said brightly. "It's been a long time. And I'm well-off. Luckier than most, don't you think?"

"You're such a positive thinker."

Ariel laughed. "Of course. Is there any other way to be?"

"Well, you can share my family from now on."

Ariel looked impishly at her. "Are they all like *you?*"

A helpless laugh bubbled out of Serena, rising from deep within her. "Touché," she managed to say between giggles.

Ariel laughed with her, and Darius looked from one to the other, amused, even though he must surely feel left out.

"Serena," Ariel confided, "is a would-be adventuress. She gets into all kinds of trouble when she's on vacation."

"Hey," Serena said, "I haven't been arrested yet."

"She came awfully close last Christmas," Ariel explained to Darius. "She was playing Mrs. Claus at the mall, and one too many little brats mouthed off at her and kicked her in the shin. So she told the parents, *all* the parents, what they could do with their little monsters."

Darius laughed heartily. "Good for you," he told Serena.

"She was supposed to go on a naked cruise this time," Ariel continued, "but the IRS seized the ship."

"Ariel!"

The young woman shrugged. "It's the truth. I know you keep saying 'clothing optional,' but I don't know what the difference is."

Darius's gaze settled on Serena again. He was smiling, but his eyes seemed to hold some deeper message, something that made her squirm in her chair. Something that felt too pleasurable for her own good. She gripped the armrests tightly and forced herself to be still.

At that moment an errant gust hit her, blowing her hair across her face and somehow managing to blow her skirt up to the top of her thighs.

"Oh!" Embarrassment filled her and she blindly reached to pull her skirt down and tuck it tightly around her legs.

"Better than Marilyn's," Darius said, a laugh trembling in his voice.

Serena glared at him through strands of blond hair. "Don't be a cad."

"Odd. That's one thing my mother has always hoped I'd become."

Brushing her hair out of her eyes, she asked, "Why?"

"My father was a very stolid Swiss banker. She spent most of his life trying to turn him into D'Artagnan."

"Poor man."

"They were very much in love." Darius's gaze strayed back out over the water, his face growing pensive, almost sad. "Anyway, now she's decided to reform me."

Serena's heart slammed. "How so?"

"She's staged her own kidnapping."

CHAPTER FIVE

"She *what*?" Serena asked, words tumbling out of her mouth. "I can't believe…who…why…I don't understand."

Darius looked at her and smiled. *That* smile again. "I don't think you'd understand my mother if you lived to be a hundred. I certainly don't. But yes, that's what she's done."

"So that guy outside your apartment, he's the kidnapper?" Ariel asked.

Darius chuckled. "He thinks so. I suspect it's more a case of her holding them captive than vice versa. Truth is, I pity the poor man. But yes, such as it stands, he's the kidnapper."

"But…why?"

"Oh, that's the easy part," Darius said with a wave of his hand. "She thinks I'm a prince."

If he'd said he had six ears, Serena couldn't have been more floored. He said it so off-handedly, as if there were no great mystery involved in a mother staging her own kidnapping because her son was, or might be, a prince.

"Ummm…" Serena said.

"Exactly," Darius replied. "Ummm…"

"I take it you don't think you're a prince?" Ariel asked.

He laughed. "No, I don't. And what's more, even if I were, I wouldn't want the job. I mean, who in his right mind would want to be the crown prince of Masolimia?"

"That place in the Pyrenees, with the awful sheep?" Ariel asked. Both Serena and Darius looked at her in stunned silence. "Well, I read something about it in a science magazine."

"Yes," Darius said. "The place with the awful sheep. And the awful weather. And the awful…everything."

"But that place is going to be rich!" Ariel countered.

Serena felt as if she had slipped into a reality warp. She'd never heard of Masolimia, but that was no surprise. There were probably hundreds of little places in the world she'd never heard of. The surprise was that Ariel *had* heard of Masolimia. And not only had heard of it, but seemed to be something of an expert on the place. That girl seemed to know entirely too much for Serena's comfort. It was almost as if she'd been…set up.

Darius nodded to Ariel. "That's what they tell me. Something about genetic research, I gather."

"Yes!" Ariel said. She turned to Serena. "It's like this. Geneticists are trying to figure out which parts of the human gene structure do what things. How much of what happens to us is inherited, how much is environmental. The old debate of nature versus nurture."

"Right," Serena said, nodding as if to say, I know this, dear. "I'm a doctor, remember?"

Ariel nodded excitedly. "Of course you are! So you know they're trying to find out if there are genetic bases for diseases. Does this gene cause cancer? Does that gene cause depression? Things like that. But it's complicated, because genes sometimes skip generations, lie dormant or some such. Plus a lot of places in the world have become so cosmopolitan, with people from all over the world adding to the local gene pool. So what you need is…"

Darius cut in. "An isolated, homogeneous population, with accurate genealogical records, so you can follow the path of genes through tens or hundreds of generations."

"And Masolimia has that?" Serena asked.

"Yes," Ariel replied. "It's a mountain principality which has had little contact with its neighbors. What's more, their traditional burial customs—going back to before the Roman Empire—use a labyrinth of catacombs, where an individual's crypt is connected by tunnels to his or her parents, siblings and children. The catacombs are a precise genealogical history of Masolimia. So a genetic research firm wants to use them as a case study."

"Which would, of course, involve a substantial payment to the people of Masolimia," Serena said.

Darius nodded. "About fifty million dollars, all told. Plus loans and investments to help modernize the place.

Quite lucrative, mother tells me. Except…the last prince died childless, and his bloodline died with him. So Masolimia has no official in charge who can okay the contract."

Serena's brow furrowed. "But surely there's a legislature or a cabinet or something?"

"Nope," Darius said. "You'd think so, but no. By tradition—and everything in Masolimia is about tradition—only the crown prince can approve contracts between the government and outside companies. No prince. No contract. No money."

"Ahhhh," Serena said, suddenly understanding. Or so she thought. "Your mother thinks you should be the next prince."

"Not quite," he replied. "She thinks I *am* the next prince. Apparently my family—her side of the family—has some connection to someone who was someone six hundred years ago. I don't pretend to understand it. Frankly, I don't care. I don't want the job."

"But what about the poor people of Masolimia?" Ariel asked.

"Yeah, what about them?" Serena echoed. He did, after all, seem awfully callous about the condition of his native land.

As if to confirm her feelings, he gave another of his patented European shrugs. "The people of Masolimia will settle on someone. It just won't be me. Not even if my mother *did* get herself kidnapped."

"Aren't you worried about her?" Ariel asked.

"Ha! The only person who worries about my mother

is God, and that's only because she wants His job. No, I'm not worried about my mother. Not by a long shot."

The sky had grown dark, the moon glittering on the waves. As if sensing Serena's disapproval of his attitude, Darius glanced at his watch.

"And I've overstayed." He stood, then reached out and took her hand, a purely polite, old-fashioned gesture that, nonetheless, sent a shiver down her spine. "Thank you for your hospitality."

He actually kissed her hand. Shiver again.

Then he turned to Ariel, repeating the kiss. "And it was a pleasure to improve my acquaintance with you, young lady. It's remarkable to meet so well-read a person."

"The pleasure was all mine," Ariel said, her voice suddenly rich with a cultured depth which lay far beyond her years. "And your choice of dinner was delightful."

Serena made as if to rise, but he held up a hand. "Please, stay here and enjoy the night air. I'll let myself out."

After the briefest of bows, he turned and strode away with a grace that was undeniably…royal.

"Wow," Ariel said, after he had left. "Just think—a prince helped you wash the dishes!"

"Hmmm," Serena replied.

THE MOON, which had been chasing the sun across the sky all day, now hung above the water, an argent orb with an amused face. Serena figured it was laughing at her, but what the heck. Ariel had gone inside to watch television, leaving her all alone on her balcony to watch the mesmerizing rhythm of silver-capped waves. The wind was now blowing offshore, leaving her untouched in her nook.

This vacation was certainly not going the way she had planned. Which reminded her, she needed to tell Marco to drop it before he did something outrageous that came back to haunt her.

Maybe, she thought wistfully, it was time to grow up year-round, not just when she was working. Yes, her job was mostly dull, but she met some very nice people. Some even had fascinating stories to tell. That should be enough, right?

Today—Ariel was right about this—she had slandered a man. In her haste to have a good time, she'd invented a dastardly criminal out of whole cloth. Instead he was an art dealer cum prince, who seemed to have a share of his own troubles.

For some reason the old song about a prince coming someday was whirling around in her head. However, so did the old joke about kissing a prince and finding a frog.

But darn it he was attractive. Everything about him appealed to her, even if he did dress outlandishly for the climate.

On the other hand, he *did* have a mother who would stage her own kidnapping to get her way. Did she want to get tangled up with that kind of family?

Yes! The thought made her laugh. He wasn't the least interested in her, but his mother sounded like a character after her own heart. In fact, his mother was the best recommendation he had.

A prince. Living next door. Well, a prince who didn't believe he was a prince. She felt a little disturbed by his cavalier dismissal of the genetic contract which could help Maso-whatever-it-was to prosper, but he was probably right. They'd find someone else to be their prince.

She could hardly blame him for not wanting the job. It would probably be tedious beyond belief. Meetings and papers and appearances, and people telling you what to do and how to behave every moment of the day....

Still... She closed her eyes a moment and indulged a Cinderella fantasy of being garbed in a beautiful gown, waltzing around a huge ballroom in the arms of a prince in a comic-opera uniform of blue and gold.

Hmmm.

Once again it was time to corral her thoughts. She had such a tendency to go off into flights of fancy, it was a wonder she'd ever made it through medical school. Or a day in her own practice.

"Hey," said Ariel, rejoining her. Apparently her program was over. "You look pensive."

"I'm facing weeks of tedium."

"With a handsome prince next door?"

Serena cocked an eye her way. "He says he's not. Don't you think he would know?"

"Actually, no. Distant line and all that."

Serena shrugged. "Doesn't matter anyway. He's determined not to be a prince. I don't suppose they can force him. Besides, who'd want to be a prince in this day and age?"

Ariel nodded. "I hadn't thought of that."

"Sounds like a boring job to me." Serena took a sip of iced tea from the frosty glass on the table beside her. "Oh, well. I'll call off Marco first thing in the morning. Can you imagine having a mother like that?"

"You mean Mr. Maxwell's? Sure." Ariel giggled. "I just have to look at you."

Serena pretended to frown at her, but she couldn't contain her own laughter. "I had the same thought."

"So what are you going to do now? Stage a bank robbery?"

"I'm not that crazy."

Ariel laughed again. "I hope not. I'd have to save you from yourself, and I'm not sure I could do that."

"You won't have to. I've been ruminating over possibilities, but it seems I'm going to have to be bored one way or the other."

"What you mean is, you haven't thought of anything that tickles your fancy yet."

Serena sighed. "I guess I have some kind of problem. Other people don't get bored the way I do."

"Other people have more in their lives. Husbands. Kids. Clubs. Maybe instead of going out to run along the beach you should join the Y. You'd meet more people."

It was lowering to admit it, but Ariel was right. Her

world had started narrowing in medical school and never really broadened again, until all she had to look forward to were her vacations. That wasn't healthy.

"But my days are so long." And they were. No matter how she scheduled them, they wound up being ten to fourteen hours at a stretch. Supposedly minor matters for which fifteen minutes had been allotted would turn into necessary surgical procedures that took longer, and so on. Even dermatologists had emergencies. And when she was done with the patients, it was time to complete paperwork, attend to business management, make calls to discuss upsetting test results. She never asked her nurse to call with a diagnosis of malignancy or other serious skin condition.

So she came home beat. If she didn't run in the mornings before she left for work, she wouldn't run at all.

"Something needs to change," she heard herself announce.

"I couldn't agree more," Ariel said. "You absolutely, positively have got to get a life."

THE WORDS WERE still ringing in Serena's head the following morning. *Get a life.* Never had truer words been spoken, and how like Ariel to cut to the heart of the problem.

She went hunting for Marco and found him as expected beside the pool, covered in layers of olive oil, browning his already brown skin.

"You know," she said to him, "you're going to make me wealthy at this rate."

He laughed. "I will come to you to cut off any trouble."

"There's going to be a lot of trouble. I'm surprised you haven't already turned into one huge melanoma."

He grinned at her, showing enviously white, although crooked, teeth. "I have good genes."

"Apparently so."

She pulled up a chair and sat facing him. On her head was a wide-brimmed straw hat that shaded her pretty well. "Listen, about what I said yesterday afternoon about our new neighbor?"

His face darkened. "The drug dealer. I have not yet seen him."

"Well, forget what I said."

"Forget it? How can I forget such a thing? My grandchildren..."

She interrupted ruthlessly. "Marco, I checked him out. He's not a drug dealer."

Marco fell silent, his mouth open, taking in her words. "No?"

"No.

"No." He nodded. "What is he?"

"A perfectly legitimate businessman." Although now that she thought about it, that prince business...had she been seriously snowed last night?

"Yes?"

"Yes." She said it firmly, despite the sudden niggling doubt.

"Okay, then. I forget it. Pah!" He waved a hand as if tossing the thought away.

"Good. I jumped to conclusions." And she'd jump right back to them if Darius Maxwell gave her any reason to.

CHAPTER SIX

THERE WAS NO Y on the island, and going to the nearest one meant crossing two drawbridges, not something Serena cared to do first thing in the morning, during rush hour. It was bad enough when she had to go to work and left every morning at six to beat the rush. No way was she going to do it on her vacation.

But Ariel's comments were still stinging, mainly because they were true. So instead of putting on her jogging outfit, she chose a white polo shirt and white shorts and picked up her tennis racquet and balls. She could practice her serve for a while, and maybe someone else would show up to play with her. Someone with whom she could be sociable.

The complex had two private tennis courts with well-maintained clay surfaces. When she arrived, a couple were already playing at the farthest court. They paid her no attention and their game wasn't of a quality to justify watching, so she grabbed a bucket of practice balls and began to hit serves.

It stank. With the first six balls she hit the net three times. Boy, was she out of practice.

Just as she moved to go gather up her balls and try again, a familiar voice said, "You're tossing it too far forward, so you're hitting it on the downswing."

Her cheeks, already a little flushed, flushed more. She turned and saw Darius Maxwell, potential prince and ruler of some nearly invisible country, standing just inside the gate. He, too, wore tennis togs and carried a racquet and balls. Lord, did he look fantastic in white, with his bronze skin.

"Hi," she said, suddenly feeling as if she might trip over her own feet.

"Good morning." He smiled, and the world lit up like noon, even though the sun was still trying to creep its way up from the horizon. "I don't mean to butt in, Serena. If I'm annoying you, tell me to go away. But if you'd like a match…"

His voice held a hopeful note she couldn't resist. "Sure. But I'm out of practice."

"So am I. But I suspect you'll get your game back faster than I will."

Not only was he a gorgeous man, but he also had a gorgeous accent. British, with a hint of something exotic.

He helped her gather the balls, then came to stand behind her while she practiced. She could feel him back there, watching. It made her nervous. Too nervous.

The other couple finished their game just then, and gave her a few moments of reprieve as they left the court. Then there was just her and Darius.

She felt wobbly. "Look," she said tartly, "you're making me nervous, standing back there and watching."

"But I'm not being at all critical," he answered. "Tell you what. I'll stand beside you and we'll *both* practice our serves."

"Fine."

It gave her great pleasure when his hit the net and hers went exactly where it was supposed to.

"See?" he said. "I'm out of practice, too."

His next ball hit the net, but so did hers. Now she was getting annoyed. She could serve better than this. Far better than this. And for some reason she felt a strong need to show him up.

She picked up another ball, drew her racquet back and slammed the ball across the court. "Bingo! Slam-dunk!"

He laughed. "Beautiful serve."

It was his turn, and this time he, too, aced it. She suddenly had a bad feeling, and turned to him. "You weren't hitting the net on purpose were you? Just to spare my feelings?"

He held his free hand up, as if to push away any such thought. "Of course not. I'm rusty."

She still felt suspicious, even though he looked as innocent as a newborn baby. Turning, she picked up two more balls and served them, one after another, perfectly. Her arm was going to hurt tomorrow, but she didn't care.

"What are you going to do about your mother?" she asked him.

"I don't really need to do anything," he replied. He

served, and watched the ball fall short again. "She's on the Riviera enjoying herself."

"But how can you be sure of that?"

"I talked to her. She didn't want me to behead her kidnappers. Besides, I recognized the country code and exchange. I called the phone company and they were able to tell me that much."

"Behead her kidnappers?" Stunned, Serena forgot all about tennis. "Would you really do such a thing?"

He shook his head, and this time when he hit the ball she could sense anger in his swing. He aced it.

"I'd never behead anyone. But I was testing her. *She* would ordinarily love the idea, if not the execution of it. Instead she told me it was déclassé."

"Oh, my word!"

"Exactly. The woman is so hung up on becoming the dowager princess of Masolimia that she'll go to any lengths. Well, I absolutely refuse to become her pawn."

"I can't say I blame you. I imagine being a prince would be an awful job."

"Exactly." He slammed another ball across the net. "I like to travel. I like my business, most of the time. I like being in the art world. Why in the world would I want to give up my entire life so my mother can preen for the rest of hers?"

Serena found herself nodding. But then she had a thought, "Still, there's that genetic thing."

"I know." He bounced a ball off the clay, caught it and looked at her. "I'm not heartless. Those people really *do* need this contract. I visited Masolimia enough as a child to know how impoverished it is. But the *real* prince will serve just as well."

"How are you going to find him?"

He hesitated, then said, "I have an idea. The problem is carrying it out."

"Why?"

"Well, it's…a little illegal."

Serena looked at him, her jaw dropping. Then, before common sense could resurrect its ugly head, she said, "If it doesn't call for hurting anyone, count me in."

SHE REALLY DID NEED someone to stitch her tongue to the roof of her mouth, Serena thought as she showered. How had she ever allowed herself to say such a thing? And now she had to meet Darius at his apartment in twenty minutes.

To plan something that was "a little illegal." As if there were degrees of illegality.

Although, in a way she supposed there were: misdemeanors and felonies. Somehow she had a feeling this was going to be no mere misdemeanor.

Good Lord, she needed to grow up!

Well, she'd just go over there and tell him she'd changed her mind. She didn't want to even *conspire* to commit a crime. She didn't want to have knowledge of a crime. She didn't want any reason to find herself in a courtroom, either as defendant or witness.

But even as she castigated herself, she was intrigued.

There were butterflies in her stomach. Her adrenaline was pumping.

And she wasn't bored. Not one whit.

AT THE APPOINTED TIME she presented herself at Darius Maxwell's door. It opened immediately in answer to her knock, and he invited her in.

His living room was full of paintings, large and small, cramming the walls and sitting on easels. The room itself was done all in white, including the furniture, as if not to detract in any way from the beauty on the walls.

Before she had done more than say hello, Serena was drawn to the walls, to the paintings. A small Rembrandt in an ornate frame. Heavens, it was real! Some artists whose names she didn't recognize. A goodness-gracious-for-real Titian.

Her jaw practically agape, she turned to Darius. "Aren't you afraid these might be stolen?"

"If they ever are, I'll know how to get them back. That's the advantage of my trade."

She nodded, believing him. "Did you collect them all yourself?"

"The more recent works. The older ones are family heirlooms. A trust for future generations."

Never once in her life had she thought that way. Of course, she didn't come from an old European family, either. "I'm surprised you brought them here with you."

He shrugged. "I'm going to be here awhile, and they

give me great pleasure. It would be a shame to keep them in storage. They're meant to be enjoyed."

"Well, I'm certainly enjoying them."

She walked slowly around the room, feasting her eyes, trying to remember each and every painting. Before she finished, however, she was honestly feeling overwhelmed. It was all too much to take in. "This is like trying to do an entire gallery in a single day."

"I know. Feel free to drop over when I'm home. I'll be glad to take down whichever painting you like so you can just sit and admire it. I often do that. This space is too cramped. Each painting really needs a separate setting."

"I couldn't agree more." She accepted his invitation to sit, feeling as if she sat in a room covered with jewels. "Listen, about this thing you're planning…"

"I know." He smiled and poured coffee from a carafe into a bone china cup. "It was kind of you to offer your help, but you don't want to get involved in anything shady."

For some reason that set her back up. "I'll be the one to make that decision, depending on what it is you're planning." Staples. She needed to staple her tongue to the roof of her mouth.

His smile deepened. "You're feisty, aren't you? Well, here's the problem. The reason the Masolimians think I'm the prince is because they followed the catacombs all the way back until they found a male branch in the late prince's line that was not yet defunct. Then they followed the catacombs along that branch and came to me.

They naturally believe, given the way the catacombs are laid out, that I'm descended from that long-ago prince, and am his only surviving male heir."

"And you disagree."

"Certainly I disagree. Is my entire future to be determined by a handful of Masolimians crawling through a network of crypts with flashlights and a ball of twine?"

"Well, when you put it that way…"

"What's more, they've made no allowance for the fact that one or more walls might have been broken through by nature or accident. They may well have followed an entirely wrong course!"

"That's possible."

"Of course it's possible," he said. "In fact, it's likely, considering how far back they had to go. We're talking about the fifteenth century here."

Serena nodded, fascinated. "That *is* a long time back."

"Long enough for something to have become bollixed. I'm hoping to prove that with as little ado as possible."

"But how? Aren't the crypts a map themselves? The only map? Isn't that why the genetics company wants the contract?"

He nodded and sipped coffee. "But I did my homework, you see. There *is* a seventeenth-century map of the entire network of catacombs. And it's here. Well, it's in St. Petersburg. Five miles from here."

"Where?" Coffee forgotten, she leaned forward, as expectant as a child on Christmas morning.

"In storage at the Kristoff Museum."

"I've been there. It's quite a place, but don't they show mostly artifacts from old civilizations?"

He too was leaning forward, looking less urbane and far more intense. "A private collector has made a conditional donation. It's a hodgepodge of works of art and artifacts collected from around the globe."

"Well then." Serena straightened. "All you have to do is ask to see the map."

He shook his head. "I wish it were that easy." Rising, he began to pace the room. "The museum won't let me see any part of the collection, because the donation is conditioned on the collection being seen by no one until the donor dies."

"Why would someone do that?"

He gave her a wry look. "Oh, I suppose because the provenance of some of the articles is in doubt."

"What do you mean?"

He lifted a hand. "Some of it is stolen."

"Oh. Oh! But…" Now Serena was standing. "From museums?"

"Probably not. Would you like a croissant or something?"

"No, thank you."

He nodded and resumed pacing. "First of all, a lot of artwork disappeared during and immediately after World War II. Someone who stole any of those items would not want to be identified while alive. Then there's another whole category of theft, having to do with archaeological artifacts. Most countries have made it illegal for such items to be in the hands of private collectors, and certainly illegal for them to be removed from their country of origin. This collection could well contain some of those items."

Serena nodded. "So the museum will lose the collection if it lets you view anything at all."

"Precisely. And I attempted to get permission from the collector directly, just to see the painting of Princess Rotunda, but he refused."

Serena blinked. "Princess Rotunda? For real?"

He smiled. "For real."

"Good grief, the poor woman!"

"Indeed."

She shook her head. "But why would you want to see the portrait of a princess? I thought you wanted to see a map."

"I do. But the map is overlaid on the Princess's portrait."

"What?"

He spread his hands and shrugged, looking suddenly very Gallic. "Apparently someone was short on materials for making the map. Or perhaps it was done purposefully. No one knows for sure. The stories I've been able to dig up conflict in all but one essential element—the map of the catacombs as they existed in the midseventeenth century is painted over her portrait like a spiderweb."

"Poor woman," Serena said again. "Did everyone dislike her?"

He chuckled, a warm throaty sound. "She wasn't very popular, that's a fact. She was married to the ruler, and is held singularly responsible for the repressive taxation that nearly starved the country to death. She was finally killed in a revolt, along with her husband, the prince—and their nephew was installed on the throne."

"You *have* done your homework."

"Certainly." He seemed surprised that she might have thought anything else.

"So you need to get a look at this painting." That didn't sound so terribly illegal.

"More than a look. I've got to get some photos of it. And if they aren't clear enough, I may have to borrow it for a while."

The "borrowing" part was where things could get hairy, Serena realized. In that context, *borrowing* was probably a synonym for *grand larceny*.

"Let's go for the photos," she said firmly.

"That would be my preference, as well."

"But…" She popped the big question. "How do you propose to do this?"

"That's where I'm going to need some help."

PABLO MENOS ANSWERED the phone reluctantly. On the best—or worst—of days, the consular phone almost never rang. Lately it had been ringing all too often, and every time it was Maria Teresa Maxwell, Soon-To-Be Dowager Princess of Masolimia.

For that reason, and that reason only, Pablo put up with the woman. He needed to be in her good graces for the future. Otherwise he might have strangled her.

"Menos," she said sharply.

"*Sí*, Doña Maria Teresa." He called her "Lady" to keep her sweetened up.

"What are you doing about my son?"

Good question, one which she had asked at least ten times in the past twenty-four hours.

"Mas and I are making plans, Doña." In fact, they were scrambling around like frantic rats trying to figure out some way to scare Darius Maxwell into believing his mother really *had* been kidnapped. "I don't suppose you'd consider parting with a finger or an earlobe?"

A shocked silence greeted his words. "Are you out of your mind, man?"

If he wasn't, he soon would be, Menos thought miserably. He was beginning to feel a great deal of sympathy for Darius Maxwell. On the other hand, there was the good of his country to consider, and in that regard Maria Teresa appeared to be his only ace in the hole.

"I'll think of something," Menos promised, though he was dead out of ideas. The man simply didn't believe his mother had been kidnapped.

"If you don't think of something," Maria Teresa said, "then *I* will."

Which, thought Menos as he glumly hung up the phone, was a real threat indeed.

CHAPTER SEVEN

THE PROBLEM Darius Maxwell faced was that he didn't want his beautiful next-door neighbor involved in anything shady. He shouldn't have told her so much, he realized, and looking at her now, drinking in her extraordinary beauty, he kept imagining her with steel bars in front of her. *Hmmm.*

Nor was her extraordinary beauty something that Hollywood would have hailed. She wasn't perfect, but to Darius's artistic eye, that was what added to, rather than detracted from, her appeal. He wished he had the talent to paint her, to capture that pensive look she wore now, or the liveliness of her eyes when she felt annoyed or happy. Her face was far more expressive than she probably realized. And he liked that.

But he didn't have time for these thoughts right now. If his life was ever to be sane again, he had to deal with this prince thing and his mother. The sooner the better.

"What I don't understand," Serena said, "is how all these people could be buried in catacombs for so many centuries. How is it possible?"

"Have you ever seen the catacombs in Rome? You

can place quite a few bodies in a relatively small space, especially if you collect the bones into ossuaries after a few years. Originally it was only the most important families of Masolimia that created their own catacombs." He tilted his head to one side. "Come to think of it, that could be a problem for me."

"Uh, yes," she said wryly, and smiled. "You must be descended from a prominent family."

"Anyway," he continued, quite sure he could deal with that problem, as well, "the catacombs in Masolimia aren't nearly as nice as those in Rome. Rather dank, hardly more than mine tunnels and earthen rooms. Beneath the surface, the country is like Swiss cheese."

"Unpleasant."

"Very. However, there's some move afoot to turn them into a tourist attraction. So far it hasn't worked. Unlike the Roman Catacombs, they're neither beautifully constructed nor historically important."

"Except for your lineage right now."

He couldn't help smiling. "Right now they are of supreme importance."

"I have to admit, I don't get this whole bloodline thing. Why should lineage automatically make one suited to rule?"

"I couldn't agree more. However, I'm not responsible for the notion. I'm merely a victim of it." Bending over the coffee table, he refilled both their cups, then sipped some coffee, staring out over the Gulf of Mexico through the glass doors he always kept closed for the sake of his paintings.

"Why can't you just refuse the job?"

He looked at her, lifting a brow. "I did."

"And?"

"My mother arranged her own kidnapping. If I don't absolutely prove that I'm not the prince, God knows what she'll do next."

WHATEVER HIS PLAN might be, Darius said not a word about it to Serena, other than what he told her about the problem he was facing. Despite her earlier offer to help, he seemed to think it would be best to keep her totally out of it.

And of course he was right, she thought irritably when she was back in her own unit. When she thought about what he'd have to do to get a look at that painting, she had visions of, well, of Tom Cruise hanging upside down, or Sean Connery teaching Catherine Zeta-Jones how to contort herself through a web of infrared motion detectors.

While she doubted the museum in question had an alarm system that sophisticated, she was nonetheless convinced that it had one. These days, practically every home had one. She had one herself. Why should a museum not have something even better?

All of which virtually guaranteed that anyone trying to break in was going to get caught.

Hence, she was going to be perfectly content to be kept out of it.

Right?

Sure.

Darn it.

Frankly, this sounded a lot more exciting than a clothing-optional cruise. Well, except for the possibility of a six-by-eight cell waiting for her.

She put that down in the "con" column of the mental list she was composing, alongside losing her practice, her savings and possibly her life itself. Not that the latter seemed even remotely likely, but cops had been known to get itchy trigger fingers.

Now for the other side of the list.

First, it wasn't as if they were really planning to *steal* the painting. A mere look would be sufficient, and indeed that ought to be a very routine thing were it not for the shady collector and his absurd conditional donation. In fact, the painting itself might well be stolen property. That fact alone gave her an idea, though she put it on the back burner for the moment and returned to her list.

Second, the people of Masolimia needed and deserved a prince, one whose mere signature could rescue them from abject poverty. While she knew nothing about the place beyond what Darius and Ariel had said, she had no doubt there were poor, dark-eyed Masolimian children going hungry tonight. Children whose lives would be immeasurably better if only their prince would come.

Third, and a not insignificant third, was her oath as a physician. Who knew what genetic diseases might be isolated in the study of the Masolimian gene pool? Who knew how many lives might be saved? The futures, the very lives of hundreds or thousands or millions might be improved if a prince were found.

Finally there was Ariel's own admonition: get a life. Serena worked fourteen-hour days and came home to a lovely but empty condo, where she knew not one blessed soul. No, that wasn't entirely true—she knew Ariel and Marco and now Darius—but this wasn't the time to quibble over details. She went away on exciting vacations, which was good as far as it went, but the people she met there were also getting away from their lives and not looking to form attachments. The more she thought about it, the more she realized she had denied herself that most essential of human needs: connection with other human beings.

In short, it was time to grow up. For the sake of the starving children in Masolimia. For the sake of science. For the sake of her own sanity. It was time to grow up and get a life.

It was time to grow up…and commit a felony.

"LET'S ROCK THIS JOINT!" Serena said as Darius opened the door.

He was certain there was some context within which her confident pronouncement bore a connection to reality. But damned if he could find it. So rather than issuing a confident counterpronouncement, he settled for something less dashing.

"Huh?"

That universal indicator of befuddlement was met by a machine-gun torrent of words:

"Okay let's do it we need plans for the museum and its security we need to know exactly where this painting is and we'll need a camera and high-speed film so we can shoot in the dark and a darkroom yes a darkroom 'coz there's no way we turn this film over to the local stop-n-crop and…"

In the manner of men everywhere when confronted by a woman for whom breath seemed an entirely irrelevant issue in the production of speech, Darius replied:

"Umm."

"My, aren't you eloquent today?" she said.

"You're doing quite well enough for both of us. Would you like to come in, by the way?"

"Oh. Yes. So…where was I?"

"At the local, how did you put it, stop and crop."

"Right. We can't go there."

"And this refers to?"

"Those one-hour-photo places!" she said, as if explaining oxygen to a Martian. "We can't take our film there. We'd be sure to get caught."

"Aha," he replied. "And what film might that be?"

She let out an exasperated sigh. "The photos of the painting, silly!"

"Right."

"Exactly!"

This called for careful consideration, something he'd always found difficult in the presence of head-strong women with inexhaustible lung capacities. Like, say, his mother. This vivacious young beauty— yes, she was a beauty, there was no denying that—had apparently been serious about her offer to help him borrow the portrait of Princess Rotunda. Moreover, she had obviously given the idea some thought, and determined that she would be an active participant. And while he'd known he'd need a confederate at some point in the venture, this was hardly what he'd had in mind.

He wondered, not for the first time in his life, if he had some kind of karmic magnetism for meddlesome fe-males. That would explain much about his lot in life. Still, this particular meddlesome female had…possibilities.

"Well," he said, tentatively, "I hadn't really…"

"I know you hadn't," she cut in, pulling out a yellow legal pad already half-covered with writing. "But I have. So let's get down to details."

She couldn't be the reincarnation of his mother, he thought, for the simple reason that his mother wasn't dead yet. Perhaps she was channeling. Yes, that would explain it. Something certainly had to.

"Umm…yes…well…quite. Let's do."

No sooner had the words left his mouth than his doorbell rang. He sighed. No doubt it was Mas or Menos from the consulate, there to issue more dire threats about their fate if he couldn't rescue them from his mother. But no. That would be too kind an interruption. Fate had his number, and it was dialing with the insistence of a telemarketer on ephedrine.

"Hi," Ariel said. "I'm here to rescue Serena."

"Hi," he replied. "From?"

"Herself."

Without another word, Ariel brushed past him and into his condo, joining Serena at the kitchen table. "So, what are we up to?"

Serena looked only mildly vexed. "*We* aren't up to anything, unless you have a mouse in your pocket."

"Yes," Ariel said, "*we* are. You need a keeper. I've nominated myself."

"Self-nomination seems to be the order of the day," Darius said blandly, feeling as if he were standing on an ice floe in a surging sea.

"Exactly," Ariel said. "So, what are we up to?"

"A museum heist," Serena said, as if she were discussing the evening's menu. "We have to get a look at a painting."

"Ahh," Ariel said. "I'm sure there's a reason we can't just buy a ticket like everyone else."

"Yes," Serena and Darius answered in unison.

"Well then," Ariel replied, apparently not needing a fuller explanation, "let's get on with it."

Not one headstrong woman, Darius thought. Not two. Three. Fate, it seemed, would not stop until he answered the phone.

"Would anyone like a bottle of water?" he asked, joining them in his kitchen. "It looks to be a long day."

IT HAD INDEED been a long day, Maria Teresa Maxwell thought with a decidedly impatient *huff*. The gown was, of course, beautiful. But now there arose another issue, the very bane of her existence. Shoes.

A childhood spent scrabbling almost barefoot over the rocky Masolimian hillsides had left her with feet that were not anatomically suited to high-heeled pumps. But she would die before she would attend her son's coronation in anything less than the finest footwear. A stunning, floor-length silk gown deserved it. *She* deserved it.

And why couldn't this incompetent cobbler recognize that simple fact?

"But, madame," he said, with the patience of Job and the wisdom of Solomon, "such beautiful feet as these, they should not be tortured into a narrow pump."

Translation: *I couldn't find a shoe to fit you if I went to a circus prop room.*

"Obviously not," she replied. "That's why I didn't go to a shoe store. That's why I came to a cobbler. A man who, unless I'm mistaken, *makes* shoes."

"Yes, yes," he said mildly.

Translation: *Shoes for humans. Not for camels.*

"So how much will it cost?"

"Hmmm…."

Translation: *How much is it worth to put up with this woman and these feet?*

"I can't go above five thousand Euro," she said.

"Yes, well…."

Translation: *That would pay for my daughter's braces.*

"So you'll do it?"

"Madame, I will make your feet beautiful!"

Translation: *What have I gotten myself into?*

WHICH WAS EXACTLY what Darius was thinking at that very moment. Between them, Serena and Ariel seemed to have committed to memory every heist movie ever made. They were speaking in code, or so it seemed.

"We'll need a Brad Pitt," Ariel said.

"He could do," Serena replied, nodding her head toward Darius.

He'd never imagined himself a Brad Pitt. Still, it wasn't so far a stretch. Just ten years. And a few million dollars. And a few billion adoring women. And…

"Yes," Ariel agreed. "He'd be perfect."

"And a Nicholas Cage."

"Angel?" Ariel asked, a sparkle in her eye.

"Driver."

"Ahh," Ariel said. "Marco!"

"My thoughts exactly," Serena said, scribbling on what was now probably an illegal pad.

"And of course a Don Cheadle."

"Of course," Serena agreed. "I don't know any of those."

"No problem," Ariel replied. "I used to date one."

And so it went, in rapid-fire fashion, Darius sitting

in silence, looking from one to the other, as if watching a tennis match. Serve. Volley. Serve. Volley. All the while feeling the hole beneath him get deeper and deeper. All the while silently cursing his mother for channeling her malevolent ingenuity into his neighbors.

By the time they had finished, both Julia Roberts and Catherine Zeta-Jones had somehow gained starring roles, and nothing short of The Great Director yelling "Cut!" would deter them from their appointed tasks.

What had begun as such a simple idea was no longer simple. But wasn't that always the way?

CHAPTER EIGHT

TOMMY MELTON'S NICKNAME was "Sparks." It had been his nickname from the time he was eleven, when he had taken it upon himself to fix his mother's garbage disposal. The plumber had just left, but not before charging her sixty-five dollars to tell her that a garbage disposal was not meant to grind up the peelings from a dozen potatoes and that of course it was going to clog. For young Tommy, this simply would not do.

And so, applying the knowledge he'd gained in the thorough study of his Radio Shack 1001-in-1 Electronic Projects kit, along with many of its parts, he had taken it upon himself to improve the garbage disposal. And improve it he had.

Yes, necessity is the mother of invention. And, like all mothers, she can get loud when electricity and water are put into close proximity.

Yes, the cost of having the kitchen rewired had far exceeded the costs of a dozen plumber calls to unclog a dozen sinks.

Yes, there was still a faint, dark smudge on the

kitchen floor where the electricity had arced before Tommy had finally mastered the problem.

But by the time he had finished, that garbage disposal would grind up the peelings from a hundred potatoes, *and* the plastic mesh sack they'd been packaged in, without so much as a hiccup. It had been a stunning victory for childhood ingenuity.

And the scar really wasn't *that* bad.

Sparks—and even his mother now called him that—had since applied his electrical cunning to any number of household problems. When his older sister complained about the glitchy automatic garage-door remote, Sparks had set himself to the task with equal vigor. Now she could open her garage door from a half mile away. And if the palm trees in their front lawn all had two stalks and sprouted fronds twice the normal length, well, that spoke to the survivability of Mother Nature.

The problem now vexing him walked on four legs and carried its own armor plating. That most annoying of Florida's yard burrowers, the armadillo. Of course, electricity wasn't always the solution. He'd read all about coyote urine, ammonia and cayenne pepper flakes. He'd even considered trying them. But coyote urine was illegal, ammonia would kill the grass, and who *really* wanted to ask the grocer to stock ten-pound bags of crushed cayenne pepper. So he'd turned back to his old, trusty, tried-and-proven methodology.

He was up to his elbows in dirt, in the process of laying conductive mesh around the foundation of the house, when Ariel appeared in the yard beside him.

"Hey, Sparks."

"Oh, hell. I mean, hello."

For reasons beyond understanding, this girl had a crush on him. She was attractive enough, he supposed. Most of the guys drooled over her. But he knew better. One look at her long, flowing blond hair, sparkling green eyes, and Playboy-perfect body, and he knew she'd been the kind of vacuous cheerleader he had come to loathe. Of course, he'd loathed them primarily because they'd seemed to find him invisible. He had, after all, been the school geek. But old loathings die hard, and despite this girl's obvious interest, he just *knew* that if he ever got into a serious conversation with her, her side of it would focus on what shade of lipstick would look good with this or that outfit.

No, thank you.

"Well, aren't we cheery today?" she asked.

"We're busy," he replied. "We have three weeks to pack for college, and an armadillo problem to solve in the meantime."

"That's right," she said. "MIT, isn't it?"

He snorted. "They wish. I'm going to WPI."

"WPI?"

"Worcester Polytechnic Institute. I'm sure you've never heard of it. It's where MIT professors go to find good ideas."

"Ah, yes," she said. "That's the college that expelled

Robert Goddard after he blew the top floor off of Salisbury Laboratory, right?"

He looked up at her, his jaw agape.

She smiled. "I read an article about the development of the Norden Bombsight. It was created at WPI, you know."

"Yes," he said, after determining that the atmosphere did, in fact, contain oxygen. "I know."

"It's a good school," she said.

"The best," he answered.

"So…"

"So…" Maybe she wasn't an airhead.

"What are you working on?"

He spread his hands with not a small measure of pride. "An armadillo repellant system."

"Electrical?"

"Obviously." Or maybe she was, after all.

"Hmmm," she said, cocking her head to the side. "You have a problem."

"And what might that be?"

"The ground. The big neutralizer, as it were. The circuit will just ground out."

"Right," he said, as if explaining relativity to a cockroach. "That's why I put the rubber landscape cloth beneath the wire mesh."

"I see," she said. "And that creates your second problem, the one you haven't solved yet."

He sat back on his haunches and looked up at her. "And exactly what might that be?"

"Water. The landscape cloth will trap water. Hello, short circuit. Number Five is not alive."

How dare she make fun of his favorite movie? And he *had* thought about the water issue. He hadn't forgotten the garbage disposal incident, after all. He hadn't earned highest honors, won the state science fair and scored a 1590 on his SATs by being stupid. Of *course* he'd thought of the water issue.

He just hadn't come up with a solution yet.

And damn her for noticing.

"Slope," she said.

"Y equals MX plus B," he replied.

"Obviously."

"So?"

"So?" she replied, twirling her hair around a fingertip.

She was taunting him, damn it! Life was dreadfully, unbelievably unfair. Her eyes flicked down to the mesh, then back up to meet his. And turn *off* those eyes!

Then, in a moment that would have made Archimedes proud to be the first streaker in history, it hit him. The heel of his hand flew to his forehead.

"Of course!" he said.

"Of course," she replied, still twirling her hair.

All he'd needed was the right equation. Of course, that the right equation had come at the prompting of an entirely too-beautiful young girl who had a crush on him was an embarrassment he would never live down.

But such was the curse of genius, he supposed. Hadn't Einstein despaired of his mediocre mathematical prowess? And hadn't Oppenheimer taken months—and more than a few mishaps—to solve the riddle of the explosive lens? So okay, he'd needed the prompting of this delightful young lady—had he *really* had that thought?—to perfect his armadillo repellant system.

"Thanks," he said.

"You're welcome," she replied. "So, what are your plans for the rest of the summer?"

"Besides packing?"

"Yes, besides that."

"I have none, really."

"Great," she said. "Then you can help me."

Something in her tone of voice set off warning bells that would've made Los Alamos proud. "Help you with what?"

"Oh, it's simple, really," she replied. "I need you to crack a museum's electronic security."

"Is that all?" he asked.

She smiled. "Well, for starters."

Okay, so she wasn't an airhead, after all.

MARCO HAD LOVED to drive fast and dangerously. Alas, those days were past. His wife had insisted they move to Florida to be near their children—defectors who had left Italy years ago for jobs in the high technology that Marco would never understand the way he understood and loved the inner workings of a fast auto.

His eldest son, one of the eight apples of his eye, had been Marco's hope of continuing in racing. Sadly, from the moment the boy had set his eyes on one of the early personal computers, all interest in racing and autos had died. The seven others, beautiful women every one of them, had of course not the least interest in things greasy. Except for men with slicked-back hair, of course. Oily weasels.

So, giving in to Giovanna's ceaseless pleas, they had moved here. He couldn't really complain. He had seventeen grandchildren of various ages, all within driving distance.

Unfortunately, the driving was made boring by speed limits. Seventy? Pah! Fifty-five? Painful.

And worse, the people here had no idea whatsoever how to drive properly. Too many of them thought they were race-car drivers…which they were most definitely not. There was a difference between recklessness and skill, between a calculated risk and a stupid risk.

Often, as he drove around St. Petersburg, he saw a tempting gap, an opportunity to dart ahead one car length. He didn't take that opportunity, of course. Long gone were the days when one car length meant thousands of lira. Now one car length was just three seconds sooner pulling into the video rental parking lot. And a mere three seconds did not justify the risk involved. Not for Marco.

But for many of the other drivers, well, heaven forbid they should let any such opportunity slip by, lest it be a permanent blot on their virility! And so they went along, darting in here, darting in there, darting, darting, like little crazed hummingbirds, sending everyone else's feet to the brake pedals and everyone else's blood pressure skyward…all for three seconds. It was, in a word, depressing.

And it was not for him. His Grand Prix days were well over. His eyes were still sharp, but for a man used to hair-trigger reflexes and a brain that could assess a situation in less than an eyeblink, he knew he was slowing down. Still better than most his age, but no longer what he had once been.

That saddened him at times in a way not even grandchildren could soothe. In his mind he was still a young man in his prime. Aging was a dirty trick.

But as Giovanna was forever reminding him, he had a family any man could take pride in. She was right, of course. All his children had married happily, his son was successful in his chosen career, some of his daughters—to Giovanna's horror—had careers of their own, while the others chose to stay at home with the children.

Yes, he was proud of them, all of them, and grateful to God and Giovanna that they had grown up so well and were now so healthy and happy.

But that didn't mean he was ready to lie down and die. Nor did it mean he had to be content.

Sighing, he rubbed a nearly invisible speck of dirt off his car with a chamois and asked God why it all had to be over so quickly. Why did seventy years seem like a cheat? Why could there not be seventy more, all of them healthy and hale. Or at least most of them?

"Hi, Marco."

He turned from his car and saw Dr. Gregory, Serena, the beautiful young woman who had the power to make his aging heart skip a beat or two whenever he saw her. In that respect he was still most certainly young, and he didn't need a pill, either.

"Buon giorno," he said, giving her his best smile, allowing himself a moment of wistfulness for the days when he could have made *her* heart skip a beat, as well.

She was smiling, her face radiant in a way he had never seen it before. Something exciting must be happening in her life. He wondered if she would share it with him.

"I need a huge favor," she said.

"For you," he said grandly with a wide sweep of his arm, "anything."

She shook her head. "You'd better hear me out first, Marco. This could be dangerous."

Ah, if there was anything more calculated to make his heart race than a beautiful woman, it was the thought of danger. "Haven't I lived my life dangerously?" he demanded, feigning insult. "Always on the edge? Taking risks that would make most men shiver in their *scarpe.*"

"Scarpe?"

"Eh…shoes. *Sì,* shoes."

"Shoes. Okay." She smiled again and tossed her head, as if to get her blond hair back from her face. "This is a different kind of danger, Marco."

He shrugged. "So, speak."

Now she looked a bit nervous, scanning the garage

area as if to be sure no one else was around. "Well, I need a driver."

At once he was offended. "A driver? Am I the man to become someone's driver? I am not a taxi driver! Not for anyone."

She shook her head quickly and leaned in close to whisper, "I need an escape driver."

Now he, too, lowered his voice, leaning even closer. "Escape? From what?"

Her eyes blinked then met his steadily. "From the police."

"Polizia?" Oh, he liked this idea very much. "But what have you done wrong?"

"Nothing. Yet."

He nodded as if he understood, but in fact he was utterly confused now. "If you have done nothing…"

"It's what I'm *going* to do."

"Ahh." He hesitated. "You are not going to kill someone?"

"No."

"No?"

"No!"

"Ahh, okay. What *are* you going to do?"

"Break into a museum."

For a few moments Marco didn't move a muscle. Then he tilted his head to one side. "To steal something?"

"I hope not. I want to take pictures. Or maybe borrow a painting for a day or two."

"But why can't you just buy the *biglietto?* The ticket?"

"Because the painting we need to see is under lock and key, and they won't allow anyone to see it until the owner is dead."

Marco frowned. "And is very important you see this?"

"Someone's future is at stake."

"*Sì.*" He nodded. "I can outrun any *macchina della polizia.*" He patted the hood of his car. "They never catch me. Never."

"But, Marco, this could be a felony."

He laughed, feeling truly youthful for the first time in ages. "Good. It will be more exciting!"

CHAPTER NINE

NO LONGER WAS Darius's apartment a pristine back-drop for his paintings. In fact, one of the most price-less of his Van Goghs had been removed from its easel, stacked against the wall and replaced with a huge pad of paper, on which things were being writ-ten by two lovely women who seem to have decided he was irrelevant.

Of course, he knew better. He cleared his throat.

Serena and Ariel stopped chattering and turned to look at him.

"It was rather my plan *not* to involve half the world."

"Well," said Serena practically, "you need someone to get you past the security systems, and someone to get you away fast. That's hardly half the world."

"True. But…" He hesitated. "The more persons we involve, the more complicated matters will get…and the more likely someone will spill the beans."

Serena put her hands on her hips. "Just how were you proposing to pull this off single-handedly?"

"I never had a chance to get that far in my plans."

"Precisely. Once you think about it, Darius, you'll realize you don't have a chance of bypassing the security measures without assistance. And if you need to get away in a hurry, you need someone who can outdrive the police."

He wasn't mollified. "I have the blueprints of the museum. I'm quite certain I could have found a way to slip in and slip out without detection."

Serena looked at Ariel. Ariel looked at Serena. In one voice they said, "Not likely."

"And even if I couldn't," he continued forcefully, "I have my own connections to rely on. Persons I know who will be trustworthy for the right price."

Ariel lifted one brow. "Are you saying we're poor judges of human nature?"

Darius looked from her to Serena and saw the same stubbornness on both faces. Female steamrollers, the two of them. They could give his mother lessons.

"Really," Serena continued. "You should thank us for helping. Much better to use persons who don't have lengthy criminal records."

"Are you suggesting I consort with criminals?"

Serena cocked her head at him. "Isn't that what you just said?"

"I said I know *of* people. I don't have cocktails with them."

"Well," argued Ariel, "we *know* these people, and are quite certain they can be trusted."

"Absolutely," Serena agreed. "Now let's see those blueprints."

PABLO MENOS WAS about as desperate as a man could be without a noose around his neck. Not only was he being threatened with dire consequences by Maria Teresa Maxwell, but he was also now being threatened by the consul himself.

"We've got to get that contract signed," the consul had said just a short while ago from a beach somewhere in Southern Florida. In the background had been the sound of giggling girls and tinkling glass and ice cubes. "Your job is on the line, Menos. Do whatever it takes."

Now, Menos didn't have the best job in the world, and he knew it. On the other hand, it was better than any job he could have held in Masolimia. If he didn't pull this off, he'd have to go back to being a petty crook.

Besides, he loved his country. And he'd be a very wealthy man once this contract was signed. After all, however low he'd fallen, he came from one of the country's most distinguished bloodlines...five or six hundred years back.

The phone rang again as he was glumly contemplating his future, and he waved at Mas not to answer it. He simply couldn't deal with Maria Teresa right now. She who sat in an expensive hotel on the Riviera driving sane men to drink.

Speaking of which... But he brushed aside the impulse to go looking for a shot of something strong and continued to brood.

"You know," said Mas, careful to keep his tone sympathetic, "this is all backward."

"Tell me about it."

"No, no," Mas said. "I mean, it's *all* backward. Instead of pretending to have kidnapped Maria Teresa, we should actually kidnap Darius, and hold him until he signs the contract."

Menos started to shake his head. Then he froze. Then he sat up straighter. "That would be a major crime."

"Here maybe. At home…" Mas shrugged. "Besides, we're already guilty of a major crime."

"What's that?"

"Extortion."

Menos felt as if the entire world were falling in on him. "We've done nothing wrong!"

"I'm not exactly sure about that," said Mas. "Telling a man we've kidnapped his mother in order to get him to do something…is that actually any better than kidnapping the man himself?"

"Umm," Menos said, with even more uncertainty than that syllable normally conveyed.

"We'll need a plan," Mas said.

"Yes," Menos agreed. "A *good* plan."

Mas sat back, a look of offense creasing his features. "Are you implying…?"

Menos held up his hands. "I didn't mean to imply anything. Except that we need a good plan."

"You'd better not."

"I didn't."

"Really?"

"Really."

Which was a lie, and they both knew it. But as every warrior knew, discretion was the better part of valor. There was a time to say "No, Mas."

FOR GINA PERTINA, working at the Masolimian Consulate was to be taken with the appropriate gravity. She was, after all, the administrative assistant. Which, when translated into reality, meant that she ran the place, because she'd very quickly realized that Señores Menos and Mas—even pooling their mental resources—lacked the horsepower for the task.

A lesser person might have believed this was unfair. After all, Masolimia didn't pay all that well. In fact, she could probably have earned more running a register at the local grocery. On the other hand, a lesser person might not recognize that the local grocery would actually expect her to show up every day. By contrast, with this job, showing up for work was pretty much optional, at least as she saw it. And since she rescued them on a regular basis, Mas and Menos knew better than to complain.

Thus it was hardly surprising that at ten in the morning on a Tuesday Gina was sitting not at her office but at the beach, reading a trashy techno-thriller and further bronzing her already golden skin. It was, however, surprising that Pablo Menos came to find her.

"We need them, um, you, at work," he said, his eyes

fixed on the trickle of sweat that ran between her full, tawny breasts.

She looked up at him and arched her back. "I'm sunning myself. I'll be in this afternoon, or maybe tomorrow."

Normally, this strategy worked to perfection. Pablo's eyes would pop out of his head, his jaw would drop open, his mouth working to find words, until finally he despaired of saying anything even remotely seemly and walked away. This time, however, he merely drooled for a moment, then swallowed and looked up at her eyes.

"It's important."

Desperate times called for desperate measures. She picked up her bottle of sunscreen and held it out. "I think my legs are burning. Could you take care of it?"

She could see the thought form in his eyes. It was a thought he'd doubtless dreamed about for the past two years, since she'd taken the job. Pablo and Gina on a beach, his hands running along her long, slender legs, working the cream into her skin, her breath quickening in unison with his, their raw, animal desires growing until they snuck away to a private place to consummate their mutual desire.

As if.

The thought, however, ought to have sufficed to send him on his way and her back to the sexual adventures of a hotshot Navy pilot and his insipidly beautiful, blond weapons officer. The pilot had been just about to devour her on the ready-room couch when they'd been yanked away to chase a terrorist-piloted, supersonic, Soviet

MIG-29 armed with a stolen, precision-guided, bunker-busting tactical nuclear weapon which was preconfigured to home in on a satellite signal providing the global positioning system coordinates for the White House.

Regardless, Pablo's fantasy did not disengage the thinking part of his brain enough to allow Gina to return to her course in the technical specifications of an F-18 strike fighter. His eyes regained something of their lost focus, and he shook his head.

"Not this morning, Señorita Gina. We have a *muy importante* consular matter that requires your…umm… attention."

"What have you screwed up this time?" she asked.

"Nothing…yet."

"But you're about to," she said.

Pablo's eyes bore the look of a deer caught in headlights. "It's Señor Mas. He has an idea."

"You're right," she replied, closing her book. "That is an emergency."

THE FRAGRANCE of coconut oil, cocoa butter and warm skin filled the consular offices. The cover-up Gina wore hardly covered much, being made of some vaguely translucent blue material that covered her to her knees but through which her hot-pink bikini showed an almost phosphorescent purple. It was not a cover-up designed to redirect the lascivious line of men's thoughts.

She sat at her seldom-used desk, tossed her beach bag to one side, sprinkling sand all over the linoleum floor, and looked at her two bosses as if they were eight-year-olds who had just committed a major faux pas.

"Okay," she said, "which one of you is thinking?"

The two men looked at one another guiltily.

"It was *his* idea," Menos said, pointing at Mas.

"But," Mas argued, "you were the one who said we must do something drastic."

"I never used the word *drastic*."

"Oh, do hush!" Even Gina had her limits. "What is this idea about?"

"You know we need to get Darius Maxwell to accept the throne."

"Of course." Gina rolled her eyes. "Do you think I live on Mars?"

"No, of course not," Menos hastened to say. Upsetting the miraculous Gina was the last thing he wanted to do. "But you know Maria Teresa Maxwell wanted us to pretend to kidnap her?"

"Yes, of course. I thought it was folly from the very beginning. How stupid are the two of you?"

Neither of them really wanted to answer that question. Finally Mas said, "We needed to do *something*. Darius *must* take the throne. And he's refused."

"Did it never occur to you that if his mother could come up with such a ridiculous plan that he's probably well aware of the kind of capers she fosters? And that he probably, for one moment, wouldn't believe you two had really kidnapped her?"

The men looked at her, dumbfounded.

"Exactly," said Gina. "And now you're thinking again, scheming on your own. How *loco* are you?"

Mas and Menos shuffled their feet. Searching for lost dignity, Menos sat at his own desk and steepled his fingers. "I'm not thinking anything at all," he announced.

"I can well believe it," Gina said. "So *you're* the one doing all the thinking, Mas?"

"I, um, had an...uh...idea, yes."

She rose to her feet and leaned over him, pressing her upper arms together. This had the effect of pushing her cleavage almost into his face, which of course was her intent. Always keep men on the defensive.

"And what was this idea?" she asked.

He couldn't decide whether to look into her piercing eyes or into her bursting bosom. Her bosom won, of course.

"Well...I...um...I thought..."

"He said we should kidnap Darius Maxwell," Menos said.

Gina wasn't sure whether he'd said that to embarrass his colleague or simply to move the stuttering conversation along. Not that it mattered.

"Was that your idea?" she asked, arching a brow.

"Umm...y-y-y-yes," Mas answered.

"Well..." she began, then took a deep breath and let it out, letting the pregnant pause come to full term, until both men were on tenterhooks, "that's actually not a half-bad idea!"

"Really?" Mas asked, stunned.

"Really?" Menos echoed, equally stunned.

"Really," Gina said. "That has real promise! So, how did you plan to do it?"

Their surprised smiles fell in an instant.

"We hadn't made plans yet," Menos said. "That's why I came to get you."

"And that," she said, smiling at him, "was an even better idea! There may be hope for you two yet."

"*Sí!*" they said in unison.

"Yes," she agreed, pursing her lips for a moment, ideas running rampant through her mind. "Okay, so we're going to need some muscle for the job. And I have just the man in mind."

LIFE HAD NOT BEEN entirely kind to Lewis Levine. From his youth in the suburbs of Trenton, New Jersey, through his high-school years in Massachusetts, he'd been ever-so-slightly on the underside of society. His parents had not been poor, exactly. Rather, they'd simply never had more than a month-to-month existence, never really getting ahead of the curve, never truly having the things they and he dreamed of when they watched the rich and famous on TV.

So, despairing of any hope of college, he'd set his sights on boxing. And that was as close as he'd ever come to success. He'd come up through Golden Gloves, though never quite to the top. He'd tried out for the Olympic team, but hadn't quite made that, either. He'd done well enough as a club fighter, picking up a few dollars here and there, waiting for his *Rocky*-esque shot at the big time.

That time had finally come in the late nineties, after a certain famous boxer had been banned because his dining habits included his opponent's ear. And so, in the space of eighty-five seconds, Lewis Levine had made a name for himself.

Alas, the name was Lead Legs.

It hadn't been his fault. He'd trained hard, but the prefight festivities had been…extensive. And, sad to say, exhausting. He'd seen the left hook coming. He'd known how it was going to feel. He'd even entertained, for a fleeting instant, the possibility of slipping it. But his legs had betrayed him. And the next thing he recalled, he was being helped out of the ring, out of the bright lights and back into obscurity.

Obscurity, on the other hand, had been kind to him. He had a nice-enough job, a nice-enough apartment, a nice-enough car, and a beautiful girlfriend. What's more, Gina had just called, and was coming to see him that very evening. She had, she said, special plans for them.

His heart leaped at the very thought.

He had set about making his nice-enough apartment as perfect as it could be. He'd even dashed out to buy some scented candles—lavender rose mist, the wrapper said, though to him they simply smelled like candied wax—and had put them in the wrought-iron sconces on the wall.

He'd spared neither trouble nor expense for dinner, patiently and lovingly roasting a leg of lamb, which he'd rubbed down with garlic salt, marjoram and black pepper. For the side dishes, he'd chosen homemade mashed potatoes and baked acorn squash.

The table was covered with real linen and set with genuine Noritake china, left him by his grandmother. The flatware was real silver. The goblets were crystal. The merlot was decanted. The roses in the centerpiece were in full bloom.

All in all, culinary school had served him well, and with those skills he hoped to, and had worked to, serve his Gina a dinner to remember forever. And then he would ask her to marry him.

When the doorbell rang he practically dashed to it, pausing only to scoop up the bouquet he'd selected to match the flowers in the centerpiece. He moved with a crisp, fluid purpose which, if he'd had it in the ring that day, might well have won him the title. But no regrets. Not tonight. Not with Gina.

He opened the door and was stunned to see her standing with two rather dubious-looking men.

"Hi, honey," she said brightly. "These are my bosses at work, Pablo Menos and Juan Mas, from the consulate. We need to talk."

So much for a night to remember.

CHAPTER TEN

"WE NEED SOME MUSCLE," Serena said.

Darius, whose home now looked as if it were the headquarters of a growing army, paintings having given way to sticky notes, lists, and other papers which had not been consigned to the floor, was appalled.

"Muscle? What in the world can we possibly need muscle for except to get into trouble? Look, the entire idea was for one man, myself in particular, to slip into the storage room and photograph the painting. Now we have getaway drivers—have I told you that I have serious qualms about a race-car driver speeding us through city streets as if it were Le Mans?"

"You've mentioned it," Serena said. She was gnawing on the end of a pencil with pristine teeth, studying yet another list.

"Well, let me mention it again." He didn't know how much firmer he could make his voice without actually raising it, and he wasn't the sort to shout, except possibly on the playing field. "I'm sorry, but that sort of speed in the streets could get someone killed. And it will most certainly attract the attention of the authorities."

Serena looked up at him. "Are you always so sensible?"

"Yes, I try to be. And now you sound like my mother."

"She may have a point."

"Oh, she always has a point. Whether it's sane or not is another question. Again, I do not approve of speeding through the streets."

She smiled. "I never said Marco was going to drive fast. But he does know how to handle a car, and that could become very important."

"I'm sure he handles a car very well at exorbitant speeds. It's his ability to drive at thirty miles per hour that I'm questioning."

She shrugged. "If he can do one, he can do the other."

Darius stifled a frustrated sigh. "As for muscle…"

"Yes, I'm glad you brought that up."

"We don't need it," he said firmly.

"Yes, of course we do."

"No."

"Yes."

"I don't want someone who'll tangle with security guards and police officers and get us all arrested for battery."

"Batt-LEO," Ariel murmured.

Darius looked at her. "What?"

"Battery on a law enforcement officer. Commonly known as Batt-LEO."

He was astonished. "Wherever did you learn that?"

Ariel shrugged. "I have a checkered past."

"I'm beginning to believe it. Look, I don't want anyone hurt, and I don't want to set up a situation where someone does get hurt."

"I couldn't agree more," Serena said. Rising from the couch, she came to stand in front of him and pat his shoulder. "But you haven't considered that you might need someone very strong to help in getting at the painting."

He opened his mouth, another objection already forming, when it struck him that she might be right. "Why?"

"Have you looked at these blueprints closely? That storage room is small. I imagine that things are squeezed tightly together, possibly in heavy crates. You aren't likely to be able to move such things alone."

He hadn't considered that possibility, and he suddenly felt very stupid. He of all people knew how carefully objets d'art were packed. For some reason he had just assumed the crates had been removed. But if the owner insisted that no one see the works until his death...

He dropped into the armchair, a man defeated. Good Lord, he might have to open every single crate...

"Precisely," said Serena. "We may need a lot of muscle and more than one night to find this painting of yours."

Maybe he should just accept the throne. Surely he could abdicate after signing the damn contract. Except he somehow seemed to remember from something he'd been told that that would be...difficult. He needed to look into that again.

"This is getting more and more complicated," he said.

"Of course it is," Ariel answered. "That's why you need us. Women are better at this sort of thing."

Serena nodded in agreement. "You'd be hopelessly lost without us."

It was one thing to act as if he were the village idiot. It was another thing to come right out and say so. Still, by the glint in their eyes, he suspected they just might be joking. At the very least, they'd certainly say so if he were to object. His mother always had. Years of conditioning had left him speechless, so he busied himself with something he could manage: ordering out for dinner.

"Do you ever cook?" Ariel asked.

She asked it as if cooking were the easiest, most natural thing in the world. Little did she know….

"Umm…no. I prefer that my meals be edible."

Ariel and Serena exchanged a look.

"You're right," Serena said, although Ariel hadn't actually made a statement with which to agree. Unless they were having conversations by telepathy. "We'll have to teach him."

"Call them back and cancel the order," Serena said.

Her tone held a breezy confidence, as if there were no doubt that he would obey. And, of course, he did. By the time he'd hung up the phone, Serena and Ariel were already rooting through his cupboards with near reckless abandon. More than once, he caught himself thinking: When did I buy that?

The results of their search were hardly heartening,

from his perspective. Several cans of clams, for a plate of hors d'oeuvres he'd never gotten around to. A box of pasta. Heavy cream that he kept on hand for coffee. Herbs from the spice rack left behind by a woman who'd tried to get to his heart through his stomach. The remnants of a brick of parmesan cheese. A bottle of chardonnay. Looking at the assembled ingredients, he couldn't imagine how they could combine to form a meal. His uncertainty was undimmed when Serena announced the night's entrée.

"Linguini and clam sauce," she said. "It's easy."

Easy? For whom?

"If you say so," he replied, his voice laden with every possible nuance of helpless confusion he could manage to squeeze into four words.

"Pah! You'll see." Ariel pointed at the pot rack. Apparently, she intended to walk him through this step by step. Equally apparently, she realized she'd have to. "First, take that large pot—yes, that one—and fill it about two-thirds with water. Yes, from the sink. No, it doesn't matter whether it's hot or cold. Yes, exactly. Now put it on the stove. Yes, the big burner. And turn the burner on high. Perfect."

So far, so good.

Under their careful tutelage, he added a splash of olive oil and a shake or two of black pepper to the water, then heard the simplest direction he'd yet encountered.

"Now, leave that alone," Serena said. "Next you open the cans of clams. You'll need a can opener."

"I know that part," he said, almost snappishly. He caught himself and added, "Back home in Europe, I had a cat."

"Had?"

"Well, I couldn't very well leave it alone with a fifty kilo bag of vittles and a tub full of water!" He realized he was overreacting—as if it were possible to overreact to these two—and explained. "I asked a friend to look after it, and from what my friend told me when last we talked, they've become inseparable."

"I take it this friend doesn't want to see you again, either?" Ariel asked, quite obviously already knowing the answer, though he couldn't imagine how.

"No," he said. "She doesn't."

"I'm sorry," the young girl said simply.

Something deep in those green eyes conveyed a true empathy and sorrow more deeply than any words could have. But this was not a discussion he wanted to have. Not now. Certainly not with these two women.

"It's fine," he said. "It's for the best, really."

"Probably so," Ariel said, her eyes still holding his fixed in her bottomless gaze. "Still, I'm sorry."

"Thank you."

Serena, who'd been watching this silently, merely reached out and touched the back of his hand for a moment. "So, you need to open the clams."

"Right," he said, relieved by the change of subject. "The clams."

He wielded the can opener like the pro he was, then

was relieved when the two women clustered around a saucepan—also the remnant of the recent woman who tried to cook her way into his affections and hadn't even made it to his bed—their backs to him, their voices murmuring like the witches in Macbeth as they toiled over it, adding this and that. He wondered if they were concocting a potion to turn him from a mouse to a man.

But of course he was a man. He was perfectly capable of standing up to his mother, and had on numerous occasions. If he could stand up to that woman, he could certainly stand up to these two petite steamrollers. It was time to stiffen his spine, lift his chin, and take charge. Huzzah!

Easier said than done of course. He found himself in the peculiar position of not wanting to offend a certain blue-eyed charmer named Serena. Who, it seemed, was not serene at all. Hmmm. She was leaching the spine from him with those sparkling blue eyes, that entrancing figure, that impish smile.

And she leached it even further when a mere half hour later she placed before him a plate of the best linguini and clam sauce he had ever before tasted.

"You need to keep some vegetables around," she told him. "This is a very unbalanced meal."

"Vegetables aren't a problem with my usual mode of hunting for dinner."

She tickled him with a laugh. "No, I guess they wouldn't be."

"This is absolutely delicious."

"Thank you," both women chimed together.

If it was a potion, it was a wonderful potion, and he ate with great gusto. It was, he was quite sure, the best meal he'd had in a long time.

"It's heavenly," he assured them.

"Thank Serena," Ariel said. "I wouldn't have known how to make it."

"You helped," Serena reminded her.

"All I did was add a pinch of angel dust." Then she dissolved into laughter, leaving both Serena and Darius to look at her uncertainly. Then eyes met and they exchanged a brief shrug. That only seemed to make Ariel giggle harder.

Afterwards, risking the possibility that the two women might decide they needed an Uzi for this job if he wasn't around to prevent it, he insisted on doing the dishes.

He could hear them talking—the living room wasn't all that far away, after all—but over the running water he couldn't make out their words. He was quite certain he'd never loaded the dishwasher so fast before. As soon as he turned it on, he headed for the other room to stand as a bulwark of common sense in the face of two women who were having entirely too much fun planning a felony.

They looked up when he entered the room. "Look," he said. "The thing is…I really don't want anyone else at risk in this venture. I would hate to see either of you or any of your friends go to jail."

"They won't," Ariel said with a certainty that only her youth could generate.

But Serena's face gentled a bit, and some of the impish sparkle in her eyes gave way to a deeper, more serious mood. "You're really concerned, aren't you?"

"Of course I am! This is my problem, and frankly, I'd rather become prince of that benighted country than see either of you get into trouble with the law."

"But what about you?" Serena asked.

"Well, I'm perfectly willing to take my lumps. Several years in prison seems preferable to a lifetime in Masolimia."

"But if you were prince, couldn't you travel?"

"That's not the point. The point is that I am not the prince, and that I don't therefore see why the entire rest of my life should be dictated by the affairs of a state I've visited for a total of eight weeks in my entire life. The proper, rightful prince should sit on the throne. He might even enjoy it."

"True." Serena nodded. "We're just trying to help."

He sighed and sat in the armchair, looking at the two hopeful faces in front of him. "I know you are," he said gently. "But I would never forgive myself if either of you were hurt in any way by this."

"I understand," Serena said. Reaching out, she laid her hand on his arm. It was somehow the most calming, yet exciting, touch he'd ever felt.

And she understood. "So," he said firmly, "I would appreciate it very much if the two of you would just forget all about this."

Silence greeted his words. At first he dared to hope

that recognition of his common sense and concern had cast them down, and they were now disappointed that they couldn't participate in this crime.

Alas, he was wrong.

"Don't worry about it," Ariel said breezily. "No one's going to get hurt."

"Of course not," Serena agreed. "That's why we're making all these plans. To be sure no one gets caught."

"But…." His heart sank. "I had a plan."

"Really?" Serena asked. "Not a good enough one, I'll bet. You didn't even think about the possibility everything could still be crated."

Point, set, match, he thought glumly. And the freight train was still a runaway.

"I'll call Lead Legs," Serena announced. "He'll be our muscle. And he's the nicest guy you'd ever hope to meet."

Darius looked at her. "You know someone named Lead Legs?"

She simply smiled. And he began to wonder what kind of crowd he'd fallen into.

LEAD LEGS LEVINE was wondering the exact same thing at that very moment. On the night when he had planned to propose, Gina had come with an entirely different and none-too-savory proposition.

"Let me get this straight," he said, taking his time because he wanted to be absolutely, positively certain he was understanding this correctly. "You're going to invite a guy to a pow-wow at the consulate, then kidnap him until he agrees to be the prince?"

"That's the plan in a nutshell," Gina said. "If we do it at the consulate, we'll be on Masolimian territory. So we're not breaking any U.S. laws. We're not going to do anything violent. You just stand between him and the door while Pablo locks it. Then we…talk to him."

"And talk and talk and talk," Pablo said, feasting on the lamb that Lead Legs had prepared so carefully for his bride-to-be. "Until he agrees."

"No violence?" Lead Legs asked.

"None," Gina assured him.

"And you're positive this is legal?"

"Absolutely. It's an arrest under Masolimian law. Once he steps into the consulate, we can effect the arrest legally. And then he's ours."

"Hmmm," Lead Legs said, rubbing his slightly misshapen chin, then the almost invisible scar over his right eye, all but removed by cosmetic laser surgery. "I guess we can do that."

"Of course we can!" Gina said.

"It will be most very good," Juan said, scooping out the last of Lead Leg's prize mashed potatoes. "Like this food. Most very good."

Yes, Lead Legs thought sadly. Most very good food. And Gina hadn't touched a bite of it. Maybe she didn't like leg of lamb. He hadn't asked. Or maybe she'd been so busy talking a mile a minute—and she'd hardly paused for breath since he'd opened the door—that she hadn't thought about food at all.

He would simply have to cook her another dinner. A

better dinner. For a better, more special night. Then, once this lunacy was over, he would kneel down, take her hand, look into her bottomless eyes, and whisper ever so softly: Would you marry me?

He could see the moment in his mind, with perfect clarity. Her heart would be softened by a fine meal and wonderful wine. They would have braved hardship together. She would smile, a soft smile at first, widening into a joyful grin. And she would say: Yes, my darling.

And they would be together, forever.

It would be, indeed, much very good.

He was in the middle of that reverie when the phone rang. Shaking his head to clear his thoughts, he picked it up on the third ring.

"Hello?" a female voice asked.

"Hello?" Lead Legs answered.

"Mr. Levine?" the female asked.

"Yes?" he answered.

"This is Dr. Serena Gregory. If you recall, I was your doctor? For the laser surgery?"

"Yes!" he answered, finally placing the voice, and recalling her fondly. She had been exceptionally gentle with him. "Yes, Dr. Gregory. What can I do for you?"

"I have a proposition for you," Serena said. "Can you meet me tomorrow, at the Pier?"

"Ummm, sure, I guess," he said.

"Twelve noon?"

"That's not a good time, Dr. Gregory. I'm a chef, if you remember. That's the middle of the lunch rush."

"How about three o'clock?" she asked.

"Yes. Three o'clock."

"Okay, great. Buh-bye."

"Buh-bye."

"Who was that?" Gina asked, the faintest tinge of jealousy in her eyes.

"It was my doctor," he said, pointing to his eyebrow. "You know…that one."

"The cute one?" Gina pressed.

"Yes, she's…attractive. But…"

"And what did she want?"

Lead Legs grimaced, feeling very much as he had when that left hook had come arcing toward him, very much as Pauline must have felt, bound to the railroad tracks by Snidely Whiplash, hoping against hope that Dudley Do-Right would come to her rescue. But against Gina, there was no rescue.

"She wants to meet with me," he said, tentatively.

"Why?"

"She didn't say."

"Hmmm. When?"

"Tomorrow at three o'clock," he answered. "At the Pier?"

"Perfect," Gina said brightly. "I haven't been to the Pier in ages. I'll pick you up at two-thirty."

"Perfect," Lead Legs said, almost glumly.

For some reason that he couldn't put his finger on, this was much very not good. Much very not good at all.

CHAPTER ELEVEN

JUST BEFORE SUNSET Ariel excused herself, saying she had to meet some friends. Alone, Darius and Serena looked at each other.

"Well," said Serena, trying to sound brisk, "I guess this is enough planning for one day. I'll see you tomorrow?"

"Wait." The word was out before he knew it was on the way. She looked at him, but nothing in her expression made him feel the least bit stupid for uttering that impulsive word. "Why...don't we watch the sunset?" he asked.

He knew she could have watched it every bit as well from her own balcony, and that she might very well tell him so, but it was the only intelligent excuse he could think of. What was he supposed to say? That he wanted to get to know her better? That he wanted a chance, just a chance, to see if this strange spark he felt around her might grow into something?

He'd successfully avoided emotional entanglements his entire adult life, but he'd never before felt this...

spark. Ever curious, he wanted to know what would become of it.

"That would be nice," she said. The imp was gone. The blue eyes that looked back at him were a woman's, deep and mysterious, full of things a mere man could only guess at. Adam, he realized, had never stood a chance.

With glasses of iced tea, they sat side by side on matching, well-padded chaises. The breeze that reached them was gentle and soothing. The clouds above were beginning to take on the spectacular orange so familiar to Floridians, that irreproducible color of a flamingo's feathers, against a turquoise sky.

When their arms accidentally brushed, Darius felt a shiver of longing unlike any he had ever known. Sexual urges were no stranger to him, of course, but this was somehow more. A different kind of yearning. Something deeper than a mere impulse to feel her satiny skin and discover her moist secrets.

Maybe he was losing his mind. It was entirely possible.

"I think I'm going insane," he announced.

"Why?"

"Because I can't believe I'm actually proposing to commit a felony in order to prove I'm not a prince."

He turned to look at her and found her smiling.

"It does sound weird," she admitted.

"Of course it sounds weird. It's the stuff of comic opera. Ordinary man on the street is suddenly informed he's a prince. He quite naturally denies it. Then his mother informs him she has been kidnapped, and a dubious figure from the local consulate of the country involved confirms it. Ordinary-man-slash-prince knows better. He's neither a prince, nor has his conniving mother really been kidnapped. But in order to save this flyspeck of a country buried in the Pyrenees, said ordinary man must now break into a museum to discover who the real prince is."

"If I were an editor, I'm not sure I'd buy the book," she said.

"Precisely," he agreed. She was laughing silently. He couldn't help himself. He laughed with her, aloud. "This is sheer insanity."

"I know it is. But I love insanity." Her eyes were dancing.

"So." He turned on his chair, looking straight at her. "Just what causes a respectable member of the medical community to become involved in such hijinks?"

"Boredom." She shrugged and looked a little embarrassed. "Ariel will confirm it. I spend so much of my life wrapped up in my work, I tend to go a bit crazy on my vacations. Unfortunately, the one I had planned was canceled by the IRS."

"So I'm a substitute."

Her eyes danced. "You could say that."

"I'm wounded."

"Well, you know what they say. Kiss a prince, find a frog."

He laughed with evident pleasure, but somehow his face moved closer to hers, anyway. Oh, he knew what he was going to do, and he could read on her face that she knew, too. "Shall we find out if I'm a frog?"

"This might be a good time," she agreed, a little breathlessly. "*Before* I wind up in handcuffs."

"I think so, too."

The breeze caught a strand of her golden hair, and he reached out with a gentle finger to brush it from her lips. Then, heedless of the metal armrests between them, one of which threatened to crack his rib, he leaned over until their lips met.

Hers were soft, velvety, pliant, open to whatever might come. And so delicious. If heaven existed, he thought, it must be amazing indeed. For to exceed this moment, this instant, when their lips touched for the very first time, when he tasted her soft warmth, was a moment to which even God must aspire.

"Ouch," she said, as their lips parted.

Oh no! What had he done wrong?

"Ouch?"

She smiled. "It's this armrest."

"Oh, yes. Mine, too. Perhaps we should…move inside to somewhere more comfortable?"

"That's a fascinating offer," she said. "And if my vacation were any less crazy, I'd certainly take you up on it. But…well…I don't want to rush headlong into… you know…"

"Yes," he said, his face falling. "I know."

She touched his hand. "I'm sorry."

"No, no, you're right."

"I'm sorry."

He looked up into those blue eyes, eyes he could lose himself in for the rest of his life. And what he saw was…honesty.

"It's okay," he said. "Things are a bit wild right now. Perhaps we should be…patient."

"Yes," she said, squeezing his hand softly. "Patient."

Which was the best answer he could have hoped for, though not the answer he'd wanted. Still, apparently she wasn't repulsed.

"So am I a frog?" he asked.

Serena giggled. "Nope. You're still a prince. To me, if not to your homeland."

He took a deep breath and let it out slowly. A prince to her. That was not at all a bad fate. As for the rest of it, well, he'd resolve that soon enough.

The idea struck them at almost the same moment.

"I should go," she said.

"Yes, it's late," he replied. "Tomorrow's a big day."

"Yes. A big day."

At the door she paused and turned to him. For an instant, it looked as if she wanted one more kiss, a soft parting coda to the music of the evening. Before he could react, she said good-night and walked away.

And his condo had never felt so lonely.

THE ST. PETERSBURG PIER reaches out over Tampa Bay from a waterfront park. Wide enough to host Grand Prix racing once a year, it sports a small shopping center and restaurant at its terminus. Serena was feeding pelicans, at a dollar a fish, when Lead Legs Levine approached with a stunningly attractive brunette firmly attached to his arm. The scar over his eye was nearly invisible. Serena had done good work.

"Hi!" Serena said.

"Hi," the woman answered, quite obviously for both of them. "I'm Gina Pertina."

"Dr. Serena Gregory," Serena said, extending a hand.

The woman took it with all the warmth of the fish Serena had fed to the pelicans.

"So…" Gina said.

"So…" Lewis echoed.

"Yes," Serena said. "So…why are we all here?"

Gina gave a terse nod. "My thoughts exactly."

"Well, I have a job for Mr. Levine."

"He has a job already," Gina said.

"Yes, I know," Serena replied. "This would be an evening job. One or two nights at most. And it's for a good cause."

"What cause is that?" Gina answered.

"It may save a country."

"Uh-huh," Gina said, suspicion evident in her voice. "Tell me more."

HALF AN HOUR LATER, having walked the length of the pier three times, the story had emerged.

"So let me get this straight," Lead Legs said, for the second time in as many days confronted with the possibility of breaking the law. "You want me to help this Maxwell guy break into a museum and steal a painting."

"Well, not steal, exactly," Serena said, remembering her own rationalizations. "We just need to look at it. And take a photograph. But we might have to…borrow it… to do that."

"And this will prove this Maxwell guy isn't the prince of this…what's the name of the place…?"

"Masolimia," Gina said.

"Right," Lead Legs said, nodding. "Prove he's not the prince of Masolimia?"

"Exactly. We just need someone who's strong enough to help us move crates and such. That's all."

"That's all, apart from the burglary issue," Gina added tartly.

Serena nodded in resigned agreement. "Yes, apart from that bit."

Gina looked at her. "And you'll pay how much?"

"A hundred dollars per evening," Serena replied. "I know that's not much for such a risk, but…it's not bad if you break it out per hour."

"It's not, really," Lead Legs said, nodding.

"It's absurd," Gina said. "Two hundred. Each."

"Each?"

"If he's in this, I'm in this," Gina said. "Period. Two hundred. Each."

Which was four times more than Serena had offered, but less than half what she'd considered offering. All in all, not a bad deal.

"It's a deal. Two hundred each."

"You're on," Gina said.

"I'll be in touch with the details," Serena answered.

TEN MINUTES LATER, after the appallingly cute doctor had driven away, Gina sipped a soft drink and looked at the man she loved.

"It's perfect."

"The soft drink?" he asked.

"No, silly. This makes it even easier to kidnap this Maxwell. And we'll get paid four hundred dollars to boot! It's perfect!"

"But what if he really *isn't* the prince?"

She looked at him as if he'd grown two heads. "Do you really think the consulate would be mistaken about this?"

Lead Legs looked glumly down at his own soft drink. "I suppose not."

"Of course not." She patted his arm, a gesture that usually drove every thought out of his head.

But in the past he hadn't been contemplating the commission of two felonies.

"OKAY," SERENA ANNOUNCED breezily when she met Ariel and Darius at her apartment late that afternoon. "Lead Legs is on board. I think that about fills out the team, doesn't it?"

Darius said nothing. He had both hands wrapped about a glass of red wine, trying to warm it from the refrigerator's flavor-deadening forty degrees to a richer sixty to sixty-five.

Ariel spoke. "So this friend of yours had no objections to getting involved in a felony?"

"Well, his girlfriend was there. She kind of pushed him into it for some extra money."

Darius sat bolt upright. "His *girlfriend* knows? Oh, my Lord."

Ariel frowned. "That's not good, Serena."

"There wasn't much I could do about it. She was attached to him like lichen to a rock. Besides, she was the one who bargained to be paid, too. She's hardly going to squeal."

Darius looked at Ariel. "I'm sure you've seen all those news reports of people who try to hire a hit man and instead hire an undercover police officer."

"Oh, please," Serena said with a wave of her hand. "Let's not get paranoid."

Darius sighed. "I'm getting more paranoid by the moment. Justifiably, I might add. Let's call this entire thing off."

"What? And have you stuck on a throne you don't want for the rest of your life?"

It struck Darius then that Serena was probably the first woman he'd ever known who would actually conspire to keep him from becoming a prince. All the others would have done their best to twist his arm into accepting the job. They'd have been so blinded by visions of diamond tiaras that they wouldn't have been able to see anything else.

This either made Serena very special or very…well, he hesitated to say stupid, because the woman wasn't in the least stupid. He settled on very special. Eccentric, but very special.

Looking at her now, he realized he wouldn't have the heart to call off this folly. The way her eyes sparkled, the vivaciousness of her entire being…he couldn't possibly cast her down. No, he'd go to jail first.

"I think," he said, "that we need to find out who this girlfriend is before we plunge ahead."

Serena started to nod, and Ariel chimed in, "I couldn't agree more. Did you even get her name?"

"Well of course. I have to write her a check."

"A check?" Darius could no longer contain himself. He slapped his forehead with the heel of his palm. "A check? Serena, plotting a felony is one thing, but leaving a paper trail to prove it is…is…"

"Abysmally stupid," Ariel said.

"Oh." Serena's cheeks flushed a bright red. "Of course."

"Well," said Darius, taking pity on her discomfiture, "that's neither here nor there. We'll pay in cash, of course. But at least we have the woman's name. We ought to be able to track her down somehow."

"Well," said Serena, "I just thought I'd call Lead Legs."

"No, no, no." Darius couldn't say it emphatically enough. "It would be a mistake to let him know we're suspicious."

It was Serena's turn to grow impatient. "Do you realize how ridiculous this paranoia is? The woman is Lead Legs's girlfriend. Why in the world would she be an undercover cop? Why in the world would anyone suspect that we're up to anything at all?"

"Oh, I don't know," he replied dryly. "Let's see. We've already involved a famous race-car driver and a dubious person named Sparks. At this point I wouldn't be surprised if half the Tampa Bay area knew we were up to something."

"Hold on," Ariel said. "First of all, Sparks is not dubious. He's just…eccentric. But brilliant. Of that I can assure you."

Darius nodded in that enigmatic, European way that said: If you say so. "And second?"

"Second," Serena cut in, "this was all your idea. We're simply trying to make it work. And with the people we've got, now it has at least a chance. Perhaps not the best chance, but a chance nonetheless."

"And?" Darius said, wanting them to finish before he continued.

"And it's the right thing to do," Ariel said.

Both Serena and Darius looked at her.

"It *is!*" she insisted. "Look, this painting is going to prove one of two things. Either you *are* the rightful heir to the throne of Masolimia or you're not. If you're not, you're in the clear, and they'll know who *is,* and the people of Masolimia will reap the rewards. And if you are, well, I'm sure that buried somewhere within you is a sense of honor and duty that would rise to the occasion."

For just an instant Darius thought he saw something more than a precocious and adventurous young woman. For just an instant, he felt as if he was looking into an abyss of light. Then the instant passed, and once again he found himself shaken by Ariel's words.

"Yes," he said. "You're right. If it turns out I am the rightful heir, I'll have no choice but to accept the position. It's like one's parents. We can't choose them, but we still have to love them."

"So," Ariel said, "this little scheme is the key of hope for the people of Masolimia. Better to be certain—one way or the other—who the rightful heir is. So no one can come back later and try to challenge the decision. And you know, with all that money flowing in, someone would."

He hadn't considered that aspect at all. But she was right. Money brought out the worst in people. He'd seen that again and again. Right now, perhaps, neither he nor anyone else wanted the throne in Masolimia. But that would all change once the contract was finalized and the country had more to show for itself than bad sheep. Then, he knew, greed would take its ugly root. There would be usurpers. With definitive proof of the royal line, perhaps the moral force of office would be sufficient to deter them. Without it, Masolimia might very well descend into civil war.

He could see it all playing out in his mind. Former neighbors and friends sniping at each other, rival families looking to settle old scores, egged on by cynical men whose only real motives were wealth and power. Images from Ethiopia and Somalia, Bosnia and Kosovo played out in his mind, recast into the poor mountain communities of his native land. The mere thought troubled him terribly.

Slowly he looked up and nodded. "Yes. We have to do this. But I want it to be understood that this is my idea, and my plan. If anything goes wrong, it's my responsibility. If my going to prison is the cost of averting a civil war, I will pay that cost. Not you two, and not anyone else. Just me. Otherwise, I scotch the entire project and find another way."

"I understand," Serena and Ariel said, in unison.

And he could tell they did understand. Whether they agreed, well, that was another question entirely.

CHAPTER TWELVE

GINA ALMOST GIGGLED as she explained the developments to Mas and Menos. For Pablo, the possibility of seeing her giggle sent a delicious thrill through his body. Okay, so she did have a boyfriend. A large boyfriend. *Muy grande. Muy, muy grande.* However, fantasies rarely include details like very, very large boyfriends who looked as if they could pound someone into dust merely for looking at their girlfriends the way Pablo was looking at Gina.

Besides, Gina seemed to go out of her way to evoke such fantasies. Like now, for example. No one had forced her to come to work in stretch shorts that hugged every nook and cranny, and a white, gauzy cotton shirt that gave much to the eye and left little to the imagination.

She could have worn the kind of proper clothing he would have seen in his homeland: rough-spun wool, dyed in the gay colors that were so popular among the women but long since faded and tinted by the ever-present, windblown dust of the mountains. Back home, it was as if, with each new garment, the women set out to break the bonds of their nearly colorless environment. And as the garment was worn, that environment reached out to enchain them once again, until their dreams of freedom were reduced to pale, dusty shadows.

This plan would change all of that. The women of Masolimia would be able to afford better fibers, better clothes. Their brightly colored dreams could take hold, and be preserved with real, automatic washing machines. Their faces would reflect their new garments, with bright smiles displaying brighter dreams of brighter futures. Perhaps one day they might even dare to dress like Gina was dressed right now.

Although, to be honest, it was rarely warm enough in Masolimia to dress the way Gina was dressed. Bright dreams were one thing. Frostbite was something else.

Regardless, Gina could have dressed in a way that did less to advertise her quite ample assets. She didn't. And there was no mistaking the way she moved, the way she would square her shoulders back as she turned in profile, or let her hips sway as she walked, or the ever so slight downward tilt of her head, all calculated to appeal to the basest urges and imaginings of the male psyche.

So, even if she did have a *muy, muy grande querido*, he didn't consider it cheating to indulge the thoughts she so obviously sought to evoke. Nor did he see any reason to sully those thoughts with that boyfriend. His fantasies were like a Porsche: fast, beautiful, exhilarating and with room for only two.

And so thoroughly engaging that he heard only one word in six, until she mentioned the portrait of *Rotunda*.

In an instant his attention left her bosom like an egg

wrenched from beneath a hen. His brow arched. "This museum, it has the *Rotunda?*"

"Yes," Gina said impatiently, as if he were a three-year-old. Which he most certainly was not. "That's what I've been talking about for the past half hour. Welcome to the conversation, Pablo."

On the one hand, he envied her boyfriend. On the other hand, he pitied the poor man. A wild mare like this would be a difficult ride indeed.

"Yes, yes," he said. "You'd been talking about some painting. But you hadn't said *which* painting until then. You're sure it is the *Rotunda?*"

"Of course I'm sure," she replied. "I wouldn't forget a name like that. Poor woman. Her parents must not have liked her very much."

"No, no! They loved her very much indeed. Back then, to be…ample…was a great beauty in Masolimia. They were very proud of her!"

Gina gave a dismissive wave. "Whatever. So, this Maxwell plans to examine the painting. That means he'll want a meeting. It makes things much easier for us."

"Examine the painting?" Pablo asked. "We must take it! It cannot stay here!"

"That's grand larceny," Gina said. "And that would *not* be on Masolimian soil. We'd all go to jail."

Pablo puzzled over the word *larceny* for an instant, until the context made it clear. "You say it is *robo?* Stealing?"

"Yes," Gina said, rolling her eyes. "Stealing. Taking

something that doesn't belong to us. Crime. Prison. Any of this making sense to you?"

"Yes, it makes much sense," Pablo said. "But it is wrong! It would not be stealing. The *Rotunda* belongs to the people of Masolimia! It was stolen in 1942, by a Vichy French officer with a petty hatred for our people. A foul man. Monsieur Voleur. Pah!"

Juan also spat in disgust. "Vile. Thief!"

Gina nodded slowly. "So this Voleur…"

"Thief!" Pablo and Juan said in unison. "Pah!"

"Right, I got that part. This guy *stole* the painting. Which means *we're* not stealing. We're recovering stolen property. As agents of the Masolimian government!"

"Yes!" Pablo agreed. "That's what I was saying. No crime. No prison."

"Unless we get caught," Gina said.

"Huh?"

"Well, you two would have diplomatic immunity. *I'd* go to prison."

That did not fit into Pablo's fantasies at all. Nor, he suspected, did it fit into her boyfriend's fantasies.

"This we cannot do," he said. He put a hand on Juan's back. "*We* will recover the painting. Alone."

"And how are you planning to do that?" Gina asked.

"Umm…"

For that, Pablo had no answer. None at all.

OUTSIDE THE CONSULATE, in the strip mall parking lot, Serena and Ariel munched on tuna-salad sandwiches from the neighboring Subway. The sandwiches were good, but Serena's mind was not on food.

"So..." she said.

"Yes," Ariel agreed. "That's the guy from outside Darius's apartment. That's the kidnapper. And she works with them."

Learning more about Gina had not been as difficult as Serena had imagined. At Ariel's suggestion, they had checked the telephone directory. Sure enough, Gina had a listed telephone, complete with address. They'd staked out her condo in the wee morning hours, waiting for her to emerge. By mid-morning they'd been growing impatient, but finally she had snake-walked her way to her car and driven to work. At the Masolimian consulate, of all places.

Serena said, "Why that double-crossing b—"

Ariel put a fingertip to Serena's lips, preventing the ugly word's escape. "It's a coincidence, that's all. How were you to know that your muscleman was her boyfriend? How was she to know who you were and what you were planning? Of course, she's going to try to use this coincidence to her advantage. But...so are we."

"How?" Serena asked.

"I'll think of something," Ariel said, then repeated more emphatically, "I *will* think of something."

"Just don't tell Darius," Serena said mournfully. "He'll have a cow."

"I can't say I would blame him."

"Me, neither."

"Heavens," said Ariel. "Let's get out of here and find an ice cream shop. This calls for some serious thinking."

THEY FOUND A BASKIN-ROBBINS, where they ordered the largest, most sinful sundaes they could, then sat at an umbrella-shaded outdoor table to eat them.

"I forgot to put on sunscreen," Serena said.

"I'm sure your skin will survive one exposure." Ariel was gorging on her sundae as if the answers to the universe lay at the bottom of the plastic dish. Serena felt singularly un-hungry, but ate, anyway, mostly for the sake of her mood. If chocolate couldn't pull her out of the pits, she doubted anything could.

"There has to be a way to use this to our advantage," Ariel insisted.

"Then you're more optimistic than I am. My word, the very people who've been claiming to have kidnapped Darius's mother now know what we're up to. How is there any way to turn that to our advantage?"

"Maybe we can *all* try to get the painting out of cold storage together."

"Hah. More likely they'll try to get to it before we do just so Darius can't prove he's not the prince."

Ariel shook her head and grabbed for a napkin to wipe away a drip of chocolate syrup from her chin. The sundaes were melting even faster than they could be eaten. "Have you considered, Serena, what you'll do if he *is* the prince?"

The question jerked Serena up short, like a sharp tug on a bridle. Shock passed through her, hot and cold. She blustered. "It doesn't matter to me one way or the other. It's not my affair."

"You've made it your affair."

"I'm just trying to help Darius out. If he's the prince for real, it's no skin off my nose."

"No?"

"Absolutely not."

"Okay, then."

Serena looked at her suspiciously. "What are you getting at?"

The younger woman shrugged as she lifted another dripping spoonful of chocolate ice cream toward her mouth. "I just wondered how committed you were to proving the man wasn't a prince."

"Well, as a friend, I'd like him to get the outcome he wants. But that's it."

"Okay." Ariel returned to gorging.

"And what does that have to do with anything?"

"Nothing. I was just curious."

Serena decided it was definitely time for a change of subject, although she couldn't understand why this one was making her so uncomfortable. "Have you got an idea?"

"About what?"

"Gina and company."

"Oh. Not yet. I think I need more chocolate ice cream."

"Buy a quart and take it home. I'm going to burn out here."

Ariel's eyes were dancing as they met hers. "Yes, boss."

Serena sighed, feeling that she had in some way been bested, but with not the foggiest idea of how.

EVENING WAS YET AGAIN settling over the Gulf Coast, filling the sky with fuchsia and orange, dappling the Gulf wavelets with bright color amidst the now gunmetal blue of the water. The disk of the sun just hovered at the horizon, a glowing orange globe still too bright to look at. But if one caught just a glimpse of it, the orb's secret was revealed in the fiery way it glistened. No benign bringer of warmth and light, but instead a nuclear furnace of flame.

But at this time of evening, too, it was possible to see just how fast the earth was spinning, for even as she watched, Serena could see the sun sinking. In minutes all that would be left of it was the reflection of its light on the clouds overhead.

When her doorbell rang, she almost ignored it, not wanting to tear herself away from the most beautiful view the world afforded. But it might be Ariel with a solution to their problem, so she went to answer it.

Instead it was Darius, holding a bottle of wine and two shimmering goblets. "I thought we might enjoy the sunset together."

A flash of panic ran through her, and she almost slammed the door in his face. She had a secret from him now, and she was terrible at keeping secrets. If he asked a single question, she didn't know if she'd be able to lie.

But slamming the door in his face would only make him suspicious. Then she found herself thinking of the kiss they had shared and how it had made her feel, and she realized that she was facing twin jeopardies, both of them arising from his mouth.

He seemed to take her silence as acquiescence, for he slipped past her and carried the wine and goblets out onto her balcony. The sun had almost disappeared now.

Having no other choice, she closed the door and joined him. Her knees felt weak, and her heart hammered as if she'd just run five miles. Oh, dear.

He filled the glasses, passed one to her with that ought-to-be-illegal smile of his and touched his to hers in toast. "May all good things come to you," he said.

Then, calm as could be, as if her world weren't in danger of shattering right around her, he turned his attention back to the sunset.

Standing beside him, glass in hand, Serena tried to recapture her earlier pleasure in the view. Instead, she suddenly noticed, as the breeze blew just right, how good Darius smelled. How…enticing. The scents of man, soap, a hint of wine….

For the sake of her sanity, she turned to put the wineglass down on one of the little glass tables, and in the process moved a couple feet away from him.

He appeared not to notice, his attention still fixed on the view.

Thank goodness. Her heart was starting to slow down, and as it did, her legs began to feel stronger. There was no reason he should guess she was keeping something from him. And, she promised herself, it was a secret she wouldn't have to keep long, because if Ariel didn't devise a solution to the problem, she herself would. Somehow. Some way.

"Is something wrong?" he asked.

She nearly jumped, but when she looked at him, he was still gazing out to sea. "Uh, no. What makes you think that?"

"You seem edgy." Then he turned to look at her, his dark eyes as dark and deep as the waters below. "Not that I can blame you. I'm feeling very selfish."

"Selfish? Why?"

"I've dragged you into a mess in which you have no stake. I should have dealt with this on my own, or simply accepted the throne."

"Don't." She ached in response to the self-disgust in his voice. "I put myself squarely in the middle of this. And as many times as you tried to talk me out of it, I insisted on getting myself deeper into it. I'm just afraid I've mucked everything up."

"No, no, of course you haven't." He faced her, view forgotten. "I was thinking too small."

"Perhaps I'm thinking too large."

He smiled. "Well, you've certainly thought of problems that hadn't occurred to me."

"They would have eventually."

"Possibly. Although I haven't been completely honest with you."

Her heart slammed. What was he about to say? That he was simply a con artist?

"The truth is," he said, "the painting of Princess Rotunda was stolen from Masolimia in 1942 by a Vichy general. His name escapes me for the moment, although, given my profession, you'd think I'd have such facts at the tips of my fingers, wouldn't you?"

"No one can remember everything." Where was he going with this?

"Well, I misled you when I said I merely wanted to take a photo of it. It's one of Masolimia's most priceless treasures, although as an art dealer I have to say it's probably one of the most abysmal paintings in the world. But as you probably know, the value of art isn't derived from some intrinsic quality, but merely the price people are willing to pay for it."

Serena nodded. "Of course. I've often been astonished at the price people will pay for some things."

He nodded and sipped his wine. "So have I. But the fact remains, in terms of Masolimian history, this painting is priceless. And it was stolen. Rightfully it should go back to Masolimia."

"Of course it should."

"So…I wasn't just going to leave it there."

She stepped toward him. Clouds still blazed in the sky even as the twilight deepened to dusk. "You were going to steal it."

"Frankly?" He sighed. "Yes."

She touched his arm. "You care more about Masolimia than you want to admit, don't you?"

He hesitated. "Odd to say, yes I do. It's not really my

country—I was raised in Switzerland and England, actually—but it *is* my mother's country. And while she seems to bear a very big grudge toward some people for the way she was treated as a child, I still grew up hearing of the beauty and peace of the mountains. I don't think she ever ceased to be homesick."

"That's sad."

"Yes, it is. But if she returns, she's bound and determined to do it wearing a tiara. And despite all her machinations, I'm beginning to think that may be the very least I owe her."

Serena was seeing an entirely different side of Darius than she had before, a much deeper, more concerned, more thoughtful side. A side that was considering making huge sacrifices for his mother. The ache in her heart deepened.

"Then, of course," he continued, "there's the well-being of the entire country. Yes, it would be lovely if I could find the real prince, but if I can't…well…" He sighed. "Am I so very awful that I don't want to live as a fraud?"

"A fraud?"

"Yes. If I'm not the real prince, then I'm a fraud, whatever benefits Masolimia may reap. Plus, as I said last night, if we can't prove the bloodline, there will be challenges. That could get ugly. And how could I stand up to a challenge with confidence if *I'm* not even sure I'm entitled to the throne? I've spent my entire life being scrupulously honest in everything I do. I've placed honor before everything. Now look at me, proposing to steal a painting."

"You'd be recovering stolen goods."

He gave a short laugh. "One way of looking at it, I suppose. But I would very much like to be certain one way or another as to whether I'm the prince. I don't want to live a lie, and that's how I'll feel if I don't know for sure. Furthermore, I'm *not* going to steal the painting. I'm going to photograph it, prove I'm not the prince, then let Masolimia know where it is. I know my mother would have loved to return triumphant to her country bearing that painting, with or without her tiara, but... honor first."

Her voice was gentle. "You've been doing a lot of thinking, haven't you?"

"Yes. Rather late in the day, I suppose. Initially I was just very angry, feeling manipulated from every direction. But I've calmed down since, and the old brain has kicked in."

He took her by her upper arms, a gentle grip. "You can't get involved in this, Serena. Please."

She was touched, very touched. But also very decided. "I'm already involved, and I intend to stay involved. But we've got to sort this out before I go back to work, or I won't have any time."

"What is it that makes a successful professional want to become involved in something so reckless, cockeyed and felonious?"

It was her turn to laugh, but more of an embarrassed

sound than a humorous one. "I was born to a reckless, cockeyed father. Perhaps even a felonious one. But he always insisted that life wasn't worth living unless you were willing to take risks. Part of me is very much like him. But I've allowed myself to get so buried in my work that…well…I feel I have less than half a life."

"You could take up skydiving."

She shook her head. "Been there, done that. Bungee jumping, too. The thing is, taking a risk simply to take a risk isn't very satisfying. I'm not an adrenaline junkie."

"Pity. That would make your life easier."

"Undoubtedly." She laughed then.

That was when he leaned in and kissed her.

If their previous kiss had been one to which God might aspire, this was one to make even Satan blush. From the first instant that their lips met, Serena wanted to be taken, possessed, turned inside out by his mouth, his eyes, his breath, his arms. A low moan began to rise from her belly.

And the doorbell rang.

CHAPTER THIRTEEN

"Sorry to interrupt," Ariel said, breezing in as if she owned the place and, worse, as if she knew exactly what Serena and Darius had been doing. "I have the answer."

And damnably impeccable timing, Darius thought. "Ahh, and what was the question?"

"Oh! Serena didn't tell you? That lady Gina, our muscleman's girlfriend? She works for the Masolimians. She's the office manager at the consulate."

"So they know." He turned to Serena. "You were planning to tell me this…when?"

"Umm…"

"I told her not to mention it," Ariel said. "Until we could figure out what to do about it."

"Yes," Serena agreed. "Why dump a problem in your lap if we don't have a solution ready?"

This was, of course, an obvious fiction. He thought about saying as much, and even opened his mouth to do so, then decided that it was two against one—and particularly *these* two against him. There was nothing to be gained. And, given what he'd seen in Serena's eyes only a few minutes earlier, perhaps much to be lost.

"So what's the solution?" he asked in resignation.

"Well," Ariel said, settling onto one end of the sofa, "as it stands right now, they think we're working for them without knowing we're working for them."

"Right," Darius agreed.

"But if you think about it, it could as easily be the other way around. They could be working for us, without knowing they're working for us."

"And how is that?" Serena asked.

"Look," Ariel said, her eyes almost flashing with excitement, "we've all been a bit skittish about the crime-cops-prison issue."

"To say the least," Darius said.

"But these two consulate guys, they don't have to worry about that. They're diplomats."

"Which says a lot about Masolimia," Darius said. "And nothing complimentary."

"Perhaps," Ariel agreed. "Although in my experience, people often have surprising strengths and talents, waiting to be unveiled."

Once again, Darius found himself distinctly unnerved by this woman. *In my experience,* she said. She was…what…barely out of high school? And yet, something in her eyes, and the words she'd chosen, touched a chord. He himself had more than once been pleasantly surprised by someone whom he'd originally written off as incompetent. Who was to say Mas and Menos couldn't do likewise?

SUE CIVIL-BROWN   159

"So...they would have diplomatic immunity?" Serena asked.

"I think so," Darius said. He looked at Ariel, who nodded for him to continue. "You told Gina what painting we were after, right?"

"Yes," Serena said, glancing down.

"No, that's good!" he said. It was as if Ariel had intentionally given him an opportunity to bring a smile to Serena's face. And that smile made him glow in a way he could not quite describe, and had never felt before. "Mas and Menos undoubtedly know the *Rotunda*'s provenance. They know it rightfully belongs to the Masolimian people."

"Which means they're going to try to recover it," Ariel said. "And they'll be doing that as official agents of the Principality of Masolimia."

"So they can't be prosecuted?" Serena asked.

"The worst that can happen is that their credentials are revoked and they're expelled," Darius said. "In short, they get sent back to Masolimia."

"I'm still not sure how this helps *us*," Serena said. "If *they* get the painting, we're no better off than we are now. Right?"

"Ahhhhhh," Ariel said. "That's the really neat part. *Then* we steal it. From the consulate!"

"Huh?" Serena asked.

Ariel turned to Darius now. "The consulate is technically Masolimian territory. Everyone thinks you're the prince of Masolimia. So we steal it from Masolimian soil. While we're poring over it to trace the bloodlines, you *accept* the throne…for long enough to officially pardon yourself and everyone else involved. If it turns out you're the prince, fine. If not, you do the honorable thing and abdicate in favor of the rightful heir. So…"

"Nobody goes to jail!" Serena said.

"Exactly!" Ariel agreed.

Darius thought for a moment. "Now all we need is a way to make sure Mas and Menos go after the painting…"

"And succeed," Ariel added.

"Yes," he said. "And succeed."

Serena nodded. "And without their knowing we're involved."

"Right," Ariel agreed.

"Right," Darius echoed.

"So how do we do that?" Serena asked.

Darius smiled. It was perhaps the first truly devious smile of his entire life. "What are moms for?"

IT DIDN'T TAKE HIM LONG to locate her. She was of course staying at her favorite hotel on the Riviera, and despite the hour, the clerk put him straight through to her room. Because it was three in the morning there, it never occurred to Maria Teresa to wonder how he'd tracked her down. In fact, at first she was hardly awake enough to recognize his voice.

"*Mamacita,*" he said, deliberately using the endearment she so despised, "I have a plan."

"Huh?" Or perhaps it was more of a groan. Either way, it seemed to contain a wordless question.

"Yes, I have figured it all out! I am going to have you out of captivity within a few days."

Now she seemed to wake up. "You are?" Her voice suddenly trilled with delight. "You'll rescue me?"

"How could you ever doubt it, *mamacita?* Of course I shall save you."

"Oh, my beloved son!" In her excitement, her voice reached heights that could shatter glass, not to mention mere eardrums. "You will take the throne."

"Actually, Mother, I'm going to prove I'm *not* the prince. Then they'll have to let you go."

Maria Teresa fell silent for a long moment. He stifled a chuckle. This clearly wasn't what she wanted, but that was the whole point.

Finally she spoke. "The catacombs…"

"Mother, the catacombs are old. A wall might have collapsed. Who knows how accurate they are now? But there is a map—the one map ever made—and I know where it is."

She gasped. He could imagine her hand fluttering to her heart. "You've found the *Rotunda?* Our priceless treasure?"

"I have." He smiled into the phone. "And I'm going to steal it for you, Mother. You can return it to Masolimia and become a cultural heroine, and I'll be able to prove once and for all that I'm not the prince."

Silence reigned. He waited, allowing her to stew,

knowing she was already trying to concoct counter-measures. Then, after an expensive two minutes or so of transatlantic dead air, he prompted, "Aren't you proud of me?"

He was quite sure that at this moment she would have liked to strangle him. But instead she cooed, "I am always proud of you, my brilliant Darius. This is wonderful beyond belief! The *Rotunda!*"

"Yes, isn't it? And I shall have it in my hands in two or three days."

"So," Maria Teresa said confidentially, "tell me all about your little plan."

The hook was set. Grinning, Darius told her everything he wanted her to know.

JUAN MAS CRINGED as the voice of Maria Teresa Maxwell thundered from the Riviera, through fiber optic cables beneath the Atlantic, and finally into the deepest, most tender nerves in his brain.

"*Sí,*" he said, for perhaps the five thousandth time in this brief conversation. If Torquemada had had a telephone and this woman, the Spanish Inquisition would have been equally effective and much less gruesome. Or perhaps more so. "*Sí,* Señora Maxwell! We know he is planning to steal the painting! We have it all figured out. We're going to wait for him to steal it, kidnap him, recover the glorious *Rotunda,* and force him to accept the throne!"

"No-no-no-no-no!" the voice yelled.

Perhaps he should explain to her that she did not have to shout to be heard. Or perhaps not.

"But Señora Maxwell…" he began. As if he had the remotest chance of completing the thought.

"You *can't* let him go after that painting!" she said. "First, he'll bungle the job and land in prison. Alas, he isn't cut out for criminal enterprises. Even if he gets lucky and does somehow pull it off, it may turn out that he's right. The painting may prove he's not the prince. And that simply will not do!"

She had a point. Two points, actually. Knowing her, she had another three or four waiting in the wings.

"*Sí*, Señora Maxwell. *Comprendo.*"

"So *you* have to steal it," she said. "And you'd better do it fast. Before he has a chance to try."

"*Sí*," Juan said, resignation burrowing into every fiber of his being like termites invading a fallen log.

"Now listen," Maria Teresa said. "He's told me his entire plan. It's actually quite brilliant. So you won't have to strain what passes for your brain to come up with a better one. You can use his plan and his people."

"Of course," Juan said. "But how do I get his people to work with me?"

"That's the wonderful part," she said. "The bimbo who works there…"

"Gina?"

"Yes, Gina. Anyway, my son described the man he's planning to use for the heavy lifting, and I'd swear it was Gina's boyfriend."

"*Sí!* It is!" Juan said.

"Perfect. So, have Gina go along when Darius gets everyone together to plan the heist. He'll tell you the whole plan. Then…you do it without him!"

Diplomatic immunity. Mas wondered if it was any good when one committed a theft. "*Sí,*" he said, his spine crumbling like the rotten wood it was.

"IT'S ALL SET," Darius told Serena and Ariel. "My mother is doing her usual thing. So now we will need your friends to cooperate with Mas and Menos, and Gina, as well."

"Well, Lead Legs is obviously no problem," Serena said. "He'll probably do anything Gina tells him to. As for getting Sparks and Marco to cooperate…they were already willing to cooperate. I don't see why that should be a problem as long as we let them know what's happening. As long as they know we're really running things."

"Ah, yes. Running things." Darius looked dubiously at the two of them. "Which of us is going to be in charge? Because I certainly haven't been allowed much input into this great scheme the two of you have contracted."

Serena felt her cheeks heat. They *had* rather steamrolled him with Ariel's wacky plan. And worse, she had kept important information from him. She didn't quite know how to apologize, either, since her transgression seemed…horrific, now that it was out in the open. Darius had more at stake here than any of them, and he should certainly never have been kept out of the loop on anything.

Ariel, for once, had very little to say. In fact, she had nothing to say.

"I think," Darius said, "that from this point on I should be in charge."

Ariel looked at Serena. Serena looked at Ariel. "Of course," Serena said.

"Of course?" He looked stunned by her easy capitulation.

"Of course," she repeated.

"Good," he said finally, clearly having accepted that he hadn't misheard. "Give your friends Sparks and Lead Legs a call. Tomorrow morning we case the joint. We go—that is, *they* go—Thursday night."

CHAPTER FOURTEEN

"WE CAN'T DO THIS," Serena said the following morning as she and Darius stood outside the museum in St. Petersburg. Traffic bustled by on the busy avenue while they waited for Lead Legs and Sparks to show up. Ariel had ducked out of this trip, claiming she needed to register for school.

Darius looked at her, one eyebrow lifted. "Cold feet?"

"Blocks of ice."

"But I thought you were so gung ho."

Damned if he didn't appear to be enjoying himself immensely. "I was. But somehow the closer I get to a felony the worse I feel."

"Well, you're not going to commit anything. Our dubious consulate employees will be doing most of the work."

"Oh, great. Darius, look at the place."

Obediently he turned and looked at the four-story building, concrete mainly, with a glass front at street level. "It does rather...resemble a prison."

"It looks like a fortress!"

"Fortresses, my dear, do not boast glass walls. Trust me, this will all be fine."

"Hmm."

He merely smiled.

Lead Legs showed up at last, a massive man with surprisingly small feet. In tow, of course, was the beautiful raven-haired Gina, who wore a knit top cut so low that the word *cleavage* took on new definition.

Darius greeted her pleasantly, even bowing over her hand. She fumed. Men were all the same, she thought. Show them a little décolletage and they suffered instantaneous brain death.

Since it was Florida, Lead Legs had chosen to show up in shorts and a tank top that revealed every tanned, bulging muscle. Gina, similarly dressed, was guaranteed to draw every eye in the building. Not exactly a covert operation, Serena thought sourly. These two would be remembered for years by the museum staff.

Then Sparks showed up. He peered at the world from behind thick glasses, and Serena was instantly sure that his lengthy beard and excessively long hair were not a fashion choice, but the result of forgetfulness. He wore a pair of khaki shorts that looked as if they'd been pulled out of the bottom of a laundry hamper, and a Hawaiian shirt that had not only seen better days, it had seen better years.

She began to wonder if they were even going to be allowed inside. Well, she and Darius would, since they wore business clothes. Darius in his usual suit with a natty ascot, she in a navy-blue skirt-suit and pumps.

Entirely too hot for standing on the pavement like this in one of Florida's abysmal winter heat waves.

"So we're all here," Darius said pleasantly, as if addressing the members of the board of a major corporation.

"Where's Ariel?" Sparks asked.

"She had to register for school," Darius answered smoothly. "Never fear, we'll keep her up-to-date."

"So what are we gonna do?" Gina demanded.

"We're here to, ah, case the joint. My cover is that I'm an art dealer here to do business. That will get me, and Serena, into the back offices without much trouble. Sparks, I want you to eyeball the electronic security, see what you can figure out for us. Mr. Levine, you and your young lady look around as much as you can manage. We need to find the best way to the storeroom on the second floor. We also need to get an idea of the habits of the security guards, how often they make rounds, and if possible how many are on duty at night."

"No prob, man," Sparks said. "These dudes like to talk."

Serena had her doubts, but kept them to herself. This whole thing had moved from the realm of imagination into the realm of reality, and her heart was hammering like the piston on an overworked engine. Why, oh, why hadn't she ever learned a sane way to cope with boredom?

"Afterward," Darius said, "we'll meet back at my

place to finalize the plan." He passed them each his business card, which to Serena's way of thinking was as good as handing the cops your fingerprints and your photo.

As the others began to move inside, she pulled Darius aside. "You shouldn't have given them your business card!"

"What difference does it make? Gina already knows who I am. But never fear, I'll collect them all when we get together at my place."

"Keystone Kops," she muttered under her breath, and began to think she might go back to work tomorrow, before she got into this any deeper. Had she lost her everloving mind?

Apparently so.

By the time she and Darius entered the museum, Sparks had disappeared somewhere into the bowels of the place, and Gina and Lead Legs were staring at a piece of cubist art as if it held all the secrets of the universe. Making a pretense at being art lovers.

Except that, as she passed, she heard Lead Legs say, "Devon was never one of the better cubists, Gina. He's more of a curiosity than a treasure."

"How come?"

"His balance and energy are always a little askew. Unsatisfying. In fact, I think he probably painted the most unsatisfying paintings in the entire history of art."

Startled, Serena glanced at Darius. His eyes gleamed back at her, seeming to dance with humor. "A lot of critics would agree with him," he murmured.

Good heavens, Serena thought. Lead Legs Levine, former boxer, current chef, was also an art connoisseur?

"Wait until he sees the *Rotunda*," Darius continued as he led her toward the reception desk at the rear. "He'll be mortally offended."

"It's that bad?"

"Let's just say the painting is on a par with Masolimian wool, which is useful only for stuffing mattresses. I hear it has about the same texture—and color—as dried Spanish moss."

"Oh."

"The artist had delusions of his own greatness. Apparently he persuaded a sufficient number of his contemporaries to join his delusion, and for a while reigned supreme in the Masolimian art world, which consisted, I believe, of two painters and a bunch of equally delusional courtiers."

A laugh nearly bubbled out of Serena, but they were within two steps of the reception desk. Within two steps of committing their deception. The realization sobered her up faster than a bath of ice water.

"Good afternoon," Darius said in his most urbane born-to-royalty accent. He proffered his card to the young woman at the desk. "I happened to be passing by and thought I might stop in to speak with your curator or business manager."

The receptionist looked at the card, looked at Darius, then said, "Please, have a seat. I'll see if Mr. Roache has a moment."

"Thank you."

The young woman disappeared through a door behind her desk, and Darius murmured, "He'll have a moment. In fact, he'll have a number of moments."

"How can you be so sure?"

He smiled and led her to the leather chairs. "Trust me, I am not unknown."

Apparently not. Almost before their bottoms met leather, a short man of middle years came hurrying through the door, the receptionist on his heels.

"Monsieur Maxwell," he said, beaming. "What an honor this is!"

"I'm truly flattered," Darius said, with a self-deprecating smile that would have charmed the scales off a cobra. "It's delightful to be here in St. Petersburg."

This time Roache gave his own self-deprecating smile, which might have charmed the scales off a garter snake. If the garter snake were sleepy. And bored.

"Well, the museums in this St. Petersburg don't rival the Hermitage, but we do our best," Roache said.

"Art is where you find it," Darius replied.

It was, Serena thought, rather like watching two fencers—one very skilled, the other a raw amateur—playing with feather dusters.

"So," Roache said after a pause, "what brings you to our little city?"

"I have a commission on a Monet. A friend in France has run upon financial misfortune and wishes to sell it.

He visited here a couple of years ago and was favorably impressed. He mentioned your name."

Roache beamed with self-satisfaction. *Touché,* Serena thought, suppressing the urge to giggle.

"Yes, yes," Roache said. "Well, of course I'd be interested. Although our endowment is…well, let us discuss particulars in my office."

With that, they were ushered back into the offices. Darius's eyes flitted about, obviously taking in details that were beyond Serena's grasp. What she did notice were the electronic keypads and motion detectors. They were obvious. It was the less-than-obvious that worried her.

Roache's office was functional, almost institutional. Serena had probably sat in these same gray-fabric chairs in a hundred different offices in the past ten years. On one wall, a dry-erase calendar set out the featured exhibits for the coming months. Behind his desk, a corkboard sported a colorful panoply of telephone messages, memos, take-out menus, and other detritus, affixed with green, yellow, red and blue pushpins. If she let her vision go a little fuzzy, it was almost reminiscent of a Jackson Pollock work. The most artistic touch—if it could be called that—was a Van Gogh calendar she herself had almost bought at a local discount store. All in all, decidedly unimpressive.

"For a relatively new museum," Darius said smoothly after they were all seated, "you've developed quite a name, Monsieur Roache. I dropped by a few weeks back and took a brief tour of the Castellan exhibit. As a curator, you're without equal."

Roache swelled with pride, and beamed at Darius. "Thank you, thank you. As you know, the Castellan exhibit was on loan from New York."

"Yes, yes, but your arrangement of the works…a touch of brilliance, I must say. Each area of the exhibit presented a mood that was at once soothing and absorbing, rather than jarring as it might have been if done otherwise."

Roache was in danger of popping his buttons, his chest had swelled so. "It was a daring thing," he said confidentially, lowering his voice. "Some art historians were gravely annoyed."

"Well, *I* think it was a stroke of genius," Darius said firmly. "Art is to be enjoyed and admired, and your presentation enhanced the enjoyment of the experience."

"Merci, merci."

Serena believed that at that instant Darius could have asked this man to turn over the *Rotunda* and Roache probably would have tripped over his own feet in his eagerness to comply.

But of course, Darius did nothing so crass. "In any event, after I checked out the exhibit, I informed my client of how you had chosen to organize it. He was quite impressed. Consequently, he feels his Monet would be in better hands with you."

Roache was still beaming, and now he practically salivated. "A Monet would be an exquisite addition to our collection."

"And, as I said, he's being forced to sell. So…there may be some negotiating room on the price. However…"

At this point Roache was practically hovering over his desk in his excitement, leaning forward and barely seeming to touch either his seat or the floor. "Yes?"

"My client *is* concerned about privacy. And about security. You see, he doesn't want it to be known he was forced to sell a family heirloom. At the same time he wants to know that wherever it goes it will be safe. Now, he knows the Metropolitan Museum of Art in New York would provide sufficient security, but insufficient anonymity, if you follow me."

Roache nodded eagerly. "Oh, I know exactly what you mean. Such an acquisition would be touted throughout the art world, and because so many at the museum would be aware of it, particularly since the purchase would have to be approved…" He nodded. "Here I can assure your client privacy. Indeed, if he wishes, we will store the painting until some future date of his choosing."

"How very generous. No one would object?"

Roache shook his head violently. "Absolutely not. We are already doing this with an endowment. I'll be glad to show you, if you like."

"I would, yes. And the matter of security?"

Roache waved his hand and smiled, his expression very like that of an alligator that believes dinner will not escape. "I will be more than happy to show you our security arrangements, Monsieur Maxwell."

As easy as that, Serena thought, feeling dazed.

CHAPTER FIFTEEN

THE GROUP REGATHERED that evening in Darius's condominium to share their discoveries and plan the break-in. An inveterate host, Darius had provided trays of meats, cheeses and vegetables with an assortment of dipping sauces and breads, and some bottles of very fine wine.

Serena couldn't believe her eyes. As if this were a party, and not the planning session for a major crime! The urge to laugh nearly overtook her, especially when it became evident that Lead Legs was torn between admiring the paintings on the walls and easels, and evaluating the food, particularly the sauces.

Gina settled into one corner of the couch, a plate of vegetables in hand, and began to survey the paintings. Serena could almost see the abacus behind her eyes totalling up the value of the assembled artwork.

Impulsively she took Darius's arm and urged him aside.

"Yes?" he said pleasantly.

"Do you realize what you've done?" she whispered fiercely.

"What?"

"You've invited a gang of thieves into your home… where they can see all your priceless paintings."

He raised an eyebrow. "But they're *my* gang of thieves."

Serena rolled her eyes, but Darius was already turning away, recommending the shrimp and artichoke dip to Lead Legs. "It's quite the best I've ever tasted," he said.

Lead Legs spooned a small amount onto a plate, then dipped his finger into it and tested it with his tongue. His eyes closed, and he rolled the small bit of dip around in his mouth as if it were fine wine.

"Exquisite," he pronounced.

"I'm glad you approve," Darius said with all the gravity of a major diplomatic exchange.

Serena began to experience an urge to run before the absurdity of these moments grew any worse.

But of course, Sparks hadn't arrived yet. Nor Ariel. Serena wondered if Ariel had wisely decided to bail out before this conspiracy moved to the point of indictment.

But as if summoned by her thoughts, the doorbell rang, then Ariel stepped in before anyone could so much as rise from a chair. "Hi, everyone," she said brightly.

"Ariel," Darius said, moving forward to greet her.

"Darius, I'm sorry I couldn't join you this morning."

"Who's she?" Gina demanded. Serena couldn't tell if she was more irritated by the arrival of someone new, the fact that Darius's door was obviously unlocked or the fact that Ariel looked absolutely stunning this evening.

"Our mastermind," Darius said smoothly. "When there's a problem, Ariel always finds the solution."

Ariel looked embarrassed. "Not really. Serena's responsible for a lot of it."

"Thanks," Serena couldn't help saying acidly. "Remind me to put you on the witness stand in my behalf."

Ariel laughed. "Well, it's the truth. Just ask Darius." She hurried over to the buffet and picked up a plate. Before long it was heaping with a bit of everything. "Wonderful buffet," she said, smiling.

Serena cast an eye on Darius. He held up his hands as if to deny everything. "Trust me. Under oath I'll swear you knew nothing at all."

That didn't make her feel any better. "Do you often lie under oath?"

"I've never had a reason to before." His eyes danced.

"Humph." His character was beginning to appear shaky, if not downright amoral.

"Where's the other guy?" Gina demanded. "Let's get this going."

"Yes," Darius said. "I may as well get out the blueprints."

Lead Legs shook his head. "I've built a three-dimensional model of the museum. Much more useful."

Everyone looked at him. "Wow," said Gina. "Where is it?"

"Right outside the door." He beamed. "Shall I get it?"

"Oh, the box outside," Ariel said. "I meant to mention it."

Seconds later Lead Legs brought a huge box into the room, balancing it as if it contained something extremely fragile.

"Wonderful," Darius said, "but before we get to that, let's start with the blueprints. The model will be perfect for planning our movements, but the blueprints will be of more help with the security problems."

Lead Legs looked disappointed, but he nodded. "Okay." He set the box carefully on the kitchen counter.

Darius had set up two card tables in the middle of his living room floor. On them was a roll of blueprints and some paperweights. Serena helped him open the roll and weight the corners.

"How did you get these?" she asked him.

"Oh, all of this kind of thing has to be filed with the building inspector. Public documents, you know."

"Including the electronic security?"

"Alas, no."

"Oh."

At that precise instant, their electronics expert deigned to appear. Sparks was still wearing the same clothes he'd worn that morning, and looked even more rumpled, if that were possible.

"Hi, gang," he said, and headed straight for the food. "God, I haven't eaten since last night. Clean forgot to." The words were followed immediately by the sound of moving jaws as Sparks worked his way down the buffet, like a horde of locusts in a cornfield.

Darius looked amused. Settling onto the couch at

the far end from Gina, he crossed his legs and allowed a faint smile to play around the corners of his mouth.

He was enjoying this entirely too much, Serena thought. Perhaps he had an instinctive criminal nature. What an appalling thought.

Finally, however, giving herself up to the pace of the evening, whatever it might be, seemed the only thing to do. She settled onto a chair and waited for the locusts to devour the food.

"All right," said Sparks, turning from the buffet. "I can knock out the electronic security like that." He snapped the fingers of his free hand, but they were evidently greasy and made no sound. As naturally as could be, he wiped them on his shorts and tried again. This time a squishy snap could be heard. It was enough to satisfy Sparks.

"How so?" Darius asked.

"Lightning."

"Lightning?"

Sparks nodded and stuffed half a fried chicken thigh into his mouth.

"You know," remarked Lead Legs from the center of the couch where he had taken up station like a brick wall between Gina and Darius, "you'd enjoy your food more if you slowed down."

"Man, eating just takes up time."

Darius cleared his throat. "Are you planning to conjure a storm at precisely the right time? And of course, direct a lightning bolt at the security system?"

Sparks smiled. Serena had to look away. No manners. Absolutely not a single one in his repertoire.

"Sparks," said Ariel, "I'll give you a doggie bag to take home as much food as you want. But *please* stop talking with your mouth full."

Silence reigned for a pregnant moment. Everyone in the room seemed to be trying to look at anything except Sparks.

"Lightning?" Darius finally prompted.

"Oh, yeah. Well, it's really simple. You know how your phone gets fried sometimes during an electrical storm?"

Everyone nodded.

"Well, it's not usually cuz lightning struck the phone line."

Now looks were exchanged.

"I'm not kidding," said Sparks.

"But how?" Serena asked.

"If the lightning hit the phone line, the damn thing would be fried. It wouldn't come back up in a few minutes when you drag your old phone out of the closet and plug it in. The phone company would be all over the place, replacing cables, tearing your house up, driving you nuts…"

"We get the idea," Gina said impatiently.

Sparks looked at her, his eyes nearly invisible behind his thick lenses, but there was no mistaking that he nearly salivated at the sight. Lead Legs reached out and took Gina's hand with unmistakable possessiveness.

Sparks swallowed and directed his gaze elsewhere.

"Lightning," Darius prompted again.

"Oh. Yeah. Okay." Sparks seemed to be grappling with disorganized thoughts. After a moment he corralled them again. "Right. Well, the reason your phone gets fried is because the charge in the atmosphere somewhere near the phone lines sets up a strong current inside the line. And that current is enough to zap your phone without burning out the wires."

Serena thought about it. "Makes sense," she said finally.

"Of course it makes sense. My God, think of the voltage in a stroke of lightning. If it hit the lines, they'd burn right out for good. If it hit your phone, the thing would probably go into a meltdown. In fact, I know it would. This guy was on the phone once when lightning actually did hit the line. It not only zapped him good, it melted the phone."

Darius shifted. "I believe you. And this takes us where?"

"It's simple. I can't zap the outside phone lines. They're fiber optic these days. But the entire security system runs on electrical impulses. Break a contact and the alarm goes off because the circuit is interrupted. All I have to do is create a magnetic field strong enough to keep the lines full of current."

"Can you do that?" Serena asked.

"Sure." He grinned. "It's a snap. There isn't a whole lot of juice running through the alarm system. I worked out the calculations. With a few car batteries and some coils of copper wire, I can keep the system juiced so it doesn't know if you open every circuit in the place."

Darius rubbed his chin. "That easy?"

"That easy. And the machines are almost finished." Sparks grinned again.

And they all looked at him in awe. Sort of.

He grabbed his plate again and resumed eating.

Chomp-chomp-chomp.

"OKAY," DARIUS SAID, assuming command of the gathering once more. "That takes care of electronic security. One of the things I discovered this morning is that there are no motion detectors. I, of course, expressed my concern about this lack, but Monsieur Roache assured me they are unnecessary because of our next hurdle—the security guard." He looked at them, one after another. "The *armed* security guard."

"Oh, no," said Serena. Her hand fluttered to her throat.

"It's all right, my dear," Darius said reaching over to squeeze her hand. "We'll deal with him somehow."

"How?"

Darius squeezed her hand again, trying to put as much reassurance into the touch as he could. "Gina," he said.

Gina sat up straighter, which had the effect of reminding all the men in the room of her great endowments. "Me?" she squeaked.

Inside, Darius wanted to laugh. The little two-timer had probably expected she could keep her nose entirely clean. Well, he wasn't going to have it. "Yes, you," he said. "You could distract any man on the face of the planet."

"Oh." In an instant she was preening.

"It's true," said Lead Legs, suddenly looking like a marshmallow instead of a muscle-bound threat.

"Aww, sweetie…" She dabbed at the corner of her eye. Whether the tear was real or pretend, Darius had no idea. Nor at this point did he care. The entire purpose of this exercise was to get Mas and Menos to do the dirty work and escape under diplomatic immunity, thus sparing everyone involved. He didn't want to see anyone in jail. However, from what he knew of Mas and Menos, the two were barely capable of getting out of bed without direction. Hence the need for Gina, who was dragging them into this, anyway.

"The thing is," Darius continued, "you can distract the security guard."

"How?"

"Claim you're being followed. He'll let you inside to protect you. Then you have to keep him distracted long enough for us to get past him to the storage room and back out again."

"Now wait one minute," Lead Legs said, his brow lowering thunderously.

"Sweetie," Gina said, her voice soothing.

"She's not a, not a…"

"I know she's not," Darius said smoothly. "I'm not asking her to do anything improper."

For a few more seconds Lead Legs looked as if he wanted to rip Darius limb from limb, and Darius had to admit to feeling a minor qualm. He might have been the best boxer in his class at Eton, but blood lust hadn't been involved in those matches.

But then Lead Legs began to relax.

"Trust me, sweetie," Gina said soothingly. "I can deal with any man on this planet. I'll get him out of the way and keep him from calling the police. And I can do it all without doing anything that would upset you."

She rubbed his arm and nuzzled his shoulder, and soon Lead Legs was a lost man. Darius felt sorry for him. He wondered if the man had any idea just how he was going to be manipulated for the rest of his life.

But it was plain to him that Gina was thrilled to have a leading role in the break-in. Which she would have had anyway, since she was planning to do it with Mas and Menos *before* his own group could act. But she seemed to like being the center of attention right now, and being a designated kingpin.

He looked at Serena and found himself appreciating all the more her concern for everyone involved. Instead of finding her qualms annoying, he found them charming and touching. She really didn't want to see anyone go to jail. Yet she was willing to go ahead with this plot to save him. Very special indeed.

Sparks was beginning to make yet another trip along the buffet. Darius was glad he'd bought enough food and drink for an army.

"So," he said. "Down to the details."

"Yes," Lead Legs said. "Let's look at my model."

With a flourish he opened the box.

CHAPTER SIXTEEN

"It's a cake," Sparks said.

"Yes," Lead Legs said, pride evident in his voice. "It's also an exact scale model of the museum."

Sparks nodded. "So…we eat our way in."

In any other context, Serena thought, that might have sounded absurd. But having watched Sparks at the buffet, well…

"Honey, it's beautiful!" Gina said, leaning forward to look and, in so doing, gathering the eyes of every male in the room to her bosom. "How did you do these glass doors?"

Lead Legs glowed. "Confectioner's glass. Very, very thin sheets of clear candy."

"Wow," Gina said.

It was impressive, Serena had to admit. He'd obviously spent a lot of time on this. What's more, he'd obviously done it to impress Gina. *Ahh,* she thought, *the things we do for love.*

That thought raised an interesting question in her own mind. Was she any different? She remembered the kiss she and Darius had shared on the balcony. She'd rationalized reasons for this enterprise again and again, but might the real reason have nothing to do with boredom or a desire to save the people of Masolimia? Might the real reason simply be that it was an excuse to be with Darius Maxwell?

As if reading her mind—and, damn it, that girl did that way too often—Ariel met Serena's eyes and said, "How sweet."

Lead Legs obviously took it as a compliment for his work, which it probably was, Serena realized. He offered a surprisingly gracious "Thank you," which Ariel answered with a brief but sincere nod.

And her eyes never left Serena's. Finally, feeling as if she were naked, Serena had to look away. "So, okay, how do we start?"

"Well," Lead Legs said, reaching back into the box, "I have some more visual aids."

He withdrew a smaller box, which he opened to reveal scale candy sculptures of the participants. Serena was not surprised to see that the sculpture of Gina was the most beautiful of all, clad in either a white tennis dress or a very short, revealing wedding dress. She suspected he'd had both thoughts in mind when he'd made it.

"Gina is supposed to distract the guard, yes?" he asked.

"That's the plan," Darius agreed.

Conveniently, Lead Legs had also sculpted a uniformed security guard, whom he placed at the museum door alongside the Gina. "So, they're there. What else?"

Ariel looked at Sparks. "Where will you be?"

"There's a parking garage across the street. I'd set up there, in my van. So that would put me…here." He placed the model of himself on the coffee table near the cake. "Yeah, right there. I can do it from there."

"And the rest?" Lead Legs asked.

"Well, we really only need three more people," Darius said. "Two of us to go in—I'm assuming that will be you and me, Mr. Levine—and someone in a getaway car outside."

He'd suggested going in with Lead Legs as sincerely as if that were his actual plan, though Serena knew better. Even as Gina nodded her agreement, Serena could see the wheels turning behind those brown eyes. Mas and Menos would be the ones going in. It was perfect.

"We'll need walkie-talkies with earphones," Darius continued, "so Lead Legs can let Gina know when we're out and in the car. Then she excuses herself from the guard, looks outside, declares that she feels safe and crosses to the garage where she joins Sparks in his van."

Gina's face scrunched momentarily at that thought, as if she were imagining the mess on Sparks's passenger seat. But the moment passed and she nodded. "And we drive away at our leisure."

"Right," Darius said. "We meet up back here."

"Sounds perfect," Lead Legs said. "Except for the actual getting in and getting out parts. Perhaps we need a few more details there?"

"Well, of course," Darius said.

And with that, Lead Legs lifted the top layer from the

cake to reveal the interior layout of the museum, each wall and door rendered in carefully carved bundt cake. He set the top layer on the buffet tray. Not surprisingly, Sparks moved in for the kill.

"This is the lobby," Darius said, pointing while he looked at Gina. "And the front counter. That's probably where the guard will be. When you get inside, ask him for something to drink. You need a cup of coffee to calm your nerves, or whatever. He'll take you here, to the employee snack room."

Darius placed her model, and the model of the guard, in the snack room. It was, conveniently, quite far removed from the storage rooms.

"And I'll keep him occupied there," Gina said.

Lead Legs still didn't seem thrilled by that prospect, but he let it pass with a curt nod. "And how do we get in, Mr. Maxwell?"

"Through this door," Darius said, pointing to the back of the museum. "The entrance beside the loading doors."

"Isn't that a metal door?" Serena asked. "It's not as if you can just kick it in."

"True," Darius said. "And had we not visited the museum today, that would have been a problem. But we did, and if you recall, I had that sneezing fit from the dust in the storage room."

"Yes," Serena said, remembering.

It had been quite the performance. The room had been dusty, of course, as all storage rooms tended to be.

But he'd taken the sneeze to Oscar-quality levels. Of course, Roache had offered to open the door, so that Darius could step out onto the loading dock and clear his sinuses. All the while, Roache had borne the stricken look of a puppy whose food dish was being taken up out of reach. His eyes had virtually screamed the thought: *No! I can't lose this deal over a dust allergy!*

"You do remember that I offered to close the door on my way back in?" Darius said, smiling.

"Of course," Serena answered.

He nodded. "But you didn't see me squirt a few drops of superglue into the dead bolt. I closed the door, but I didn't turn the bolt closed. And now it won't close."

"That's fine," Serena said, "but I don't think it will help much. They've probably already called a locksmith to fix it. And worse, once the locksmith pries the mechanism open and sees it was bonded with superglue, they'll be on notice."

Darius offered her one of those smiles that made her heart skip a beat and her blood run cold, all in the same instant. He had entirely too many kinds of smiles, and they had entirely too much effect on her.

"I'm sure they'll get it fixed, once they notice it's broken. But I closed the door, and shook the knob to show that I'd locked it. Roache nodded, and led us out of the storage room, then made a big show of locking the inside storage room door. They're not expecting any deliveries until Monday, so I doubt anyone will check the back door until then. So...we have five days."

Gina had been nodding throughout, obviously taking in every detail of the plan. "So there's just a regular knob lock on that door right now?"

Darius nodded. "And not a very good one. A credit card should be sufficient to slip it. Sparks takes out the electronic security, so there'll be no alarm when we go in. You keep the guard busy. In. Out. Ten minutes, tops."

"And where exactly is the painting?" Lead Legs asked.

Something in his eyes sent a shiver of delight through Serena, though she wasn't sure what or why. She glanced over at Ariel, who merely smiled faintly, as if she already knew what was going to happen. Fey girl. She probably did know. She usually did.

"Here, in a crate," Darius said, pointing.

"In this crate?" Lead Legs said, touching one of the pulled-taffy models he'd built.

"Yes," Darius said.

"You're sure it's this one?" Lead Legs asked again.

"I'm quite positive. Yes, that one."

Lead Legs lifted the crate out and handed it to Gina. "I guess it's in that one, then."

Perhaps love truly is blind, Serena thought. Or perhaps Gina had been too distracted by her own thoughts to be following the nuances of the conversation. She merely looked at the model crate and nodded. "Good."

"*Very* good," Lead Legs said, smiling.

"Yes, it's a beautiful model," Gina said. She turned the crate over in her hand. "The taffy looks just like wood. Amazing."

"Yes," Lead Legs said, still smiling. "Amazing, what's in that crate."

"The painting," Gina said, nodding. "The lost treasure of Masolimia."

"Certainly a treasure," Lead Legs said, nodding eagerly.

The woman was either unbelievably dense, unbelievably distracted or unbelievably cruel, Serena thought. Even a blind man in a night fog could have seen what was coming.

"I wonder if he did a model painting," Ariel offered by way of suggestion.

"He just might have," Serena agreed.

"He's modeled everything else," Darius added, obviously having caught on, as well.

"Oh, all *right*," Gina said, and cracked open the taffy.

For a moment she didn't move. Didn't even breathe. Slowly her eyes rose to meet Lead Legs's.

He smiled. "Would you marry me?"

Gina upended the crate over her open palm. Out fell a diamond ring.

"Oh! Larry!"

Ariel glowed. Serena was almost sure she could see a shimmering aura around the young woman, one that probably matched the glow she felt in her own heart. Even Darius smiled wide.

"Yes!" Gina said.

"Yes?" Lead Legs asked.

"Yes!"

"Yes," Sparks agreed. "So that's settled. Can we eat the museum now?"

SERENA REMAINED after everyone else had departed. She kicked off her shoes and tucked her feet up beneath her while Darius brought her a cup of coffee.

"What do you think?" she asked.

Darius stretched out on the couch, propped up against the arm. "I think she's going to do it."

"How can you be sure?"

"Well, I can't be, of course. But I'm fairly certain. It was something about the way she attended to details when we did the walk-through. Remember, I'm an art dealer. I make my living in part by reading people. And my read on Gina is that she's going to advance the schedule, and dazzle Sparks into working with her and those two from the consulate. Judging by the way Sparks was looking at her, she won't have to dazzle him very much."

Serena nodded, but internally she felt a…pinch, for lack of a better word. A pinch in her heart as she thought of Gina. Compared to that woman, she was merely pretty. A blond dormouse with almost invisible curves. How could any man, including Darius, not drool over Gina?

No one had ever drooled over Serena. Never. She'd always been too bookish, too smart, too wacky. What a combination. Her own mother had told her not to let the boys know she had a brain, but to pretend that the boys were smarter. It hadn't worked.

Serena had rebelled at the whole idea of pretending to be something she wasn't just so a boy could feel like a big deal. It wasn't that she bragged when she aced the math and science tests—in fact, she never mentioned her grades—but she hadn't been able to bring herself to act as if she were wowed by some dork with the intelligence of a boiled peanut.

She sighed, lost in her thoughts.

"Something wrong?" Darius asked.

"No." She lied and smiled as if she meant it. "That Gina is really beautiful, isn't she?"

"If you like a full-blown rose. I personally prefer buds."

Something in his eyes made her heart slam. Suddenly frightened, she looked down at the cup in her hands. Never in her life had a man served her coffee in a bone china cup and saucer rimmed with gold. It was clearly a coffee cup, taller and narrower than a tea cup, but every bit as elegant.

She stole a look at Darius and found him still staring intently at her. Did she have something on her face? Nervousness made her hand tremble a bit. "These cups are beautiful," she said finally. Like him. Elegant.

"Thank you. I picked them up in New York last year. I like their simplicity."

But his eyes were saying something else. Serena felt her cheeks warm. "You…have good taste."

"Yes, I do." He smiled, a warm expression. "Taste is one thing I have in ample quantity."

"I'm sure you have other qualities."

"Oh, yes." The corners of his eyes crinkled as his smile deepened. "I'm loyal to a fault, once I give my loyalty. Which, I confess, I don't do too readily these days, having been stung more than once."

"Unfortunately that seems to be part of growing up."

"Yes, doesn't it?" His expression changed, the smile vanishing.

"I'm surprised you're not married."

He tilted his head to one side, his gaze once again seeming to penetrate her. "I could say the same about you."

"Oh…well…" She fumbled, embarrassed both that she had dared broach the subject and that she had no answer other than, I've never had the opportunity.

"I very nearly married once," he told her. One corner of his mouth lifted. "As I said, I'm loyal to a fault. I didn't believe my friends when they told me she was cheating. Until I found her in flagrante, as they say."

"Oh, I'm so sorry!" Her heart went out to him. She couldn't imagine how painful that must have been.

"I felt terribly stupid, I can tell you. But I'm not sorry. It taught me a few things, and later I was able to appreciate what a narrow escape I had."

She smiled gently. "You have a very positive outlook."

"What other kind is there to have?" He laughed and put his cup and saucer on the end table. "For example, I have every confidence that the *Rotunda* will have been stolen within the next thirty-six hours. And that within twenty-four hours after that we will have heisted it yet again."

"What if they ship it before then?"

"Trust me, my dear, I've considered all possibilities."

He rose and walked toward the kitchen, where he began cleaning up the evening's mess....which meant disposing of it into garbage bags. Serena immediately went to help him.

"You know," she said, "I'm feeling sorry for Lead Legs."

"I'm not." His eyes danced. "He's getting the woman of his dreams, and from what I saw of her this evening, she reciprocates fully."

"But he's going to be involved in this mess...."

He shook his head. "If I know people as well as I think I do, I can virtually guarantee you that Lead Legs won't even enter the museum."

"Why not?"

"Because if anyone is going to get caught in the process of this robbery, I can assure you, Gina intends it to be Señores Mas and Menos."

"How can you know that?"

"Call it instinct. I think that woman would very much like to give her employers a hard time. And it would only be a minor hard time, given their diplomatic immunity. No, I think she has it planned that they'll be the fall guys if anything goes wrong."

Serena passed him another paper plate. "I imagine you're right."

"Of course I'm right." He laughed, his dark eyes dancing. "Oh, this couldn't have worked out better if I'd been able to plan it this way."

Serena couldn't help but laugh with him. After all, one of those men from the embassy had tried to convince Darius that his mother had been kidnapped. He deserved a small bit of satisfaction.

"But what about Marco?" Serena asked, suddenly remembering the race car driver.

"I purposely didn't invite him tonight. I don't want him involved in Gina's toils. We'll need him to get away from the embassy, though."

Serena nodded. "Thank you. Sometimes I think I should never have asked him. He's a grandfather, for heaven's sake!"

"Don't worry, my lovely bud. He won't pay for *my* crimes. I promise."

My lovely bud. Every other thought flew out of her head. He had called her his lovely bud!

He touched her chin lightly with his forefinger then resumed the cleanup. "As for you," he said, "we're going to have to find a better way to deal with your fits of boredom. We can't have you turning decent men into felons for the rest of your life."

She didn't know whether to laugh or cry. She was still too stunned. Maybe it had been a slip of the tongue.

But maybe it hadn't.

CHAPTER SEVENTEEN

GINA WOKE EARLY in the morning beside Lead Legs, feeling better than she had ever felt in her life. The dear sweet man beside her had at last proposed marriage, and she held up her hand to admire the huge marquise-cut diamond that she was sure he had spent entirely too much on.

They were going to have to talk about practicing economy eventually, but not today. Today was golden, and her beloved Larry was going to become her husband just as soon as she could arrange the wedding.

But in the meantime she had to deal with this mess at the consulate. Turning, she dropped a gentle kiss on Larry's brow. Poor man needed his sleep. Tonight he would be cooking again, which meant he'd be going in to work at noon to prepare things, and he probably wouldn't escape the restaurant kitchen until nearly midnight. People had no idea how hard the great chefs worked.

But Gina did, and she loved her man all the more for it. Sometimes she wished she could be more like him, but the simple fact was, her job didn't pay her enough to work her cute little behind off. Once they were married, she would go to work for Larry, and they'd be together all day every day.

But right now she needed to marshal those two fools at the consulate. Masolimia, the country of her father's birth, needed rescuing, and neither Mas nor Menos were capable of dealing with any of it.

AT THE CONSULATE OFFICE the two squirrels were waiting for her, both of them looking rather hangdog.

Gina breezed in, tossing her purse and beach bag on the desk farthest from the door. "She called again?"

"Of course she called again," Menos moaned. "Three times during the night. How did she ever get my home telephone number?"

Gina didn't bother to tell him that she had given his number, and Mas's, to Maria Teresa simply so the woman wouldn't bother *her* all the time.

"Well, if she calls again, tell her we're going tomorrow night."

Mas shuddered. "So soon?"

"Sooner, even," Gina said. "We're actually going tonight."

Menos muttered something unintelligible in Spanish and hastily crossed himself. It was strange, thought Gina, how fast that man got religion when, for as long as she'd known him, he'd never set foot inside a church.

"Tonight," she repeated. "I have one little detail to take care of first. Then I'll come back here and tell you exactly what to do. Trust me, I have it all worked out. It'll be a walk in the park."

If either of them understood the English idiom, she neither knew nor cared. She had more important things on her mind.

Ten minutes later she emerged from the back room clad in a scandalous red bikini with a semisheer cover-up and red sandals with heels at least five inches high.

"How do I look?" she asked, twirling before them. Their dropped jaws gave her the only answer she needed. "I'll be back in an hour or so."

Menos shook himself partly out of his preoccupation with the delicacies practically spread before him. "You're going to the beach?"

"Nah. I don't have time for that this morning. No, I'm going to take care of something for tonight. When I get back, I want you both ready to get your instructions."

The men nodded as one, still virtually speechless.

Gina gave them a little wave, then went out to get into her car.

Sparks was next on her list. And she had absolutely no doubt she could bend him to her will.

ARIEL HAD TO SUPPRESS the giggle, lest she be found out. She'd expected Gina to show up at Sparks's place today. Thus, yesterday, she'd made arrangements to do some yard work for Sparks's elderly neighbors. The neighbors who had a lovely privacy fence, ideal for spying on a young man being bedazzled by a young woman.

And to give her credit, Gina certainly was dazzling. To Sparks she must've been a centerfold fantasy come to life. Tanned olive skin, raven-black hair, big brown eyes, luscious curves, and everything just packaged in that crimson bikini with matching high-heeled sandals, ever-so-slightly and thus more enticingly hidden beneath a gauzy white cover-up. Ariel nodded. Exactly what she'd imagined Gina wearing. Funny how that worked out.

AT THAT MOMENT Sparks was still trying to breathe life into his jaw muscles, lest it hang slack through the entire conversation. He simply nodded as Gina made her pitch to move the job up a few days…and do it without Darius.

"You understand this treasure is important to the people of Masolimia?" Gina asked, with the tiniest flick of her head that sent her hair flipping over one shoulder and her breasts jiggling.

Nod-nod-drool.

"So it's important that it be recovered by the government of Masolimia and not some art dealer who will merely sell it for a profit."

Nod-nod-drool.

"The painting was stolen, you know? Back in World War II. The people of Masolimia are merely getting it back."

Nod-nod-drool.

"So you'll help?"

Sparks was just about to nod again when his trans-mandibular joint sprang to life, and his jaw snapped shut. Yes, it was a stolen painting. Yes, it rightfully belonged to the people of Masolimia. Yes, yes, yes…

No. This woman had already had a boyfriend. A fiancé, in fact. A large fiancé. So while she may have appeared in his side lawn like an adolescent mirage, she was just that…a mirage. Ariel, however, was real. And Ariel would be profoundly disappointed with him if he were to double-cross her friends.

"But…" he began.

ARIEL'S MOUTH COMPRESSED to one side. Trust Sparks to get an attack of loyalty. It wasn't exactly surprising. He was a good young man, with a good heart, even if his head often was spinning away in an electronic galaxy far, far away. When he did visit earth, he did so with kindness and sincerity. And loyalty. All admirable qualities, in any other circumstance. But in this circumstance…

She closed her eyes to the scene and let her mind drift away into thought.

"I UNDERSTAND," Gina said. "You're quite taken with that young woman…what's her name?"

"Ariel."

"Yes. She's very pretty."

"Yes, she is. And very nice."

"She seems like it," Gina said, smiling. "And you'd

feel awful about letting her down. That's what you think you'll be doing, isn't it? Letting her down?"

"Not just letting her down," Sparks said, trying to pull his eyes from her cleavage to her face. "It would be a betrayal of her and her friends. Betrayal is wrong."

"You're right," Gina said. "If you betrayed Ariel, that would be very bad. But you're not betraying her, or her friends. You're actually helping them."

"How is that, exactly?" Sparks asked.

"What they're planning to do is illegal," Gina said. "My fiancé and Ariel's friend Darius…if they were to be caught…they'd go to prison."

Sparks had thought of that much already himself. But Ariel had never steered him wrong, in all the time he'd known her. He trusted her, for reasons he could not fully understand himself. He was sure she had a good reason, some worthwhile cause that justified the risk. That's why he'd gone along with this from the outset. But yes, there was the risk of prison.

"And if they got caught," Gina continued, "then the authorities would want to know how the security system was bypassed. How long do you think it would be before the cops got on to you?"

"Probably not very long," Sparks said. "I knew there were risks. But how is it any different your way?"

"Ahhh," Gina said, reaching out to brush a fingertip across his cheek. "See, that's the thing. My people are officers of the Masolimian Government. They couldn't go to jail. The worst that could happen is their diplomatic privileges would be revoked and they'd be expelled back to their homeland."

"Good for them," Sparks said. "That gets your fiancé and Mr. Maxwell out of danger. But it doesn't help me."

"Sure it does," Gina replied. "Because I'm sure the grateful government of Masolimia would be willing to offer political asylum to someone who'd helped to recover one of its priceless treasures. Really, Sparks, this is safer for everyone involved."

She had a point, Sparks thought.

GINA HAD A POINT, Ariel thought as she listened. Now she needed Sparks to soften that iron-clad loyalty of his, and realize that this really *was* the best way to get the painting out of the museum.

Blatant sex appeal hadn't worked, not that Ariel had expected it would. Appeals to Sparks's self-interest hadn't done the trick, either, not that Ariel had expected they would. But they'd set the stage for what she knew would work. She closed her eyes, listened and drifted off in thought once more.

"LOOK," GINA SAID. "Your friend Ariel, she seems genuinely fond of this Darius Maxwell. Not *that* way, but in a friendly way. And of course you know I'm fond of my Larry. As frightening as he appears, he's a soft, cuddly sweetheart of a man."

Sparks nodded.

"So we have two *decent* men, one of them my fiancé,

another the friend of someone you obviously care about, who will be putting themselves into considerable danger if they follow Maxwell's plan. If we do it my way, there's no risk for either of them. You won't be betraying Ariel. You'll be protecting her friend. And her, as well."

"Her?" Sparks asked.

He hadn't considered Ariel to be at risk here. She wasn't participating in the break-in.

"Yes, her," Gina said. "It's called conspiracy. She knows all about this plan. She's the one who recruited you to help, isn't she?"

"Well, yes, but…"

"That makes her as guilty of the crime as you or Larry or Maxwell," Gina said. "Ariel could go to jail if we do it Maxwell's way and things go wrong. And while she would never know it, *you* would know that you could have protected her, kept her out of danger. That would be an awful burden to carry in prison, don't you think?"

Sparks's heart squeezed.

ARIEL'S HEART SQUEEZED. She knew what he had to be thinking, what he had to be feeling. If she could have spared him this inner conflict, she would have. But she knew nothing less would have overcome his good nature. Blinking back tears, she listened.

"YOU'RE RIGHT," Sparks said. "I couldn't do that. Not to her. Not to your fiancé. Not to her friend. I'd feel terrible about it for the rest of my life."

"This really is the best way," Gina said, her face trying to offer comfort and solace. "For everyone."

"Yes," Sparks agreed. "So when do we go?"

"Tonight. If you can be ready."

He'd already done most of the fabrication on his Rube Goldberg machine. It would be a busy afternoon, but yes, he could manage.

"Okay then, tonight."

"Be in the parking garage at 10:00 p.m.," Gina said.

"Right," Sparks said. "On one condition."

"Yes?" Gina asked, her brow furrowed.

"When all of this is over, you let *me* tell Ariel what I did and why. I owe her that."

Gina smiled. "You are a dear young man."

ARIEL SMILED. Yes, Sparks, you are a dear young man. Dear beyond all words.

CHAPTER EIGHTEEN

"THEY'RE GOING TONIGHT," Ariel said, sitting at Serena's dining room table. "At ten o'clock."

Serena nodded and turned to Darius. "Just like you planned."

"Yes," he said, his face drawn.

Ariel's face, too, was heavy with tension. Serena had no doubt that her own was, as well. It was one thing to plan. It was another thing to know that in just six hours, people they knew would be going into harm's way. And something else again to know they themselves were going to turn those efforts on their ear twenty-four hours later. The heady excitement of the scheming and planning had given way to the solemn, daunting prospect of waiting.

"She's not such a bad woman," Ariel said absently, staring out the window. "Gina, I mean. She has a good heart, I think."

"You're probably right," Serena said, also looking out, watching pelicans flit over sun-speckled waves in search of food. Now and then one would rise up, flip over in midair, and plummet into the water, to emerge a moment later shaking its beak. "I'm sure you're right."

"What a sight we are," Darius said. "Sitting here like we're on death row."

"Yes," Ariel agreed.

"Yes," Serena echoed.

"I always hated waiting," he continued. "I remember my first really big acquisition. I'd been commissioned by a private collector who loved Renoir, and one had just come on to the market. Or we hoped it had."

Distracted, Serena looked over at him. "I don't understand."

He gave another of his patented European shrugs. "There's a lot of forgery in the art world. There are painters, brilliant painters, who spend their careers mastering the techniques and styles of the old masters and creating beautiful forgeries. Some even do originals in the style of a known master, mixing their own paints from authentic pigments, finding old canvases, the whole nine yards. Then they sign the master's name to the painting. Suddenly a beautiful, original work of art, which would have been worth a few hundred dollars at most, is worth a few million."

"Is that illegal?" Serena asked. "I mean, if it's an original painting, how is it a forgery?"

"It's not illegal," he said, "until they sign Monet's name to it. Or whomever's. But then the painting will be represented as an old master's, when in fact it's the work of a new, probably unknown artist. An artist whose work couldn't get a showing under his own name. It's sad, in a way, that the name on the painting matters more than the painting itself. But that's the way in the art world."

"So this Renoir?" Ariel asked. "Was it a forgery?"

Darius leaned back in his chair. "We didn't know. That was the thing of it. It wasn't cataloged, but a lot of authentic old paintings aren't. They were painted for a private sponsor and remained out of circulation, handed down through generations, until the descendents ran upon hard times and had to sell off family treasures. Then, for the first time, the painting enters the public world, and we in the art community have to figure out whether it's really an old master or simply a forgery."

"And there are things you can test for, I'm sure," Serena said. "Carbon-14 testing or some such?"

He nodded. "We can test the pigments, the canvas, even how many layers of paintings were done on a canvas. Artists often painted over other works. Ones they weren't satisfied with. It saved on materials."

He took a break to refill a glass with iced tea, then returned. "So, there I was, sitting in the foyer of a chemist's lab in Berne, reading Swiss financial magazines by the stack without paying them any attention, waiting, waiting, waiting. With a nervous client sitting beside me, popping mints in his mouth in rapid-fire succession."

"Had he put any money down yet?" Serena asked.

"Not a lot," Darius said. "Only my expenses, and of course he'd split the costs for the testing. But he'd fallen in love with the painting. I couldn't blame him. It was beautiful. Stunning. Alive. Beautifully preserved and cared for."

"So why not buy it, anyway?" Ariel asked. "If he was in love with it, I mean."

"I suspect he would have. But of course, not for the price he'd have paid for an authentic Renoir." He paused and chuckled. "In a way he should have been hoping it was a fake. Then he could have gotten a painting he adored for a far smaller price. But…to own a newly discovered Renoir…that was his dream. So he sat there, chewing on mints, until the entire room smelled like a candy factory. And I read. And we waited."

"So?" Serena asked. "Was it real?"

He nodded. "Every test we knew of confirmed it. So either it was an authentic Renoir, or the forger had done everything right, down to the age of the canvas and the kind of resin used for the varnish. Which is possible, if one has the right budget and enough diligence. But we and the lab pronounced it an authentic Renoir, and my client paid three million U.S. dollars for it. Of which I earned ten percent."

"And a reputation, I'd imagine," Ariel said.

He smiled almost sheepishly. "Yes, and a reputation. It established my career. And I've been scrupulous about protecting that reputation ever since."

His face darkened, and Serena could read the thought. "Until now," she said.

"Yes. Until now."

"Don't lose faith," Ariel said. "We're doing the right

thing, for the right reasons, in the right way. It will all work out fine."

Looking into her eyes, Serena found it impossible not to believe her. But there was believing, and then there was *believing*. And between, there was only waiting.

SPARKS WAS ALSO PLAYING the waiting game, watching as Gina walked up to the front doors of the museum and tapped on the glass. In his hand he held a remote control, based upon a common garage-door opener. He would push the button—disabling the museum's security—immediately after the guard let Gina in and before the guard was in a position to see his monitor console. Just in case there was any flicker in the sensors when his machine kicked in.

All of this, of course, assumed that Mas and Menos hadn't messed things up at the back of the museum. Sparks had put the override circuit in place earlier, but having met the principals in tonight's adventure, he was certain they would find something to do wrong. In the meantime he watched Gina, and waited.

FOR THEIR PARTS Mas and Menos had decided to spend the waiting time productively. Specifically, they argued about which of them should have to take the next call from Maria Teresa Maxwell.

"*¡La mujer está loca!*" Mas said. "And she's making me crazy, too. You have to take the next call."

"No," Menos said. "I endured an entire day of her while you were here scouting out a parking place. An entire day of sandpaper dragging over every nerve in my body. Even now, look!"

Menos held out a hand, which shook slightly. Then he pulled back his collar. "And look here! She's giving me hives. No. You take the next call."

Mas popped another antacid tablet, chewing furiously. "I'm going through half a bottle of these a day. Longlasting relief, ha! It lasts only until she calls again, or I remember the last call. My stomach feels like I've been swallowing razor blades."

"I'm ready to swallow razor blades," Menos said, "rather than talk to her again. It's *your* turn."

"No, it's *your* turn," Mas countered.

And so it went.

THE PLAN WENT AWRY almost from the moment Gina tapped on the door. She'd rehearsed this scene in her mind, exactly how she would smile at the guard, exactly how he would smile back, exactly how she would pose, exactly how he would leer, exactly what she would say, exactly how he would respond.

And all of those rehearsals had one, single, common, overriding thread. The guard was a man.

This guard wasn't.

Gina wasn't looking up into the acne-scarred face of a college student working extra hours to buy his girlfriend a pizza, nor at the grizzled, sagging jowls of a retiree who was supplementing his Social Security check. Instead, she was looking straight-on, or even down a little, into the clear blue eyes and almost-undetectably lined skin of a thirtysomething woman.

Time to change plans.

"Hi," Gina said, offering a mollifying, I'm-sorry-to-be-a-bother smile. "I hope you can…um…I think I'm being followed."

Gina angled her head back up the street, though of course no one was there when the woman peeked out.

"I'm probably being silly," Gina added.

"No," the woman said. "Not at all. I know the feeling. We can't be too careful."

That *we*, naturally, referred to the Eternal Sisterhood of Anxious Women, which included almost every female in the country and probably the world. It was an immediate us-against-the-big-bad-world bond, and the answer to a thousand age-old questions, such as why women go to the restroom in pairs.

It wasn't the emotional hook Gina had planned to use, but it was equally effective.

"Come in," the guard said. "I'll call the police."

"No, no," Gina replied, shaking her head in a don't-I-feel-silly way. "It's probably nothing."

"You're sure?"

Gina nodded in a no-but-I'm-being-brave manner. "Yes. I just need to get a grip."

The guard nodded an I-know-the-feeling-sister. "Well, come on in, anyway. Take a few minutes."

"I couldn't impose," Gina said.

"No imposition at all," the guard replied. "I'm stuck here, anyway. I could use the company."

"Okay, but just for a few minutes," Gina said.

The guard locked the door behind them. "Can I get you a cup of coffee?"

"Thanks," Gina said. "That'd be nice."

SPARKS PUSHED THE BUTTON on the remote, then whispered into the walkie-talkie he'd customized for the job.

"She's in. System disabled."

Either Mas or Menos should have heard the signal. Would have heard the signal. If they hadn't still been arguing about who should take Maria Teresa's next call.

"NICE NIGHT, THOUGH," the guard said. "I'm Sheryl, by the way."

"Janine," Gina said. "Nice to meet you."

"Likewise," Sheryl said, guiding Gina back toward the cafeteria. "I hope you like it strong. I have to, to stay awake all night."

"If I can bend a spoon with it, it's just right," Gina replied, even though she hated strong coffee.

"A woman after my own heart," Sheryl said, and smiled.

Gina's heart rose into her throat. She'd rehearsed exactly how to handle that kind of smile…from a male guard. But from this woman, it caught her by surprise.

"Well, we women have to stick together," she said, hoping her own smile and breezy tone covered the momentary shock that must have flickered across her face.

"Oh, definitely," Sheryl replied.

MAS AND MENOS might have spent the entire evening arguing in their truck behind the museum, had their spat not gone physical.

Menos tore his shirt open and leaned forward. "Hives, I tell you!"

Mas waved a hand dismissively. "Those aren't hives. Those are mosquito bites."

"They're hives!"

"That," Mas said, poking Menos's chest, "is not a hive. It's just a bite."

"Don't you!" Menos said, swatting Mas's hand away and leaning forward. "They're hives."

In leaning forward, he'd pressed against the talk button on the walkie-talkie.

SPARKS JUST ABOUT JUMPED out of his skin as the radio crackled to life.

"Pooh on your hives!" he heard Mas say.

GINA COUGHED as the sound came through the tiny earpiece hidden beneath her hair.

"Pooh on your ulcers!" Menos replied.

"Something wrong?" Sheryl asked. "Is the coffee okay?"

"It's fine," Gina said. Actually, it could probably be used to surface a road. "I just swallowed wrong."

At that moment Sparks pressed the page button, which transmitted a loud, squealing alarm. This had two notable effects, one expected, the other not.

"WHAT WAS THAT?" Mas asked.

"The radio?" Menos replied, equally unsure.

"OUCH!" GINA CRIED, bringing a hand to her ear.

"Are you sure you're okay?" Sheryl asked.

THIS TIME, Sparks didn't whisper. "Are you two planning to do this anytime soon? She's in, and the system is disabled. Go!"

"OH," MAS SAID, picking up the radio. *"Gracias."*

"DE NADA," Gina replied, pressing her ear again. "It's nothing. Just a bit of an ear infection. I guess the heat of the coffee…"

Sheryl nodded understandingly. "I have some ibuprofen in my purse."

Yet another artifact of the ESAW: analgesics always at hand. Gina kept some in her own purse, but decided to let Sheryl be gallant.

"Thank you," she said. "That would be nice."

"No problem," Sheryl replied, with another of those smiles. "No problem at all."

"NO PROBLEM," Mas said. "We go now."

NO PROBLEM? Sparks thought. Nothing *but* problems with those two. Well, at least they were finally going. Now if his bypass would just work correctly…

"THERE'S GUM ON THE DOOR," Menos said, pointing. "Americans and their litter."

He took out a knife and reached to scrape it off. The knife had just about touched it when Mas saw the tiny wires leading out of the wad of gum.

"No! That is the machine!" he said, pointing to the wires.

"He made it with chewing gum?" Menos asked.

"I guess he likes *MacGyver*," Mas answered. He took out a credit card. "Now we open the door."

CHAPTER NINETEEN

"THEY SHOULD BE GOING NOW," Ariel said.

Serena glanced at her watch. "Yes."

Darius merely nodded. He affected a casual air, but Ariel could tell he was nervous. So was she. She was worried about Sparks, mostly. As young males went, he was pretty good. A prize catch, in fact. She would feel terrible if anything happened to him. But there was nothing she could do except to wait.

"It will be fine," Serena said.

"Yes," Ariel said. "It will."

She hoped.

NO ALARM, Gina thought. At least, no alarm from the security system. There were other alarms ringing in her head, having mostly to do with the quiet, disarming smile that never left Sheryl's face.

"So, busy day?" Sheryl asked.

"You have no idea," Gina replied.

MAS HAD SPENT two hours that afternoon practicing with a credit card at the back door of the consulate.

He'd discovered there was a knack to this. Slide the card in, jiggle it a little, a little more pressure, another jiggle. And the door popped open, easy as pie.

"Let's go," Menos said.

LET'S GO! Sparks thought. This entire operation should have been finished by now. Well, not really. But at least further along. Count on those two Masolimians to be too busy arguing to hear his signal. Now they were running late, and he was sure Gina was having to think fast to keep the guard in hand. He hoped Mas and Menos had remembered to take the walkie-talkie with them.

GINA WAS HAVING to think fast, but not to keep Sheryl in hand. Quite the contrary. She'd handled pickups by guys a thousand times. But there was something about the way Sheryl approached it. Totally different. Subtle but unmistakable. And infinitely more difficult to duck away from.

"Whoever it was got you pretty spooked," Sheryl was saying. "You're still on edge."

"Maybe it's the caffeine," Gina said.

Sheryl nodded. "Yes, I guess extra strong coffee wasn't exactly the best idea to calm someone down. My apologies."

"It's okay," Gina said, needing to keep the woman here, looking for a safe avenue of conversation. "So, have you worked here long?"

"A few months," Sheryl said. "It's not too bad. I have

a lot of time to read. And think. Have you read Chastity Bono's book?"

Gina had seen it in a bookstore. The back cover described it as a poignant love story between the author and a woman who ultimately died. Sort of *Love Story*, but true, and lesbian.

"I've seen it," Gina said, choosing a neutral, middle course between disinterest and active response. "I didn't buy it, though."

"It's sad," Sheryl said. "So sad."

"Yes," Gina said. "Sad."

MENOS WAS NOT QUITE SAD, but not happy, either. "The radio. We forgot it."

"Damn," Mas replied, turning from the door.

"No," Menos said. "You go ahead. I'll go back and get it."

Mas nodded and stepped into the storage room. He pushed the door closed behind him, then reached for his flashlight. As his shin made contact with a pallet in the darkness, he realized he could have sequenced that better.

Cursing silently, he turned on the flashlight and pointed it down at the pallet. As if to get even, in an understandable but utterly futile gesture, he gave the pallet a sharp kick, at which point the Law of Unintended Consequences began to take effect.

There would have been no unintended consequences, but for the carelessness of a museum employee named Brian Stork, who had, earlier that afternoon, placed a replica clay pot from the pre-Colombian Inca exhibit on that very pallet, rather than back on the shelf where it belonged. Mas's initial stumble had begun the pot's wobble. His kick had amplified that wobble, and gravity did the rest.

In a busy restaurant kitchen, the sound of the clay pot shattering on the floor might have been lost in the background noise. In a silent and ostensibly unoccupied museum storage room, it reverberated along every aural neuron in Mas's brain, leaving him with much the same expression one would expect in a cartoon character whose head is inside a bell when it is rung.

"Damn!" he said.

"DAMN!" GINA SAID, hearing the faint crunch of something breaking. She knew Sheryl had heard it, as well. Gina pointedly scooted sideways and looked into her purse. "I sat on my sunglasses."

"Oh, sweetie!" Sheryl said. "You *are* having a bad day, aren't you?"

Sweetie? Gina thought. *C'mon, guys. Hurry!*

WHICH WAS EXACTLY what Menos was trying to do, having returned to the back door with the radio in hand. Except that Mas had closed the door. Locking him out.

Menos had not spent two hours that afternoon practicing with a credit card at the back door of the consulate. So he had not discovered the knack. His Bank of

Masolimia Visa card was the first to shatter. Next came the MasterCard. Then the red retail card he'd gotten just after accepting the consulate posting, when he'd discovered the joys of American shopping. He was down to his gasoline company card when the door opened.

"What are you doing?" Mas asked, looking at the plastic confetti on the ground.

"You locked me out!" Menos said.

"Why didn't you knock?" Mas asked.

"Right, and let everyone know I'm trying to get in?" Menos countered.

OH, GET ON WITH IT! Sparks thought.

OH, GET ON WITH IT! Gina thought, though the thought was most definitely not directed at Sheryl, who at that moment had chosen to casually brush a hand across hers, but instead at what she suspected were her bumbling partners.

"LET'S GET ON WITH IT," Menos said.

Mas nodded agreement, and they stepped once again into the darkness of the storage room.

"Watch the pallet there," Mas said, an instant before Menos let out a strained, almost silent whimper as his shin also connected with the pallet. "And watch for the broken crockery."

Crunch.

"So where is this damn painting?" Menos asked.

"It should be right over here," Mas said. "In this crate. If our information is right."

"Something ought to go right soon," Menos said.

SOMETHING OUGHT to go right soon, Gina thought. So far as she could determine, everything about this plan had gone sour. Except for the alarm. At least that had worked right. Or not, as it were.

Now if she could just deal with Sheryl for another few minutes without having to pick out china patterns.

THINGS MIGHT HAVE GONE very right very soon if only Mas hadn't had a problem with right…and left. Gina had distinctly told him the crate was short, thin and to the right of the door.

So naturally Mas turned them left. Straight into a crate the size of a small walk-in closet.

"That's it," he said with trepidation.

"*Por Dios*," Menos muttered. "We need a…what do you call it?"

"Forklift," Mas muttered back. He took the radio from Menos's hand and keyed the mike. "We need a forklift."

OH GOD! Gina was starting to panic. A forklift? Darius had distinctly described the crate as half the height of a man, nor more than three feet wide. The *Rotunda* was not a huge painting. Darius had been sure that two men could carry the crate without any trouble. Of course Darius had been thinking it would be himself and Lead

Legs. And Gina had opted to keep her sweetheart entirely out of this scam.

But her panic over her two bumbling, inept, hapless employers didn't come anywhere near the panic she felt as Sheryl moved to a closer seat.

"What's wrong?" Sheryl asked as she covered Gina's hand with her own and squeezed. "Janine, you look as if your world is going to fall apart!"

Which, thought Gina glumly, was exactly what it was doing. Piece by piece, Mas by Menos, Sheryl by Sheryl.

Biting her lower lip, Gina decided it was time to do the best acting of her life. She turned her hand over and gripped Sheryl's tightly…about as tightly as if she were a drowning victim.

"It's…it's my *husband,*" Gina said, and let the tears begin to fall.

"IT'S NOT SUPPOSED TO be this big!" Mas hissed.

"I know," Menos whispered back, snatching the radio back, his teeth clamped so tightly an alligator would have envied his bite. "*Ay, caramba,* Mas, you've messed up!"

"*I've* messed up? I was told the crate was half the height of a man. Does that look like it's half my height?"

"*Estúpido,* it's the wrong crate!"

"No, it's not! She distinctly said to the right of the door."

Menos slapped his forehead, then slapped Mas with equal vigor. "*¡Tonto! ¡Estúpido! ¡Derecho! ¡Allí!*" He pointed to the opposite side of the room.

"Pero…" As soon as the argumentative *but* left Mas's mouth, he clamped it shut. "Oh."

Muttering under his breath, Menos turned the flashlight in the other direction. And there, as promised, was the crate, thin, half the height of a man.

Mas spoke. "Gina said we should open the crate and cut the painting from the frame."

"Idiot! I'm not going to commit such an act of sacrilege. That's why I brought the truck. We'll take the whole thing."

"But if we take the crate, the museum will know the painting is gone."

Now it was Menos who lifted the walkie-talkie to his mouth. "Cancel the forklift. We had the wrong crate. Now we have the right one."

GINA RELAXED.

SPARKS RELAXED.

"BUT," MENOS CONTINUED, "Mas doesn't want to cut the painting. He says it would be sacrilege. He wants to take the whole crate."

GINA WAS SHAKING NOW, but with rage, not fear. She should have known those two *locos* would be unable to follow directions. Now, instead of just taking the painting one way or the other, they were going to stand there and dither about *which* way to do it.

"What is your husband doing to you?" Sheryl asked.

Gina looked at her, trying to collect her thoughts. "He's…um…having an affair!" Then she burst into some very real tears.

ACROSS THE STREET Sparks was getting antsy. He wasn't generating a whole lot of voltage from these car batteries, but he sure as hell hadn't calculated on them having to last more than half an hour. What the hell were those two dumbbells up to? Arguing about *how* to make the heist?

For the first time since interrupting their prior argument, he keyed his mike and spoke. "I don't care if you cut the painting, take the frame, take the whole crate, or take everything in the warehouse. Just get it *done… soon! ¡Apúrate!*"

"YES!" GINA SAID ALOUD.

Fortunately, Sheryl had just answered her statement about the affair with "Are you sure?" It was, Gina thought, perhaps the only fortunate coincidence of the night thus far.

"Ohh, you *caught* him?" Sheryl asked. "How humiliating."

"It's terrible," Gina said, once again not answering Sheryl, but instead the voice over the radio.

WHICH HAD BEEN the voice of Menos, who, having found a hole in the crate, had made the mistake of shining his flashlight through it and looking at the *Rotunda*.

"*¡Es terrible!*" he said, not realizing he was still holding the microphone open.

SPARKS, REALIZING their mike was still open and that they had not heard his prior admonition, pressed the page button again. The squeal overrode their open mike.

"OUCH!" SAID MENOS, who, because he was holding the flashlight to the hole, and because he was holding the radio in the same hand as the flashlight, and because he was peering through the very same hole, had his ear right next to the speaker.

"OUCH!" SAID GINA.

"Yes," Sheryl agreed, taking Gina's hand. "Ouch. I am so sorry. Men are pigs."

"Some men, especially," Gina said.

"WHAT?" MENOS SAID into the radio.

"WOULD YOU GET the hell *out* of there sometime soon?" Sparks said, now sure he had their attention. "Women have given birth in less time than this is taking."

"*Sí, sí,*" Menos replied. "We go now."

They hefted the crate. They walked their way back to the door. *Whack* of knee hitting pallet. *Crunch* of pottery underfoot. And out the door. To the truck. Heft. Slide. Ahh. *Finito!*

"We're done!" Menos said into the radio.

"FINALLY," GINA SAID, then, realizing she once again had responded to something not from Sheryl, "finally, I decided I just couldn't take his lies anymore."

"I know the feeling," Sheryl said, squeezing her hand. "My ex went to the Michigan Womyn's Music Festival last year. Because she liked music, she said. Then I saw the video from the festival. She was…"

"Caught," Gina said.

"CAUGHT?" MENOS SAID, looking over at Mas as he started the truck. "What do you mean, we're going to get caught? We're finished."

Mas simply held up his own undamaged credit card.

A lightbulb went on over Menos's head, not the proverbial lightbulb, but a real lightbulb—the truck's overhead light—as he opened the door. He returned to the back door of the museum and gathered up the shattered evidence of his life as a lock-pick.

"We're done," Mas said into the radio when Menos returned. "We've got it."

"THEY'VE GOT IT," Sparks repeated, just in case Gina hadn't heard.

WHICH OF COURSE she had. And just in the nick of time, because Sheryl had chosen that moment to scoot her chair a bit closer. Close enough that their thighs were brushing.

"Listen to me," Gina said. "I'm blubbering like a silly fool. And I've taken up too much of your time. I should just go home and tell him. Tell him exactly what I think of him."

For a moment Sheryl seemed about to protest. Then she straightened up and looked directly into Gina's eyes. "Yes, girl, you do that. You go home and tell him *exactly* how it's going to be."

"I will!" Gina said.

"Sisterhood!" Sheryl said.

"Sisterhood!" Gina agreed.

"But before you go," Sheryl said, "let me give you my phone number. In case, you know, you need moral support."

"Uh, thanks," Gina said, managing a bright smile.

At the door, though, Sheryl remembered something. "Wait! What about that man who was following you? Are you sure you should go out there?"

The sooner the better, Gina thought. But for the first time since this evening began, the budding Sarah Bernhardt was unable to conceal a look of guilt.

Sheryl saw it. She smiled. "You came in here just to see me, didn't you?"

Gina flushed, not with embarrassment, but with annoyance. She lowered her head, pretending to be embarrassed when what she really wanted to do was kick someone's shins.

"It's okay," Sheryl said gently. "I'm flattered. You have my number."

"Yes," Gina muttered, then made her escape as fast as if all the devils of hell were on her heels.

FIVE MINUTES LATER, Gina climbed into Sparks's van.

"I thought they'd never finish," Sparks said. "I was afraid my batteries would die."

"I was afraid *her* batteries wouldn't," Gina replied.

"Her?" Sparks asked.

Gina shot him a withering glare. "Don't even ask. Just drive."

CHAPTER TWENTY

THAT NIGHT, as Serena sipped hot chocolate in bed, she thought about the two kisses she'd shared with Darius. She could get very accustomed to such kisses. Was either of them really considering a future beyond this adventure?

No, of course not. Their lives and backgrounds were too divergent. The chemistry was there…oh, how the chemistry was there! Remembering his kisses was enough to make her insides light up like a roman candle. She crossed her legs tightly, trying to ease the tingling at the apex of her thighs, but that only served to make it worse.

"No." She said the word aloud, talking to her empty bedroom, because the mere act of speaking her thoughts aloud forced her to look at them more clearly than she ever could if she just let her mind drift.

"First," she told herself sternly, "your lives are utterly incompatible." Of course they were. He was an international art dealer, accustomed to traveling all over the world as his job required. He probably hadn't bought that condo next door, but simply leased it for however long he thought he needed to be in the area. So in a few months he might be packing up to return to European capitals, or wherever.

But she was firmly planted right here. Her life was here, such as it was, and she wasn't about to give up the practice she had so painstakingly built. She might claim it bored her to tears—and truthfully, it often did—but she still believed that she was fulfilling an important purpose, one that often satisfied her to her very soul. Yes, some of what she did was purely superficial, but those superficial things made people feel a whole lot better about themselves.

And she did treat some very serious diseases, from cancer to psoriasis, that could make a person's life a living hell. And she had saved more than one teenager's face and social life from the ravages of acne.

So she *was* proud of what she did. She couldn't give it up.

Wouldn't give it up.

Besides, she asked herself, what would a worldly man like Darius Maxwell see in a provincial mouse such as herself? He no doubt knew Europe like the back of his hand. He had lived in both Switzerland and England, and for all she knew, in New York and Los Angeles, as well.

This area was a mere backwater by comparison, no matter how often city leaders tried to bill Tampa as America's *next* great city.

By contrast, she had lived her entire life in Florida, and the farthest she had ever traveled was the Caribbean.

So. What could they possibly have in common, other than a little chemistry and a felony?

All of a sudden feeling very grumpy and a little despondent, she put aside her cocoa, turned off the light and scrunched down in her bed.

"No hope," she said into the darkness.

Which was just as well. Why in the world would she want to become involved with a prince?

OVER IN TAMPA, not far from the port, next to a train track that seemed to have become inordinately busy at this very late hour, the conspirators were unloading the truck.

Sort of. They were having a heated, though quiet, argument about whose shins got the worst barking, and whose shoulders were sorest from hefting the painting in its heavy crate.

Arguing, too, about whether Gina had been right about cutting the painting from its frame, rather than wrestling the entire thing onto the back of the rental truck.

They were parked at the rear of the consulate, the back door of the storage room wide-open to receive the precious booty. A freight train rumbled slowly by on the other side of the truck, no quieter for taking its time. The argument rose in volume.

And was brought to an instant halt by the sudden appearance of swirling red and blue lights.

The two of them jerked around and were instantly blinded by the brilliant beam of a police car's spotlight.

"Raise your hands and don't move," the car's occupant ordered over a loudspeaker.

The two Masolimians were too frozen to do anything else. Well, except for their mouths. Mas muttered to Menos out the corner of his mouth, "It's all *your* fault."

Menos might have tried to reply, except then a second car appeared behind the first.

There was no escaping the fact that they were now in deep guacamole.

"THANKS, SPARKS," Gina said cheerfully as Sparks dropped her off in front of the embassy. "I'll let Darius know we have the painting."

"Uh, sure," said Sparks, who'd already let Darius know. It was beyond him what was going on, but he didn't really care. His contraption, in the back of his rusty van, had done the job required of it. Maybe it looked like a Rube Goldberg machine, all those batteries cabled together with a huge copper coil that resembled the nose cone of a Saturn rocket.

He had no doubt that his big darling had probably knocked out the security systems for a three- or four-block radius, but he wasn't worried about that. After all, no other thieves knew what he was doing, so it was unlikely anyone else had taken advantage of the downtime.

Then he noticed something besides Gina's assets. "Uh, Gina?"

"Yes?"

"Um...behind the building? It looks like the cops might be there."

Gina turned and said something very expressive that Sparks was glad he couldn't understand. Then she turned to Sparks. "Get out of here now."

He was only too happy to oblige. He'd signed on to make a dandy machine, not get himself arrested. He sighed and returned his thoughts to Ariel as he hit the pavement. She'd be very proud of him.

GINA HAD MOVED to Tampa as a child, and while Spanish was spoken in her home as she grew up, she'd adopted English as her native tongue. Her father had been a dockworker, though, and her preference for English hadn't kept her from learning enough Spanish curses, imprecations and naughty language to fill a phone book.

As she stormed up to the building, she used more than half of them. Grabbing her key from her purse, she unlocked the consulate's front door, flipped on all the lights, then continued her *blitzkrieg* toward the back of the offices and the storeroom.

Trust those *imbéciles* to make a mess of something as simple as unloading a truck. Trust those *locos* to make such a deal out of it that the police came! And now, as usual, she was going to have to save their scrawny hides from disaster.

Reaching the storeroom, she saw the back door was open. All she could see was the side of the rental truck, but Gina had never been short on inspiration.

"Mas!" she called. "Menos! What's taking so long? I want to get home to bed. Just bring the damn thing in here…."

Her voice trailed off as she stepped out the door and pretended to become aware of the police for the first time. "What's going on?"

"Miss, put your hands up and move away from that door." Two officers with guns were facing Mas and Menos, and she realized she was in the line of fire.

Another woman might have quailed. Another woman might have meekly obeyed. Not Gina. She wasn't made of the quailing type of stuff.

"What the hell do you think you're doing?" she demanded of the policemen. "This is the consulate of Masolimia, these two men are diplomats, and all they're doing is unloading a shipment we received tonight." She had to shout to be heard over the deep rumble of the passing freight, but shouting was exactly what she felt like doing. This entire night had already been trying enough.

The two cops exchanged looks, but their guns didn't lower.

Gina put her hands on her hips. "Just how long are you planning to hold two diplomats at gunpoint? And how are you going to explain it to your superiors after I have the consul-general call to complain?"

Now it was the officers who began to look uneasy.

"Look," said Gina, trying to sound reasonable despite having to yell to be heard, "I'm willing to forget all about it if you will just let these two men get on with their legitimate business."

Menos took that moment to open his yap. "I'm not going to forget about it," he bellowed. "This is an insult to Masolimia!"

"Shut up," Mas begged. "They have guns!"

"Oh, be quiet both of you," Gina said, coming around to the end of the truck. "Why haven't you shown these officers your credentials?"

Menos was in no mood to become calm, now that he saw the light at the end of the tunnel. "How am I supposed to show them when they won't let me put my hands down?"

"Which pocket?" Gina demanded.

Menos's eyes grew huge. Apparently the idea of Gina's hand in his pocket had a greater effect than facing two loaded guns. He stammered.

"All right," Gina said, *really* in no mood for this crap, "I'll find it."

She patted his pockets, sure she was driving him insane, until she found the bulge of his wallet. "There," she said, reaching in. Menos quivered.

Out came the wallet. She flipped it open and in the window pocket was the diplomatic identification card issued by the State Department. She tugged it out and passed it to the officer.

He accepted it, and while his buddy kept his gun on the trio, he turned and read it in the glare of the floodlight.

Finally, after a minute both agonizing for Mas and

Menos and irritating for Gina, he turned back. "Looks real to me."

"Of course it's real," Gina said tartly as the caboose passed by and the level of noise began to lower to something less than standing directly behind a jet engine. "Now, can we get on with our work?"

"Sure," said the first officer, holstering his gun. "Need some help with that crate?"

Mas turned ashen. Menos looked as if he wanted to run as fast and far as he could go.

Gina was well aware of the irony as she said sweetly, "That would be wonderful, Officers."

Five minutes later, with the aid of two of Tampa's finest, the stolen *Rotunda* was settled into her new home in the back room of the consulate.

Twenty minutes later Maria Teresa had received the good news.

"Now," said Mas to Menos, "maybe she won't call us four times every night."

"Si Dios quiere," Menos replied. *God willing.* It was the most fervent prayer he had offered in years.

"Now," said Gina, dashing their hopes of going home to bed, "let's open it and make sure we have the *Rotunda.*"

The men exchanged looks. Let her eyes bear the strain—neither of them had the fortitude for a second look at Masolimia's greatest treasure.

"And afterward," Gina said serenely, "the two of you take the rental truck back. Anybody have a crowbar?"

THE KNOCK ON SERENA'S DOOR was quiet, almost tentative. Thinking it must be Ariel, Serena climbed out of bed. Wearing nothing but her knee-length sleep shirt, she padded across her living room to the front door. Peering through the fish-eye lens, she saw not Ariel but Darius.

Her heart slammed, first with delight, then with fear. God, had something gone wrong? Quickly she worked the dead bolt and chain lock and opened the door.

"Darius?"

"Sorry to bother you," he said almost sheepishly, "but I'm so jazzed I can't sleep. I hoped you might be awake, as well."

"I am," she said, stepping back and inviting him in. "I don't know if I'm jazzed or what, but I've been lying in the dark watching the moonbeams make patterns on my ceiling. Can I get you anything?"

"I'm fine, thanks."

She closed the door and locked it behind him. "If you don't mind, I'm going to get a bottle of water. I'm thirsty."

"Sure. In fact, that sounds good now that you mention it."

She smiled at him. "Have a seat."

Of course she was wearing her favorite ratty old T-shirt, the one she'd slept in so many times it was almost worn-out. The fabric was so soft and thin, now, it felt better on her skin than satin.

Of course she wasn't wearing the one negligee she

had, something purchased on impulse last year when she'd been dating that cardiac surgeon and things had appeared about to become serious. Well, they *had* had four dates. That was a record in her book.

He never made a pass at her, though, and there was never a fifth date. Six months later she ran into him and he introduced her to his boyfriend. How very lowering.

Now a royal (maybe) European hunk (definitely) was sitting in her living room at two in the morning, and she was wearing a T-shirt that should have been consigned to the rag bin years ago. Even the message on the front, Dare To Be Different, had become almost invisible.

Oh well, she thought as she reached into the fridge for two bottles of spring water. It was pointless, anyway. He'd come over here because he was restless, not because he particularly wanted to be with her.

Back in the living room, she found him sitting on one end of her sofa. She handed him a bottle of water, then sat on the opposite end, legs curled up beneath her.

He lifted his bottle in toast. "To a great scam."

She raised her bottle, too, took a sip and said, "To a great heist."

"Yes, there *is* that facing us." He sighed, and he suddenly looked so weary that she ached for him.

"Are you all right, Darius?"

"I'm fine. I'm fine." He smiled crookedly. "I'm sorry, but at the moment I'm feeling rather appalled with myself. I've not only conspired to commit a felony, but I'm about to pull a double cross."

"One has already been pulled on you," she reminded him.

"That doesn't relieve me of responsibility for my own actions."

She nodded and impulsively scooted closer to touch his hand, which lay on the back of the couch.

"What's more," he said, "I'm beginning to take this more seriously. For the sake of that benighted country, the contract must be signed. It's no longer merely a matter of whether it might disrupt my life. It's a matter of knowing the truth as swiftly as possible so the contract will be ironclad. Think how awful it would be if I sign it and it turns out someone else is the prince. The research firm might back out. Or sue."

Serena nodded. She hadn't really thought of these things before, but she was impressed that Darius had. "You're a very good man," she told him.

"I'm not so sure of that right now. But I set it in motion, so now I have to carry through."

"It's my fault," Serena said, hanging her head. "I was the one who stuck my nose in and started planning a huge heist."

"We're quite a pair, aren't we?" he said with a quiet laugh. Then, startling her, he turned his hand over and clasped hers.

Instantly a feeling washed over her like warm surf on a sunny day. Her hand felt very…right…in his. There was a pleasant comfort. She ought to have been terrified, thinking about everything that could, and no doubt would, go wrong. She ought to be cautioning herself, telling herself to slow down, hide, stay away, stay safe inside the shell of a life she'd built for herself.

Instead she simply felt…right. For the first time in a long, long time.

"What is it?" he asked, looking into her half-closed eyes. "Are you sleepy?"

"Umm…no," Serena said. "I'm just…comfortable. Very comfortable."

"Comfortable is good," he said.

"Mmmm, yes. It is."

She couldn't decide if she wanted him to kiss her or not. On the one hand, at that moment, with this man, she felt so totally kissable. On the other hand, at that moment, with this man, she knew that a kiss would lead to more, and more, and more. And while the thought of making love with Darius Jacobus Maxwell III was infinitely delightful and attractive in its own way, so was simply sitting here, hand in hand…comfortable.

"I can't decide what I want to do," he said, still looking at her.

"Neither can I," Serena answered.

"I mean…I want to…but…"

"Exactly. This is so…"

"Comfortable."

"Exactly," she said.

"Maybe it's that today has been so wild. Hell, the last two weeks have been wild."

Serena nodded. "Yes, they have. And now *we* have a chance to be wild, and I want to, and yet…this feels like an island of peace in the middle of a topsy-turvy ocean. Just this."

He leaned a bit closer, and their shoulders brushed. Without really thinking about it, she tipped her head over onto his shoulder. He slid his other arm around her, still holding her hand, and they sat in silence. Comfortable, blissful silence. No wild adventures. No waiting to hear if people they'd come to care about were now in jail. No worrying about whether he was a prince, or what that might mean for Masolimia. Only the comfort of his warm arm around her, his hand in hers, her cheek nestled on his shoulder, feeling his chest rise and fall with each slow breath, the faint scent of his aftershave mixed with the musk of maleness.

She closed her eyes and let her mind roam far, far away, to a world where she could feel exactly *this* forever. It wasn't realistic, of course. There were no happily-ever-afters in the real world. There were always problems, challenges, stresses, triumphs, heartaches. Without them, she supposed, moments like this would have no meaning. It was the sweet contrast of the tension of the day and the relaxation of this moment that made it what it was. Still, it was nice to daydream.

In her daydream he held her like this, on the floor, on a fur rug, their backs propped against pillows, watching a fire crackle in the fireplace. Outside, through the windows, snow was falling. Big, white, fluffy flakes. She hadn't seen snow in years, of course, and somehow that made it even more special in her fantasy. Beside them on the floor sat glasses of wine. A rich, heady merlot. There was faint music around them, strings gently dancing on a soothing melody.

They were naked.

She imagined what his body looked like. Soft, light curls of black hair over his chest and down the center of his belly. Curls that caught the firelight and almost seemed to sparkle. Long, muscled legs. Broad shoulders. Arms that bespoke strength without the narcissistic overkill of body-built bulges.

His eyes were fixed on hers, pupils wide in the low light, his face soft as their lips met. And she melted into him, her breasts pressed to his chest, her pelvis snuggled up to his, as their lips met, touched, parted, tongues dancing ever so lightly, breath shared, hearts shared, souls shared.

It was a beautiful daydream.

As his face turned to her, his hand slid up to lift her chin, and their lips met.

It was a beautiful daydream.

And it was real.

CHAPTER TWENTY-ONE

"THIS IS, WITHOUT DOUBT, the worst painting in the history of art," Gina said.

Mas and Menos couldn't deny that statement. Yes, the *Rotunda* was a national treasure. Perhaps that said a lot about their homeland. But there it was. Horrid.

The artist—if that word could fairly be applied—had posed the princess in a very straightforward way, her face slightly turned to the left. Although the portrait ended—mercifully—just below her bust, Gina could tell that the princess had her hands crossed in her lap. Yes, the pose was just fine.

After that the artist had run into trouble.

The trouble seemed to have started when the artist mixed his colors on the palette. Unless the princess had been half jaundiced and half iguana, that yellow-green tinge to her skin couldn't be right. And while she'd once met someone with brown eyes that almost looked orange in certain light, they weren't *that* color of orange. Perhaps the artist was color-blind.

The composition wasn't too bad, if you considered it likely that the princess had a large growth on her right shoulder. Or perhaps she'd been wearing padding beneath her dress and it had bunched up. Throughout the sitting. And he hadn't noticed until he was finished. He had paid special attention to her cleavage, and cleavage she had in abundance, owing principally to the fact that she had *everything* in abundance. But, out of courtesy to his subject, he could have omitted the mole. Or at least he might not have painted it so vividly, including the three hairs that trailed out like a baby Medusa trying to escape.

The princess had apparently had a fondness for the bottle, as it was once quaintly put. Looking closely, Gina could see the tiny network of blood vessels beneath the skin on the face, neck and bosom, as if the princess had wandered into a reddish-blue spider web and it had stuck. Again, out of courtesy to the subject, the artist could have omitted those details. But he hadn't. In fact, he had painted them in loving detail.

Her dress was, perhaps, reflective of her culture and her times. Or perhaps she enjoyed looking like a monk who'd bought his habit as a child and refused to give it up, even though he had to pour himself into it. The material appeared to have been a coarse brown wool, made coarser by regular wear and by being stretched over a woman several sizes too large for the garment. If the princess could have breathed, Gina wasn't certain how she'd have managed it.

The crown jewels were supposed to have been the focal point of the painting. And they might have been, if they had not been set in so dismally tarnished a silver crown. The primary stone appeared to be a ruby, or perhaps a giant pimple. Gina couldn't tell for sure. The surrounding spray of emeralds, irregular in shape and placement, most closely resembled the remnants of a sneeze.

Yes, if she'd seen a more horrid painting in all her life, she couldn't remember it. Beyond any doubt, this painting must have been the product of a vendetta.

"Our treasure," Mas said, shaking his head.

"Yes," Menos agreed, also shaking his head.

"Wow," Gina said.

For all its apparent ugliness, however, Gina found she couldn't stop looking at the canvas. Each viewing brought out some new flaw. The princess's hair had either been full of grease—not unusual in that day as a way to ward off lice—or the artist had painted it with a trowel.

There was an energy in the painting, to be sure, but it was the energy of a sick person attempting to vomit. Perhaps that, too, reflected the artist's state of mind when he'd been working. If the portrait were any guide, the princess certainly could have served as a purgative. Or perhaps the artist had simply disliked her and had gone out of his way to make her and her portrait as hideous as could be imagined.

"What happened to the artist?" she asked.

Mas shook his head. "He died tragically. Run over by a wool cart."

"Twice," Menos added.

"Twice?" Gina asked.

"It was at night," Mas explained. "Apparently the driver of the cart wasn't sure what he'd hit, so he backed up to check."

"Ahh," Gina said.

"A terrible accident," Menos said. "Terrible."

Accident, my eye, Gina thought. Someone got even. And rightly so.

"Of course," Mas said, "once he died, his work was in high demand. And this was his masterpiece. The most prized work of the best artist ever born in our country."

"It's certainly…compelling," Gina said.

"It hung in the palace for over two hundred years," Menos said. "Beneath it was a tribute to the artist, including the story of his tragic fate."

A warning to future royal portraitists? Gina wondered. The Masolimian equivalent of a head on a pike?

"So when do we ship it back to Masolimia?" Gina asked.

"Ahhh," Mas said. "We will take it back *personally.* We leave on Saturday."

Two days, Gina thought. *Two days that I'll have to look at this…this…this!*

Saturday couldn't come soon enough.

ARIEL SAT ON A ROCK, looking out at the water. Sparks was beside her, looking up at the sky as if trying to figure out how to hotwire the stars together. But it was nice to know he was safe, even if he never truly inhabited the same world as the remainder of the human species.

"You did good tonight," she said, having pried the story out of him.

He smiled. "I did well. Whether I did *good* is, I guess, an open question. I helped someone break into a museum and steal something. Is that *good?*"

"The painting belongs to the people of Masolimia," she said. "It was stolen from them. You helped them recover it. That was good."

"I committed a crime," he said. "Not a prank. Not some April Fool's joke on a teacher. A crime."

"Yes," she said. "You did. But I suspect God will know your heart, and your reasons, and forgive you."

He dropped his gaze from the heavens and turned to her. "Do you think so?"

She nodded and kissed him, a peck on the cheek. "Of course. God can forgive anything."

It pained her that his heart was troubled. She had no doubt that they had done, and were doing, the right thing. But of course he couldn't be privy to her certainty. And that, more than anything else, pained her. She couldn't just tell him. He would have to learn that on his own, in the fullness of life and experience.

She reached over and began to scratch his back lightly, using only the tips of her fingernails, through his shirt. As expected, he sighed happily and turned his back this way and that, like a bear against a tree. She simply continued scratching and let his movements direct her fingers. It was a small comfort, she thought, but a comfort nonetheless.

As she scratched, she closed her eyes and let her thoughts drift to what he must be thinking and feeling, puzzling out in his mind. He would be weighing, evaluating, judging himself and his actions against his own, high, harsh standards. And finding himself lacking.

Yet he lacked for nothing. He loved, loyally and honestly and with the quiet sort of commitment that fills in the tiny cracks of the passing days. He took wonderful care of his mother. He helped his neighbors. He was kind and thoughtful—when his mind wasn't a million miles away—and if he had any vices, they were the common vices that naturally accompanied late adolescence.

He was just fine, worthy of love and forgiveness, mercy and blessings untold.

His movements beneath her fingertips slowed, softened, until he was still and relaxed. Finally he turned to her.

"Ariel?"

"Yes?"

"May I kiss you?"

She smiled wide. "Of course you may, my lovely young man. It would be my delight."

DELIGHT WAS PRECISELY what Darius was feeling at that very moment. The delight of a beautiful woman, soft in his arms, their skin slightly slick from their languid, gentle exertions.

"You are so beautiful," he said quietly, in the near darkness.

"All cats are black in the dark," she said, smiling impishly at him.

"Don't say that! Serena, you *are* a beautiful woman. Outside, inside, through and through. Beautiful."

He felt the gentle shiver run through her, felt her melt even closer to him. They had barely begun, yet it seemed to him that it had always been this way.

The strangest of sensations, one he had never before experienced, his own desire a heavy, throbbing weight in his groin, but reluctant to move forward, as if every second of this night needed to be savored and drawn out to its fullest degree.

Passion filled him, yet an even deeper hunger demanded satiation. Running his hand over her back and bottom, he felt once again the graceful curves, the satin of her skin. Skin that was misty now with the desire he had awakened in her again and again, yet had not fulfilled. She seemed as content as he to draw these moments out, even when he gently lifted her to a pinnacle where she rocked against him as if seeking harder touches, deeper touches.

Her hand, too, ran over his back and down to his bottom, a delightful caress that caused him to shiver. At some point the dam would break, but for the first time in his life, he was content to wait for it to happen on its own.

It was as if these minutes were a precious time of learning. A time of discovering how she responded to each touch and caress. Her breasts, he had found, were exquisitely sensitive, causing soft moans to escape her. And she had touched him in the same way, discovering for both of them the same sensitivity. To think he had never known that about himself.

As time slipped away, every touch seemed to become more erotic, even though they didn't change physically. Their internal climates were changing, he realized vaguely as the heat within him continued to build. Inside him a new world was opening, a world he had never before shared with anyone. Barriers were falling, dissipating, vanishing, until he began to feel that the boundaries between them no longer existed. Her touch became his, his reaction became hers, their hungers became one.

What had been languid became feverish. No longer able to restrain himself, he slipped his hand between her legs, and parted her moist petals. She arched, and this time a groan escaped her, a deep, taut sound that seemed to rise from her very toes. Her hand found his shaft, stroking gently, and the same groan escaped him.

Mouths replaced hands. He sucked on her breasts until she was writhing against him, until finally she moaned, "Darius…please…"

He rose above her, between her parted legs. She tilted to receive him. The throbbing that filled him, the burning, the ache, seemed to flame in every cell of his being. With one slow thrust he entered her.

She cried out, one sharp sound.

And he knew.

Somehow…she had never done this before.

The realization pierced the fire, reaching him, stopping him.

"Serena…"

Her eyes fluttered trying to open. "Don't stop," she whimpered.

Thank heaven. Because buried deep within her wet warmth, he wasn't sure he could have stopped.

Propping himself on one arm, he reached down between them and found the nub of her passion. She was going to make this journey with him. At each new height he wanted her with him.

And with each moan he drew from her, he knew he was bringing her along.

Higher. The ache within him growing hard and driving, forcing a rhythm to his movements.

Until finally, at long last, thought was gone, buried in the explosions that rocketed him over the top. Distantly he heard her cry join his.

SHATTERED. Darius had tucked Serena against his side, her head on his shoulder, and she lay there now, listening to his heart slow, to his breathing calm.

Shattered.

It wasn't exactly the right word, but it was the one that kept coming to her mind. It was as if the last hour had taken her apart and put her back together again, a different person. The tiny twinge of soreness was merely a reminder of the bigger walls that had been breached. She savored it, hugging the feelings close, never wanting to forget a single moment of this night.

"How are you feeling?" he asked huskily. His hand lifted from her shoulder to stroke her tousled hair.

"Fabulous," she answered on a sigh.

"You're sure?"

She heard the concern in his tone and dragged herself far enough out of paradise to say, "I realize it's unusual to find that a woman of my age has never...well..."

"Why *is* that?" he asked.

"I just... I don't know." She sighed. "I rarely had time to date. Relationships never developed. I don't know. It wasn't a conscious plan." Nor did she want, at this juncture, to tell him that she'd avoided sexual involvement largely because she'd never felt she'd met the right person. She didn't want to scare him right out of the bed.

But then he astonished her. "This may as well have been my first time, too," he said quietly. "I've never— *never*—had an experience like this before."

She melted into him again, as happy as a sleepy kitten, and hoped all of this could happen to her again, soon. With him.

For now she could, and would, forget all that loomed ahead of them.

IN THE WEE HOURS of the morning, a red Ferrari pulled up behind the Masolimian consulate.

"Just wait here," Sparks said to Marco.

Marco sighed. If he was to be the getaway driver, it certainly wasn't for this odd-looking young man who needed to be dropped head-first into the nearest bathtub. But Ariel had asked him, and for Ariel he would play taxi driver. Sparks, she had said, had some important work to do.

Marco didn't like this section of Tampa. It was too near the working shipyards to be a truly desirable neighborhood. Although, he reminded himself, that was prejudice speaking. Some of the nicest parts of Tampa were also close to the port.

But this area. He looked around and shuddered, and wished he were safely back on the key in his comfortable condominium.

Sparks grabbed a black nylon backpack out of the nearly useless back seat and left the car. Marco drummed his fingers on the steering wheel, watching as the young man went to the back door. Was he going to break in?

But no. Sparks set the black bag down and pawed through it. Moments later he removed some small object which he then stuck to the wall near the door with a wad of—Mamma mia, was that plastic explosive?

All of a sudden Marco wished he hadn't agreed to help Serena. But he couldn't believe Serena would be involved with something as dastardly as a bomb. Would she?

His knuckles whitened as he gripped the steering wheel. Maybe he should get out of here now. Just leave Sparks and his bomb…

Sparks now took something else out of his bag and fiddled with it. Another minute passed, then he grabbed his bag and came back to the car, where Marco was gritting his teeth.

"Okay, dude," Sparks said as he tossed his bag in back and slid into the front seat. "Let's go."

But Marco didn't move. He couldn't leave that bomb there.

"No."

"No?" Sparks looked at him.

"No."

"Why the hell not?" Sparks demanded. "The job's done."

"Bomb," said Marco.

"Bomb?"

"Bomb."

"What bomb? Is there a bomb in the car?"

Marco glared at him, then pointed to the back of the building. "You cannot leave a bomb."

Sparks gaped at him. Then laughed. "That's not a bomb."

"No?"

"No."

Marco frowned. "It looks like—"

"Dude, it's not a bomb. It's an electronic circuit is all. And it's stuck to the wall with Silly Putty."

"Silly Putty?"

"Silly Putty."

"What's that?"

"Believe me, it doesn't explode. So could we please get out of here now? I'm not into blowing things up. Ever."

Marco stared hard at him, then decided this distasteful young man wasn't lying. He shifted the car into gear, and with a squeal of tires they were off.

Ordinarily Marco wouldn't have driven in such a fashion in town, but he felt he owed fright for fright. And glancing quickly in the direction of Sparks, he realized that the young man was looking, ah, just a little bit scared.

Grinning, Marco headed for the southbound I-75. At this time of night, no one would be on it. He could teach this young man a thing or two about speed. And fear.

CHAPTER TWENTY-TWO

SERENA AND DARIUS might have slept late, except the phone rang at 6:00 a.m., startling them both out of happy dreams.

Groaning, more from habit as a physician than from desire, Serena rolled over and picked up the receiver.

"'Lo?" she mumbled.

"That Marco is a madman!" Sparks shrieked at her over the phone. "He had us doing over 150 miles an hour!"

"That's why he's the getaway driver."

"But we didn't need to get away! There was nobody there. All I did was install the circuitry."

"Mmmm."

"He's a madman, I tell you. We don't need him at all."

"We might," Serena said sleepily. Then a finger trailed down her spine, causing a delicious shiver to run through her. "Can we talk about this later?"

"Believe me, we will. I want a meeting today, before we go."

"Sure," Serena sighed, as a hand reached around to cup her breast and tease her nipple. Another delightful shiver ran through her.

"What time?" Sparks demanded.

"Um...I'll check with Darius. Call me back in a couple of hours."

"Okay." The phone on the other end of the line was sharply disconnected, the emotional equivalent of a door slamming.

"Something wrong?" Darius asked drowsily, as he nibbled the nape of her neck.

"Later," she answered, and gave herself up to him.

REALITY, HOWEVER, could not be held at bay forever. Later, as Serena made them a hearty breakfast, the heist planned for that night reared its ugly head.

It was Darius's fault, of course. Trust a man to get practical an hour or two too soon.

"Who was on the phone?" he asked, swiping a strip of bacon from the paper-towel-covered plate where a half dozen were draining.

"Sparks." She sighed and started cracking eggs into the frying pan. The microwave dinged, announcing the grits were ready. "He thinks Marco is a madman and shouldn't drive for us."

"Why's that?"

"Apparently Marco was doing 150 last night."

Darius shrugged. "I've done that on the Autobahn. No big deal."

"It was for Sparks, evidently. He wants a meeting before we go ahead tonight."

"Whatever it takes to calm him down. We certainly can't do anything without Sparks."

She gave him a half smile and answered, "Somehow I think he knows that."

"Probably." Darius swiped another piece of bacon. "He's calling back, right?"

"Yep."

"Then tell him we'll meet at three. I'll gather up the others."

She raised a brow at him. "Not Lead Legs?"

"Certainly not. That would be…a mistake, I think."

"Me, too."

He took another piece of bacon.

"Do you want me to make more of that?"

He looked at the bacon strip in his hand, then at the plate. Then he gave her his most winning smile. "If you wouldn't mind, please?"

"SO IT'S BASICALLY the same plan?" Sparks asked, as the five of them sat around Darius's kitchen table.

"Well, except for Gina's vamp routine," Serena said. "We won't need that, because there's no guard at the consulate."

"Except for Mas and Menos," Sparks said.

Ariel shook her head. "They're not usually there at night. They usually go clubbing in Ybor City, then back to their apartment." After a pause, she added, "I've been watching them for the past few days."

"All of that might change, now that they have the *Ro-*

tunda there," Darius said. "We have to consider the possibility that they'll be there, hovering over it like mother hens, making sure no harm befalls it."

"Like us, for example," Serena said with a smile.

"Exactly," Darius agreed. "So, if they are there, that's where you enter the picture."

"Me?" Serena asked.

"Yes. You speak Spanish."

"I took two years of Spanish in college," she said. "That means I speak Spanish like a two-year-old. Your Spanish is much better than mine, I'm sure."

"That may be," Darius said. "But I'm the heavy lifter. It's my job to get the painting out...while you distract our two Masolimian patriots."

"If necessary," Serena said.

"Yes," he said. "If necessary."

"And Marco?" Sparks asked, looking over at the older Italian. "Tell me he's not going to drive that way again. I aged ten years in ten minutes."

Marco feigned offense, although he was clearly pleased that his driving had had the desired effect. "We were not in danger, young man. I know how to drive."

"You drive like a lunatic!" Sparks said.

Marco smiled. "That was always my edge."

"Your edge?"

"Didn't you know?" Ariel said, patting Sparks's hand. "Our friend Marco was a Grand Prix driver. A champion, in fact. You were in good hands."

"I can't tell you how relieved I am," Sparks said, his

voice dripping sarcasm. "So our getaway driver is going to pretend he's back on the race course?"

"Only if necessary," Marco said.

"And if we run into the police?" Sparks asked. "Are you planning to outrun them, too?"

"Hardly. I can outdrive any car, but I can't outdrive a radio. No, for the police, I turn it over to Darius."

"And I make the appropriate explanations," Darius said. He'd already prepared a story and run it by Serena. She'd made a few changes, and they'd settled on it. Now he simply smiled. "Trust me. It will be very persuasive."

"Which leaves only one tiny detail," Ariel said. "When do we go?"

"Tonight," Darius said. He glanced at his watch. "In about four hours, in fact."

"Then I need a nap," Sparks said. "I didn't sleep at all last night. If I'm going to be any good to you, I need to hit the bed for a while."

"That," Serena said, winking at Darius, "sounds like a capital idea."

GINA RETURNED to the consulate balancing a pizza box in one hand and a six-pack of high-caffeine cola in the other. "As promised," she said, "food and drink. Enough to keep us all awake and alert. Just in case."

"In case what?" Lead Legs asked.

He'd introduced Mas and Menos to the wonders of poker, and at present had a monster pile of the pretzel sticks they had been using for currency. Mas and Menos appeared relieved that Gina had returned.

"Yes," Mas said. "In case what? Nobody knows we have the painting."

Gina frowned. "I'm not sure I fully trust Sparks. He might have said something to them."

Menos blanched. Bad enough they'd had to commit thievery, but the idea of having to face the future prince of Masolimia after having helped to double-cross him…he could think of more pleasant things to do. For the first time, it occurred to him that by interfering with Darius's plan, he might have committed treason. *¡Dios mio!*

Mas spoke. "Surely they won't try to steal the *Rotunda* from us. That *would* be a crime, and they don't have…how you say…immunity."

"True," Gina said. "But something about last night was just a little bit too pat. They're going to try something. And I'll bet this is it. What's more, I'll bet they try it tonight. So…we wait for them."

"And then?" Lead Legs said.

Gina smiled. "And then we're back to Plan A. We kidnap Darius."

SINCE IT WAS STILL broad daylight, not the witching hour for thieves, con men and desperate Masolimians, Gina and Lead Legs headed off to the beach, leaving Mas and Menos to protect the *Rotunda* and deal with any misguided tourist who might show up seeking a visa.

It was exactly the moment Menos had been waiting for.

"We're in deep doo-doo," he told Mas, but in Spanish.

Mas looked at him as if he'd lost his mind. "*¿Por qué?* For what? We solved the problem, and Maria Teresa is no longer badgering us. How could life be any better?"

Menos scowled at him. "*¡Tú eres un tonto!*"

"I'm not stupid!"

"*Sí,* you are! You have not thought!"

"About what?"

"Exactly."

Glowering at each other, the two men sat in silence. The only sound in the office was that of the air-conditioning, which, thank goodness, was working well for a change, if only because Gina had insisted on having it repaired so the painting wouldn't become damaged. For Mas and Menos, no one cared. Which seemed only right to the two diplomats.

Finally Mas could stand it no longer and he asked, "What have I forgotten?"

"You have forgotten that Darius Maxwell is the prince of Masolimia!"

Mas went off into a long snickering laugh. "Of course. I have forgotten the very thing that has given us both ulcers!" Now he hooted, and held his sides as if he had just heard the funniest joke in the world.

Menos simply glared at him until at last even Mas couldn't wring out another cackling laugh. Silence again reigned. This time Mas refused to be the first to speak. But Menos was past caring who could outstare the other. Finally he said, "Have you considered that we have committed treason?"

Mas started to laugh again, but the sound was cut off midchortle and became a strangled gurgle.

Menos smiled with evil pleasure. "See? You are stupid, as I have said. We are *both* stupid."

"We didn't do anything wrong."

"No? Did we or did we not help Gina to steal the very painting that our prince wanted? Did we or did we not help her to double-cross him?"

Mas stopped breathing. Then, "He won't know…."

"*She* thinks he does. *She* wants us to stay here all night to protect the painting from him. From *him!*" Expressively Menos drew his finger across his throat.

Mas quivered. "But she said it was necessary, so that he would assume the throne."

"Pah! I spit on her!" Figuratively, of course. Not even Menos would actually spit indoors. "To say we have kidnapped the mother of the prince, when in fact we have not, is only a small thing. But now she is talking about kidnapping the prince *himself!*"

Mas quivered again, this time as if he were racked with ague.

"You may not be very fond of your head," Menos continued relentlessly, "but I am very fond of mine, and I like it right where it is."

Mas shook his head. "There are no more beheadings in Masolimia."

"That was under the *old* prince. This is a new prince!"

Mas groaned.

"Diplomatic immunity!" Menos spat the words. "Yes, that keeps us from getting arrested here. But it doesn't protect us from our own prince at home."

"He won't…he wouldn't…"

"Are you sure?" Menos waited for an argument, but Mas couldn't seem to collect enough words—or ideas— to muster one, so he plunged ruthlessly ahead. "Say he doesn't behead us. Or throw us in a hole for the rest of our days. What do we do if he takes away our jobs and *banishes* us forever from Masolimia? Who *else* would be stupid enough to hire *you?*"

Mas bristled, at least he bristled as much as he could when verging on death by terror. "Or you," he said, trying to sneer.

Menos ignored the insult. Considering its source, it was beneath notice. Besides, he had bigger fish to fry, which was an English idiom he preferred to the more banal Spanish *Tengo cosas más importantes que hacer.*

The *pescado* he was frying at the moment was a desperate need to find a way to end this folly before he lost his job, his country and his head, not necessarily in that order.

"What do we do?" Mas asked finally.

"I'm thinking."

That answer was enough to make Mas shudder even more than the thought of beheading. So far all *thinking* had done was get them into serious trouble. Action was what they needed.

For a long time he considered how far he could flee and how fast, and what he could possibly do to survive if he did.

The future looked grim indeed, but little did he guess it was about to get even grimmer.

CHAPTER TWENTY-THREE

MARIA TERESA MAXWELL received the news of the recovery of the *Rotunda* with very mixed feelings. On the one hand, it was wonderful to have retrieved a national treasure, and at so auspicious a time, the recovery planned by none other than the soon-to-be prince. It would certainly go a long way to allay any lingering political issues. After all, he would undoubtedly have the support of the Masolimian people after that little triumph. On the other hand...

On the other hand, there was no way she trusted Mas and Menos to bring the painting back to Masolimia. No, it was unthinkable. They were planning to book it as standard airline cargo! That meant it would probably end up lost in Botswana, at best, or stuck in Madrid customs, or any of a number of unthinkable possibilities. No, that simply would not do. She would have to handle this personally.

So, no matter that it was midnight in the Riviera, she picked up the phone and called her travel agent. At home. No doubt interrupting his ménage à trois involving the man's wife and receptionist. Maria had seen the way they all looked at each other. So she considered herself killing two birds with one stone as she dialed the phone, listened to the ring, and then heard her travel agent's breathless and none-too-happy-to-be-disturbed voice.

"Oui?" he said.

"Hello, Gascon," she said.

"Madame Maxwell?" he asked. *"Quelle heure est-il?"*

"It's four minutes after midnight," Maria answered, stubbornly refusing to appease his linguistic preference for French—rather presumptuous for an international travel agent, she thought. "As you doubtless knew, having checked the bedside clock when you answered the phone."

That was a calculated guess, but a reasonable one. Still, it had the desired effect. No one liked to believe that others could see—or even surmise—what happened behind the privacy of bedroom doors. Especially not when they had been caught in *flagrante delicto,* as it were.

"Well, yes," Gascon answered. "I did. So what is so important that it can't wait until the morning?"

"I need to fly to America," she said. "Specifically, to Tampa, Florida. And I need to leave within the hour."

"That's simply not possible," he replied. "There are no flights out of Nice until the morning."

"No commercial flights," she said. "I know. But I have no intention of flying commercial. I need a charter. Your commission would be…considerable."

She was sure he had visions of illicit activity dancing in his head. Not only the illicit activity in which he had been engaged right up to the moment of her call, but also activity of the criminal sort. No, she was hardly "the type," but in the Riviera, one often found less-than-savory characteristics in those who didn't seem to be "the type." That was part of the area's charm, in fact. And if Gascon suspected as much of Maria Teresa, well, she was not about to disabuse him of that notion.

"How considerable?" he asked.

"Shall we say…twenty thousand Euros…above your usual percentage of the charter fare?"

"Hmmm," he said.

She could practically see the thoughts turning over in his mind, as one desire gave way to another. He was the sort of man for whom involvement in something shady—however peripheral his involvement might be—would be a badge of honor. That there was nothing shady involved was simply a delicious irony, of which she would be aware and he would not.

"Perhaps arrangements could be made," he said. "Give me a half hour."

"Make it fifteen minutes," she said. "As I said, I need to *leave* within the hour. I'm sure you can…get your staff together quickly."

After all, she thought, *they're right there in the bed with you!*

"Yes, yes," he said. "My staff is always on call. Fifteen minutes, then. I will call you back."

"Fine," she said, hanging up the phone.

As she set to packing, Maria smiled. The charter fee,

and the extra twenty thousand Euros, was a small price to pay for the opportunity to see to the *Rotunda* personally. And for the opportunity to ruin Gascon's evening. Not a bad price at all.

AT THE MOMENT that Maria Teresa's flight left the runway in Nice, Darius and Serena met their accomplices in the condominium parking garage. Once again, Sparks had his van, although it was much cleaner tonight than it had been the night before. After all, Ariel would be riding with him. She probably wouldn't have said anything—she wasn't the type to say such things—but he'd have been mortified if she'd had to sit amongst his customary mess. So, rather than the afternoon nap he'd planned, he'd spent the rest of the day with a thirty-gallon trash bag, a vacuum cleaner, and finally that interior and dashboard polisher that left a high sheen and a slick residue.

"Everyone knows the route?" Darius asked for perhaps the fourth time.

"Yes," Marco said, smiling. "Sparks and I were there earlier today. We'll be fine. Just relax. All of you. Compared to the museum, the security at the consulate is laughable. This will be a piece of cake."

"And the museum was a whole cake," Sparks said, hoping the reference to Lead Legs's model would lighten the mood.

Marco, who hadn't been at the meeting, simply looked on blankly. Darius, Serena and Ariel gave stiff laughs. Not a time for humor, Sparks decided.

"Well, let's go," Darius said. He turned to Sparks and Ariel. "See you when it's over."

Sparks and Ariel climbed into the van and circled out of the parking garage. He and Ariel would be across the street, monitoring the radios and operating his antisecurity device. Serena and Darius would ride with Marco in Darius's Ferrari four-seater. Marco would wait in the car while Serena and Darius went in to get the painting. Then they'd meet back in Serena's condo. Simple. Easy.

"You're nervous," Sparks said, glancing across at Ariel.

She tried to smile, but it came off more as a grimace. "I just don't trust Gina. If it were only Mas and Menos, we could count on them to do something stupid and make it easy for us. But Gina…"

"You don't like her?"

"Quite the contrary," Ariel replied. "I do like her. And I respect her. For all that men get lost in her bosom, they miss the intelligence in her eyes. She was an excellent ally. I'm simply afraid she'll be every bit as competent a foe."

"So you think she'll have some surprises waiting for them?" Sparks asked, as they wove through traffic.

"Definitely."

"Why didn't you say something?"

For a moment her thoughts seemed a million miles away. She had a way of doing that, he'd noticed, as if she were accessing a dimension of time and space beyond ordinary human perception. It was eerie, truth be told. But it was also beautiful. For in those moments, she had a radiance that made every fiber in his being glow.

When she returned, it was with a look of faint sadness. "Because sometimes things need to happen with difficulty. Or else we don't fully appreciate them."

It was an odd answer, he thought. Then again, she had always been prone to odd answers to simple questions, even in high school. Surprisingly, he usually discovered—after the fact, and often much to his consternation—that her odd answer had been not merely accurate, but the most elegant possible summary of what had lain ahead. It seemed that way to him, at least. To the other students, she had simply been…spacey.

"Is it hard?" he asked. "Being…I don't know…what are you…psychic?"

She glanced over and smiled. "I don't know that I'm psychic. It's just…sometimes it's as if I can see how the pieces are tumbling together. How they're going to line up when all the tumbling is done. That's all."

"It's a marvelous gift," he said. "But it makes me a little nervous sometimes."

"Why?"

"Well," he began, then paused for a moment, both to consider his answer and to negotiate the interchange onto I-275, which would take them up through St. Petersburg and across the bay into Tampa. "I work with things. Science. I know if I drop an apple, it's going to fall. Gravity. I know if I send a current through a wire coiled around an iron bar, it will create a magnetic charge. The apple doesn't have to decide whether to respond to gravity, and gravity doesn't have to decide whether to act on the apple. The current doesn't have to decide whether to move through the wire, and the iron bar doesn't have to decide whether to become magnetically charged. They just are. It's the nature of physics."

"But?" she asked.

"But people are different. We *do* make decisions. I have to decide whether to drive on to the consulate and help with this cockamamie scheme or whether I should just whisk you off to Sanibel Island for a weekend of frolicking on the beach. Darius and Serena have to decide whether to go into the consulate. Marco has to decide whether to wait for them. Gina and Mas and Menos have their own decisions to make. And if any of us decides to do something strange, well, then everything changes."

"And if I can see how the pieces are coming together," Ariel said, "then you and the rest of us are reduced to falling apples, copper wires and iron bars? With no real power to change the course of our lives?"

"Yes," Sparks said. "Something like that. Exactly like that."

Ariel nodded and smiled. "Well, perhaps you might consider whether the apple, or the wire, or the iron bar really *do* make decisions."

He looked over at her. "Umm…"

"Maybe," she said, "just maybe, there is consciousness in everything. Sentience. Life force. From the electrons in that copper wire, all the way up to you and me. For some of us, like the apple, the decisions are pretty simple. Fall, don't fall. If it doesn't fall, it might save itself from smashing on the ground. But in not falling, it would upset something the rest of us all rely on. So, it decides to fall. Sacrificing itself for the good of all of us.

"In that sense," she continued, "we trust the apple to fall, and it honors our trust. Darius trusts you to drive over to Tampa, and you trust your machine to disable the security at the consulate when we get there. You honor his trust, and the machine honors your trust. All I really do is predict who can be trusted, and when, and how. I'm not *always* right. I do get surprised by life. And sometimes in delightful ways I had never imagined. Like…meeting you."

Sparks blushed crimson. The way she explained it sounded so…simple. But then, her explanations always sounded simple. And usually that simplicity masked a bottomless wealth of subtlety. And yet, all of those thoughts had flitted away in the instant she'd said *Like…meeting you.*

He'd never considered the possibility that he had been as wonderful a surprise for her as she had been for him. But there it was. She'd said it. And he…trusted her.

"Thank you," he whispered. "Likewise."

As daylight gave way to night, she reached over to take his hand. The taillights of the cars ahead were a flickering, glowing, red ribbon, guiding them on. And on they went.

"YOU'RE NOT GOING anywhere!" Gina said sternly. Lead Legs stood between Mas and Menos and the consulate's exit door, his arms folded, looking, Mas thought suddenly, like Hercules defying—whoever it was Hercules had defied.

"We are leaving," Menos said stoutly, although there was a crack in his voice. "We are not going to commit treason."

"Treason!" Gina's eyes widened, then she laughed. "Oh, you are so priceless, Menos. Just priceless."

He looked confused, all his laboriously organized arguments scattering to the four winds. *"¿Qué?"*

"How can this be treason?" Gina asked, still laughing.

"Because…because he is *el príncipe!*"

Gina stepped toward him, hands on her hips. *"Not,"* she said, "until the coronation."

Menos's head jerked back as if he had just been struck. He stammered, *"Pero…pero…. But…his naci- miento!* His birth!"

She shook her head. "His birth entitles him to the job, but he isn't the prince until the coronation. No way."

Even Mas appeared to find this explanation strange. He looked at Menos, who looked at him.

Finally Menos collected himself to say, "If that is true, then we can make anyone the prince!" His own brilliance startled him for a moment, causing him to nearly smile.

The smile was never born, however, because Gina stepped toward him, wagging her finger under his nose just the way his mother used to. "Listen, buster…"

"¿Qué es 'buster'?" Mas asked.

"Shut up, Mas," Gina said. "Menos, let's get this straight. He may be *entitled* to the throne by birth, but he doesn't have it yet, and he won't have it until he's crowned. So nothing you do now is treason…as long as you are acting in the best interests of Masolimia. Right now the best interests of Masolimia involve getting that contract with the genetic company signed as quickly as possible. Do *you* want to be responsible for your countrymen starving to death?"

Menos blanched.

"I didn't think so. Now get your skanky butt in back, and protect that painting with your life. Your *life,* Menos. Because it's one of the greatest treasures of your benighted country. You have a duty to make sure that it is *not* stolen again. Not by anyone. Not even by the *future* prince of Masolimia. Am I clear?"

"But kidnapping…" He was looking lost and getting more lost by the moment.

"Kidnapping! It's not kidnapping, it's *repatriation.*"

"Repatriation?"

"Exactly. I knew you'd understand. Now don't let me hear any more of this nonsense. Your country is depending on you, and you'd better not fail."

CHAPTER TWENTY-FOUR

THE MINUTES until the heist both dragged and raced for Serena. *Heist.* Lord, until a week ago, the word was hardly in her vocabulary. Now it was in her head all the time. What was she coming to?

Darius sat across from her in the back seat of the Ferrari. Marco drove quickly but with calm assurance. He was the only calm one among them. Darius, she realized, looked no happier about this than she felt. He wasn't the sort of man who would do this, either.

And she was beginning to forget all the *good* reasons behind this. All she knew anymore was that she would do whatever was necessary to put this matter to rest for him.

And then he would get on with his life, whether that meant traveling the world as an art dealer or assuming the throne of Masolimia. Either way, she would be left behind.

In that regard, these minutes seemed to be speeding by with all the relentlessness of a rapid freight train. On the other hand, wanting this whole night safely behind them was making the clock hands drag.

"She's going to be waiting for us," Darius said. "*They're* going to be waiting for us."

"Then maybe we shouldn't do this. What if Gina calls the police?"

He shook his head. "She's not the type. The last thing on earth she wants to do is have me arrested."

"Why?"

"Because then she'd be responsible for postponing my ascent to the throne. Because then she might have to explain how *she* came by the painting. No, I don't think we'll see police involvement."

Serena nodded slowly. "Then we should be fine."

He smiled wryly. "I'm not looking forward to arguing with Lead Legs."

"Well, there *is* that."

"Yes. There *is* that."

Serena sighed. "Then maybe we shouldn't do this, Darius. I don't see how it can possibly work. They'll outnumber us. How in the world are you and I going to hold off the four of them?"

"We won't have to," he said with a crooked smile. "I have a plan. After all, I never wanted the painting in the first place. I only wanted to *look* at it."

"Oh. *Oh!*"

His smile widened. "You don't have to come with me, if you don't want."

Her whole mood had shifted. "I wouldn't miss this for the world." Then she laughed.

"And now that they've tried to keep it from me, I want that look more than ever."

MARIA TERESA MAXWELL, like most Europeans, was accustomed to a rather speedy trip through customs. In Europe the borders were very much like the border between Canada and the U.S. Present your papers and go.

However, these days U.S. Customs was not easy. Well, it had never been terribly easy for foreigners, but now it was all but impossible. Apparently a Swiss passport was a suspicious thing to be possessed by an olive-skinned, dark-haired woman. Well, she would be ready for them. She looked out the window at the blackness of the Atlantic, and considered which of several stories she might spin to pass quickly through customs and get on to the consulate.

The simplest, of course, was that she was coming to the States to visit her son, an art dealer. But that wouldn't do. First, the theft of the *Rotunda* had probably been discovered by now. Announcing that you had come to visit an art dealer, in a city where an art theft had just occurred, was likely to raise eyebrows. More than that, however, it was just *too* simple. It lacked, as the French would say, joie de vivre. And what was life, if not to be enjoyed?

Obviously, she couldn't tell the truth—that she was coming to claim and return to her homeland a painting that had been stolen fifty years prior, and stolen again the night before. On the other hand, she had found that the most believable fictions often carried with them a germ of truth. It was simply a matter of choosing the right germ.

"On the left, Madame," the pilot said over the intercom. "The Azores."

"Merci," she said without really looking.

Yes, the Azores Islands were something of Europe's last gasp before the vastness of the Atlantic. Yes, passing them meant she was nearly one-third of the way to Florida. She supposed that mattered to many European tourists on their first trip to the United States. To her, it meant only that she had barely four hours to finalize her thoughts and plans. Then, after all of these weeks spent hovering behind the scenes, she could finally step onto the stage.

She was, at heart, an actress. The stage was where she belonged. On this night the stage was in Tampa, Florida. And there she would be. Just as soon as she decided what to tell the functionaries at customs.

ON THEIR WAY to the consulate, Marco, Serena and Darius had to drive through Ybor City, Tampa's famous and historic cigar district. These days not only were cigars hand-rolled here by many small businesses, but the city had become a famed night spot.

Life began after dark in Ybor. The sidewalks were crowded, every club and bar blazed with inviting signs. Founded by cigar manufacturers who had left Cuba for Key West, then Key West for Tampa, Ybor's main street charmed visitors with its Cuban flavor at any time of day, and at night promised endless hours of entertainment and some of the finest Cuban and Spanish food to be found anywhere.

Marco expertly dodged slightly drunk revelers, and got them through as quickly as possible. The Port of Tampa loomed only a couple of blocks away, but as the country's twelfth largest port, that was only its beginning. Away from Ybor, around the head of Tampa Bay, lay the working piers where everything from petroleum to phosphates to food and cars entered the country, and equally prodigious exports departed.

It was in that area that Masolimia had placed its consulate, rather than near Ybor and all the channelside cruise ship berths. The rationale for the decision was as clear as mud, but there it was.

"There it is," said Marco, driving slowly past a low strip mall that contained an import-export firm, a hardware store and a lawyer's office. On the very end hunkered the Masolimian consulate, in dire need of paint and a new sidewalk. The neighborhood around, however, showed more care, containing as it did the offices of shipbuilders and repairers and some recently renovated older homes. In short, the building was an eyesore with train tracks right behind it.

"Ah, for urban planning," Serena muttered.

Beside her, Darius chuckled. "It somehow seems so apropos," he answered.

Maybe to him it did. "I think it needs a bulldozer."

"Well, if I turn out to be the prince, maybe I'll oblige you."

Serena had to laugh, but Marco interrupted her.

"Prince?" he said. "You are the prince of Masolimia?"

Darius started to shake his head, but before he could respond in any way, Marco plunged on.

"I knew the old prince," he said, his voice conveying warmth. "We used to race together. Well, against each other. He was a great driver, the best. All that practice on the narrow mountain roads of your country," he added.

"It's not my country yet," Darius said, but Marco appeared not to hear him.

"We had some great times together, the prince and I. I called him Gio, because his name was Juan, and when he could escape his bodyguards, we went drinking and gambling together."

"Really." Darius didn't exactly sound enthralled.

"Oh, *sì*," Marco said, his voice conveying nostalgia. "He was very good at poker, as good at poker as he was at driving. We had a competition going, to see who could win the most races." He sighed. "I went to his funeral last year. Very sad."

"Yes, very," Darius said. "I wish he'd lived a lot longer."

"Very generous," Marco said. "Maybe you and I play poker some time, yes? Or race?"

"No racing," Darius said firmly. "But maybe poker. I'd enjoy that."

"Good."

Serena looked at the man beside her, surprised. "You like to gamble?"

"Poker isn't exactly gambling," he replied. "It's a game of skill. If it weren't, you wouldn't see the same faces at the final tables so often in the tournaments."

"Oh."

He looked at her. "Do you play?"

"Only a little. For me, it's definitely gambling."

"Then someday I'll teach you the finer points of the game. You have the right mind for it."

"Hmm." She had never in her life wanted to gamble anything. She didn't even buy lottery tickets.

"We'll play for chips, not money," he said. "It's every bit as much fun."

"If you say so."

He laughed. "For a woman who barged into my life and helped plan the theft of a painting because she was bored, you're amazingly straitlaced."

She didn't know if she liked that at all. "I am not."

"Well," he said meaningfully, reaching over to squeeze her thigh, "you're not as straitlaced as you used to be."

"Humph."

Marco had driven them past the consulate, down a few side streets, and now brought them back by it. "It looks empty."

The windows were definitely dark, and there was no movement to be seen anywhere.

"Still," said Darius, "I want to watch the place for a while."

He put the headset on his head, and keyed the radio. "Sparks?"

"Yo."

"Can you see the rear?"

"Clear as can be. We're in position."

"Okay. We're going to sit out front and watch for a while. Nothing before midnight."

"Gotcha."

Marco backed the car into a parking slot across the street in front of a shipping firm. Two other cars sat in the lot, making them less conspicuous. In one of the cars sat two men, using a penlight to look at something that might have been a map. Marco waved at them, and one of them waved back.

"Now," Darius said, "we'll see if anyone's home."

MARIA TERESA MAXWELL's plane was the last to land at Tampa International Airport for the night. At home it was nearly six in the morning, but here it was coming up on midnight. She had wanted to arrive at a more reasonable hour, but what was one to do? Not even a host of imprecations sent heavenward could shorten the distance from Nice to Tampa.

So here she was, feeling rather bedraggled, staggering into an airport with her maid at her heels, too much champagne in her blood and too much caviar to mix well with it in her stomach.

She was not, at this moment, a happy woman, and woe betide the customs official who gave her any difficulty.

Her maid was, as always, a paragon of efficiency, arranging for a porter to unload the six trunks and suitcases Maria Teresa had brought along for herself, and the maid's own two. Then down the stairs and across the tarmac to customs. Why was there no convenient car awaiting her as there would be elsewhere? Had these Americans no sense of her importance and wealth?

Apparently not. Customs was winding down for the night, and the woman on duty didn't look at all happy to see Maria Teresa's mound of baggage.

The customs agent took the passports from the maid, Elena, then looked suspiciously at the two of them. "How long are you planning to stay?"

"Only a few days," said Maria Teresa, with a regal wave of her hand. "I have come to see my son."

"It looks like you're moving in with him."

"One must always be prepared for whatever occasion arises."

"Humph." The officious woman looked at the passports again.

Maria Teresa wanted to wallop herself in the head, for not having remembered to use her well-manufactured story. If she hadn't been so fatigued, she wouldn't have blurted the truth.

"What does your son do here?"

"He is *visiting*, also," Maria said. "He is the prince of Masolimia!"

If she expected this declaration to smooth her way, she was sadly mistaken.

The customs official looked at her again, and this time her expression was clearly suspicious. "Your passport says you are Swiss."

"I am. As is my son. But he is the long-lost heir to the throne!"

"Now I've heard everything," the woman said. And instant later she was speaking into a radio. A few moments after that, Maria Teresa and her maid were surrounded.

Well, thought Maria Teresa irritably. The germ of truth hadn't worked. So now it was time to add the lie. *"Escuche,"* she said sternly. "My son is ill and needs to return home. I've come to get him. Call the Masolimian embassy. They will confirm it."

THE RINGING of the telephone came as a shock to several people. First to Mas, Menos, Gina and Lead Legs, all of whom, despite their intake of pizza and heavily-caffeinated cola, had dozed off.

"What the—" Gina and Lead Legs began in unison.

"¡Infierno!" Mas and Menos concluded as they jerked awake and promptly smacked their heads together.

THE NEXT SHOCK came to Darius and Serena, who at that moment were poised by the back door, she with a flashlight, he with a credit card.

"Is that a phone?" she whispered.

"Yes," he said, his heart sinking in his chest. "And someone's answering it."

"Damn," Serena said.

"Exactly," he replied.

"EXCREMENTO," MAS SAID, holding the phone to his ear.

"Exactamente," Menos replied, already knowing who was calling, who was always calling, who seemed

to be unable to let a single hour go past without calling, even though she hadn't called all evening. Which, come to think of it, was so suspicious that he knew what would come next, almost before he saw Mas's face fall like a quail hit by birdshot.

"*¿Qué?*" Mas said, apparently still too shocked to switch from his native language to English. "*¿Qué?*"

"What is it?" Gina said, her dark eyes suddenly alert.

"*¿Qué?*" Mas repeated into the phone again.

Gina once again tried to get his attention, this time punctuating it with a sharp kick to his shin. "What?"

"*¿Qué?*" Mas said, looking over at her.

"WHAT?" SERENA SAID, looking at Darius, who had his ear pressed to the door.

"Well, either I'm listening to an episode of *Fawlty Towers,* or confusion reigns within." He winked. "It could be either."

For Serena, it was as if a dam of anxiety had broken. She didn't simply giggle. She laughed.

Loudly.

"Shhh," Darius said.

"SHHH," LEAD LEGS SAID, putting a finger to his lips and pointing to the back door.

Gina nodded and turned to Mas. "Give me the phone," she whispered.

From the reaction, she could as easily have asked Mas to give her an angry rattlesnake. He handed it over, not merely without hesitation but with vigor. Menos nodded sagely, understanding. He knew who was on the phone, and he would have done the same thing. Let Gina deal with the virago.

"Masolimian Consulate," Gina said calmly. "How may I help you?"

As she spoke, Lead Legs moved to the back door. He listened for a moment, then pulled it open with a flourish.

Darius, who had been leaning against the door as he listened, tumbled inward. Serena, who had been leaning against Darius, followed.

"That's correct," Gina said, turning to face the back door. "Yes, ma'am. As a matter of fact, he's right here."

CHAPTER TWENTY-FIVE

SPARKS LOOKED AT ARIEL. "Something's wrong."

"Perhaps," she said. "At least they're in."

"That door was opened from the inside," he said.

She nodded. "Yes, it was."

"You were right. Gina is there."

She nodded again. "That would be my guess."

"And you're not worried?" he asked. "When we were driving over here, this was exactly what you *were* worried might happen. Now it's happened, and you're *not* worried?"

She smiled. "Exactly."

Somehow, somewhere, in some universe of infinite, circular possibilities, that made sense. Here, now, in *this* universe, Sparks wasn't so sure. He reached for the door handle.

"Shhh," Ariel said, reaching over to rest a hand on his. "Let things happen."

He considered resisting but decided against it. She had always had a sense for these things. He wasn't sure if he believed in a higher power. But he believed in Ariel.

"Okay," he said. "We'll do it your way."

She patted his hand. "It's not my way, Sparks. It's simply the way things are. The way things need to be."

He still wasn't convinced. On the other hand, there were worse things than sitting in a van with a stunningly beautiful woman whose hand was resting on his. He settled back in his seat and watched.

"Good," she said.

"GOOD," GINA SAID into the telephone. "We'll see you soon, then."

She hung up the telephone and looked at the startled twosome still untangling themselves on the floor.

"Guess who?" she asked.

"I don't have to guess," Darius said, having seen the faces of Mas and Menos, and knowing only one who could elicit that particular expression of horror. "My mother."

"Right in one try," Gina said. "How convenient."

"Convenient?" Darius asked.

"Of course! She's coming here for the painting, and for her son. Might as well have both of you in one place. We wouldn't want her to have to chase all over the area looking for you."

"No!" Mas and Menos said in unison, the mere thought apparently setting them off into spasms of terror.

Darius felt sorry for them. He truly did. He at least had almost four decades of experience dealing with his mother. They were ill equipped. She had probably made their lives hell for the past few days—or weeks, or months. Knowing his mother, these two would probably have nightmares for years to come.

And all because of him.

"Well," Serena said, rising to her feet. "I guess we're all here."

"I guess we are," Gina said, eyeing her suspiciously.

"And I don't suppose you're going to let us leave," Serena said.

"No," Gina said. "I don't think so."

"Fine," Serena said. "Then we may as well look at this silly painting that's caused so much trouble."

Mas looked at Menos. Menos looked at Lead Legs. Lead Legs looked at Gina. Gina merely shrugged.

"I guess you're a glutton for punishment. But, okay—" she walked to an easel that stood against one wall, and grasped one corner of the sheet that hung over the frame "—here she is. Miss Masolimia."

"ABSURD!" Maria Teresa said as she stood at the curb while two skycaps and Elena wrestled her bags into a taxi. "In the south of France, I would have a limo waiting."

"That may be," the taxi driver said calmly. "But this isn't the south of France."

"Obviously not!" she said. "But I would think a bit of class would be available."

The driver laughed as he closed the trunk. "This is Florida, ma'am. Class is clean flip-flops. So where are we going?"

"The Masolimian consulate," she said, climbing into the back seat. "I assume you know where that is."

"No, ma'am, I don't," he said, and closed the door. Then, to the skycap, he added, "But I'm sure I'm going to find out."

The skycap grinned. "Better you than me."

Maria Teresa knocked on the window, then rolled it down. "Well?"

"Yes, ma'am," the driver said. He circled around the cab and settled in behind the wheel. "So where is this consulate?"

"How would I know?" Maria said. "This is your home, not mine!"

"Not a problem, ma'am," he said, picking up the radio.

He would rather get his directions from the dispatcher, anyway. The less he dealt with this woman, the better. Oh well, he thought. At least she wasn't from up north.

DARIUS HAD NEVER SEEN the *Rotunda*. He had seen a single thumbnail photograph, in the collection catalogue. But that had been mercifully reduced. And slightly, but mercifully, out of focus. This was full size and clear.

And horrible.

"We know," Gina said. "Trust me, we know."

"It's…" Serena said, as if searching for words.

"I've seen worse," Darius said. Seeing the shock in Serena's eyes, he nodded. "Really, I have. You would be amazed."

"I thought art was…"

"Beautiful?" he asked. Serena nodded, and he continued. "Well, eye of the beholder, as they say."

"And some beholders have astigmatism and color-blindness," Gina said.

"Perhaps," Darius said. He grew quiet for a long moment, studying the painting, tipping his head right, then left, standing back, approaching it close, then standing back again. "But not this painter."

"No?" Serena asked.

"No," he said. "Believe it or not, this is quite good. Amazing, in fact."

"Oh please," Gina said. "Spare us the art-snob, you-just-don't-understand school of art appreciation. Anyone can see it's horrible."

"Oh, it is," Darius said, smiling. "As a portrait of Princess Rotunda, it's abysmal. But that's not what it is. Not really. And for what it is, it's amazing work."

"So what is it?" Serena asked.

"A map of the Masolimian catacombs," Darius said.

"Well, yes, I knew that much," Serena said.

"And," Darius added, "a brilliantly encoded history of the people who built them."

"What?" Serena asked.

"What?" Gina echoed.

"*¿Qué?*" Mas and Menos said.

"WHAT?" SPARKS ASKED, rolling down his window.

"Something's wrong," Marco said, having left his

car and walked over to the van. "They've been in there way too long."

"Ariel says it's fine," Sparks said.

"Do you, now?" Marco asked, looking across at her.

Ariel nodded. "Well, yes. I suspected Gina would be here tonight."

"So did Darius," Marco said. "He and Serena were talking about it on the way over here."

"So," Ariel said, "things are going as expected."

"That's one way of looking at it," Marco said. "But shouldn't we go in and see what's happening? See if we can help?"

"Only if you want a violent confrontation," Ariel said. "And I don't think anyone wants that. There are times to act and times to let events act for you. This is a time to let events act for us."

"You're sure?" Marco asked.

Ariel nodded. "I don't think anyone wants to *harm* anyone here. So there's no reason to worry."

Marco seemed mollified. "I guess you're right."

"Want some coffee?" Sparks asked, holding up a thermos.

"I should get back to the car," Marco said.

"Why?" Sparks asked. "It's not like they're coming out anytime soon."

"True," Marco said. "Okay, sure."

"Hop in," Sparks said. "The back seat is clean."

"Very clean," Ariel said.

Ahh, Sparks thought. *She noticed!*

Marco climbed into the back seat of the van and took the proffered cup of coffee.

"This is going to be a long night," he said.

WHICH WAS THE EXACT THOUGHT running through Tom Kelly's mind as he wove through Ybor City. Okay, he was a cabdriver. And as a cabdriver, he saw all kinds of people from all over the world. Businessmen. Tourists. Relatives coming to visit, or impose, depending on one's point of view. Americans of all geographic origins. Japanese. Brits. Europeans. Happy people. Anxious people. Miserable people. Polite people. Rude people. He'd seem them all.

Or he thought he had, until he'd had the terrible misfortune to be first in the queue when Maria Teresa Maxwell emerged from the terminal. He knew now why the Europeans loved to put gargoyles in their architecture. They were marking the passage of this woman.

"Pathetic," she said, looking out the window. "This is what passes for culture in America? Eighty years and you call it historic," Maria Teresa said. "In Europe, something eighty years old is considered novel. Honestly, you have no understanding of history."

"No, ma'am," Tom said. "I've never been to Europe."

"Pity," she said.

"My wife agrees with you," he replied. "She wants us to visit the old country. Ireland."

"Irish," Maria said, as if she were pronouncing a block of cheese unfit for human consumption. "I might have known."

On another night, with another fare, he might have let that go. But his wife had, just that afternoon, and for the third time in a week, complained about his working nights. Never mind that his driving a cab had been her idea. Never mind that he'd only been on the job for four months and didn't have the seniority to get day shifts. Never mind that the night shift paid extra, although not enough to make up for the smaller tips that nighttime fares usually gave.

His nerves were still raw from the spat, and he was in no mood to hear some haughty European windbag put down his proud Irish heritage. And so, knowing he ought to keep his mouth shut, knowing she would probably complain to the company and he'd lose his job, knowing he was making a big mistake, he pulled the cab over to the curb with a squeal of brakes and turned in his seat.

"Lady, don't you *ever* talk down the Irish. My people preserved civilization while your people were busy dying of plague. We were starved, denied freedom of worship, denied our own land, and we survived it all. So if you want to find out how we survived it all, you just keep complaining. And you'll see what the Irish really are."

Much to his amazement, the woman did not reply. In fact, after a momentary pause, she sat back in her seat and actually smiled. She peered at the nameplate on the dash. Finally, she spoke.

"I like you, Tom Kelly. You have spunk."

Of all the tactics she could have chosen, this was the one for which he was totally unprepared. Had his jaw dropped any lower, he'd have had to unfasten his seat belt to retrieve it. A long moment of silence passed.

"Thank you," he said. "I think."

"You think, therefore you are," Maria Teresa replied. "Now, if we're finished with the lovely tour of your city, could we get to the consulate, please?"

He wasn't sure if she was being sarcastic or sincere. He decided on sincere, if only because he'd had enough fights for one day.

"Certainly, ma'am. I am at your service."

"Quickly, please," she added.

"Is there a condensed version of this?" Gina asked, interrupting Darius's explanation of the history and culture of Masolimia during the thirteenth to fifteenth centuries. "I don't mean to be rude, but…"

"Yes," Darius said. "I can get long-winded."

"I was fascinated," Serena said.

"Wonderful," Gina said. "Ask him for the unabridged version tomorrow. In the meantime, if we could cut to the chase, please."

"Certainly," Darius said, somewhat put off by Gina's manner, but that was more than balanced by Serena's reply. More than balanced. With a smile in Serena's direction, he continued.

"So, here we reach 1489, and for the past three hundred years, Masolimia has been something of a through way for French and Spanish armies. Of course, there's no guarantee that it won't happen again, so the court was understandably reluctant to do anything so bold as to openly assert a cultural heritage. Instead, at the behest of Prince Tímido, and much to the horror of his wife, the royal portraitist was commissioned to celebrate the newly established Masolimian independence in the most obscure manner possible. And thus we have…the *Rotunda.*"

"You're saying he messed it up on purpose," Gina said.

"Exactly. The hump on the princess's shoulder represents the mountains in which Masolimia is located. The greenish-yellow hue of her face mirrors the pale greens of springtime in that semiarid area. The orange of her eyes calls to mind the sun rising and setting in freedom. The plain, worn wool dress—she actually wore a lovely green for the sitting, I'm told—reflects the work and struggle of the Masolimian people to win their liberty. The featureless hair, painted with broad sweeps of a knife, connects past, present and future in a seamless whole, as if the invasions and occupations of the past were mere blips on an unbroken history. It's quite amazing, really."

"And the pimples and veins," Serena said, nodding with a practiced dermatologist's eye, "they aren't real. Their shapes and patterns don't fit the blood vessels of the face and neck. They are the map of the catacombs?"

Darius smiled. "Precisely, my dear. The family histories of Masolimia, to that date, reflected in the face of the reigning princess. As if all of Masolimia lives in her and the prince."

"So how do we decipher the map?" Serena asked.

"My earliest ancestors were this mole," he said, pointing. "The three hairs represent three brothers, the first citizens in my family line, refugees from southern France, who lay in the same tomb."

"And the royal line?" Gina asked.

"Begins with the pimple on her nose," Darius said. "Now all we need to do is follow the lines. And connect the dots."

"Sounds simple enough," Serena said.

AND IT MIGHT HAVE BEEN, but for what was happening in the parking lot at that very moment. For just as Marco was leaving the van to return to his car, he saw the two men who had been parked near him approach. Figuring they hadn't found what they wanted on their map, he politely waited to help them with directions.

But before anyone spoke, the two men in street clothes sprang from surveillance into action. Drawing weapons, they spun Marco against the side of the van.

"Police. Everybody out."

"What's going on?" Sparks asked, dumfounded, his head hanging out the driver's window.

"You tell us," the cop said. "Parked in a deserted lot, late at night. This guy comes up to the window, then sits in the car for a few minutes, then leaves? That sounds like probable cause to me."

"Me, too," the other cop agreed. "Looks a whole lot like a drug deal."

"Yup," the first cop said. "So let's just see what you have in that van."

Oh please, Sparks thought. What else can go wrong?

It was at that moment that the taxi skidded into the parking lot and Maria Teresa Maxwell burst out.

CHAPTER TWENTY-SIX

"AY, MADRE DE DIOS!" Maria Teresa shrieked as she saw the men with the guns holding that poor little man against the side of the van. "*¡Socorro!* Help! *¡Ladrones!* Thieves! *¡Agarren a los ladrones!* Stop, thief!"

"Shit," said one of the men holding Marco against the van. "Police!" he shouted, but the word was utterly lost in Maria Teresa's shrieks.

Tom Kelly leaped out of the cab, the only weapon he had in his hand. It was a piece of thick PVC piping he could claim was for a repair job at home, but which still could function as a fairly good weapon.

"What the hell?" he said as he saw what was happening at the van. Two scruffy men were holding a small elderly man against the side of the van, and each of them held guns.

"I'm calling the police," he shouted.

EVEN INSIDE THE EMBASSY, largely because the back door was still open, the uproar in the parking lot could be heard. Darius cocked his head to one side, looking quizzically at Gina. "My mother?"

Gina nodded.

"She's *here?*"

Gina shrugged. "Not part of *my* plan," she told him.

"Oh my God," Serena said, suddenly grabbing Darius's arm. "Someone just shouted that he was police."

Darius sighed. "Then it's most definitely my mother. Excuse me a moment, please?"

"LADRONES!" Maria Teresa shouted, joined now by the shrieks of her maid. "Leave that poor *viejo* alone!"

As Tom Kelly reached into the cab for his radio mike, Maria Teresa grabbed the PVC pipe from his hand and charged forward, ready to do battle.

"No!" shouted Sparks, visions of this innocent woman being laid out bloody on the pavement for the crime of trying to help. "No!"

"Police," shouted one of the cops again, but Maria Teresa still charged forward.

Then into the bedlam came a voice that froze everyone.

"Mother!"

Maria Teresa stopped midstride. *"Mi hijo?"*

"Basta ya. Ellos son policías."

"Policía?"

"Sí."

Maria Teresa eyed the two armed men suspiciously. "No uniform?" she asked in English. "No badge? They just grab this old man…."

"I'm not an old man," Marco said. "Not unless you're an old woman."

Maria Teresa bridled. "I was going to save you."

"You were more likely to get yourself shot," Marco said. Shaking himself hard, he broke loose of the policemen who were now looking as confused as anyone. "I am Marco Paloni, the most famous Grand Prix driver of all time, and I would not come within a mile of drugs!"

"Marco Paloni?" Maria Teresa repeated, her eyes widening. She dropped the pipe.

"Marco Paloni?" the cops said in unison.

"My God," said the shorter of the two, "you were my hero when I was growing up."

The other said sarcastically, "He still tries to drive like you."

Marco smiled graciously at them both, as a man who was merely receiving his due. "I am honored."

Maria Teresa, who never liked to be second fiddle to anyone, announced, "And I am the dowager princess of Masolimia."

"Really?" Marco asked. "Then Darius over there is your son?"

"Precisely."

"Unfortunately," Darius said. "However that may be, officers, this *is* consular property, and I *am* the Prince of Masolimia, so I'm afraid I'm going to have to ask you to let me sort out this mess myself."

The officers exchanged looks. "Why all the suspicious activity?"

"Because," said Darius, "my friends came to protect

me. There is the rumor of a kidnap attempt against my person."

"Well then," said the shorter cop, "you need us."

Darius studied them thoughtfully for a moment. "Yes, of course, you're right. But I need your assistance *off* the consular grounds. I'm sure you can understand. If you'd resume your watch, I'd be very grateful. In the meantime I have a family situation to sort out."

"Ah."

"Well, okay," said the taller officer. "You need us, we'll be right across the street."

"Thank you." Darius gave them an utterly European bow. Mollified, the officers returned to their car.

Darius's lips compressed. "Everyone inside. Now!"

"Darius!" his mother objected.

"Move. *¡Ahora!*"

"What about me?" Tom Kelly asked. "She hasn't paid me."

"You come inside, too," Darius said. "I'll pay you for the entire night. She's going to need transport back to the airport come morning."

"Darius!"

"Mother, shut up."

Maria Teresa's mouth closed with such force that the clack was heard by everyone. Tossing her head, she marched in the direction Darius pointed, her maid trotting on her heels. Tom Kelly followed them.

Then, with a wave, Darius indicated that Marco, Sparks and Ariel should follow.

"We're going to sort this out and we're going to sort it out now," he said firmly.

Ariel grinned. "It's about time."

UNDER DARIUS'S DIRECTION, Lead Legs brought the painting out to the front office, where there was more room and more light.

"As you can see," Darius told Gina, "it is no longer necessary to kidnap me. Or let my mother pretend she has been kidnapped."

"Pretend?" Maria Teresa asked. "You have no idea what I went through to escape my abductors! I filed away a lock. I crept…"

"Mother, enough. You were at the Ritz. If you needed help escaping from there, the place has certainly changed in the last year."

Maria Teresa once again fell mercifully silent. With an angry movement of her head, she directed her maid to bring her a chair. Then she plopped down, looking for all the world like fury chained.

"This," said Darius, looking at his mother and pointing to the painting, "is the *Rotunda*."

"*Dios mío,* they should have beheaded the painter!"

"Exactly what I thought," Gina agreed. "But apparently it's all symbolic."

"I," said Darius's mother, "should never have allowed *anyone* to make me look like that. I would have… shot him!"

"Rotunda wasn't given any choice," Darius reminded her. "This was her *husband's* idea."

"Then I should have shot him."

Darius smiled faintly. "I never knew you were so bloodthirsty, *ma mère.*"

"What do you expect? You've driven me to distraction for weeks now. Why won't you acknowledge the truth?"

"I will. Once I am certain it *is* the truth. Which is why we are now going to study this painting and follow the catacombs."

"And how, exactly, are we supposed to make sense of these lines?" Maria Teresa asked, peering at the painting. "It's like the web of a drunken spider."

"Ahhh," Serena said, stepping forward to look closer. "I think that's where I can help."

"You?" Maria Teresa asked.

"You?" Gina echoed.

"Me," Serena said. "After all. I'm a dermatologist. I'm used to looking at lines on skin."

"She's got a point," Darius said.

"A *doctor?*" Maria Teresa asked, beaming.

Darius merely shrugged and smiled in a *Hey, even a blind squirrel finds an acorn now and then* kind of way. His mother nodded approval, but his attention had already returned to Serena, who was now examining the painting, her fingers tracing over cheekbones and the line of the nose, under the eyes and across the forehead.

"I'll need a pencil and paper," she said. "When it comes to skin, I think better with a pencil moving."

She first sketched the face. Darius was surprised to discover that she had a talent for drawing, though he supposed it made sense that a dermatologist would be part artist. After all, they painted on the canvas of the human face, where everyone would see their work. In a matter of minutes, the form of Princess Rotunda appeared on her page, and she began to trace—in surprisingly accurate detail—the web of lines with which the painter had desecrated a princess and celebrated a people.

"Can't we just follow it on the painting?" Maria Teresa asked.

"Sure," Serena said. "If you want me to deface the painting by writing on it."

"No!" Mas and Menos shouted in unison.

"Heavens, no!" Maria Teresa agreed.

"I didn't think so," Serena said. "So…we have to do it this way."

Soon there were eleven people huddled around, glancing from page to painting to page to painting, offering advice in the manner usually reserved for a game of solitaire.

"There's another line across her chin," Tom Kelly suggested, pointing.

"And don't forget this one, on her throat…oh, you've got it already," Lead Legs said.

Darius was surprised that Serena could handle so much…help…with grace and courtesy. Most of the time, she even said, "Thank you." Most of the time, she even managed to make it sound sincere. She truly was an amazing woman, in so many ways.

She had also managed, almost immediately, to get the measure of his mother. That had never happened before. Always, *always,* when he met someone and introduced them to his mother, the sparks flew almost immediately. And always before, the someone had slunk away, out of his life. And always, his mother had said, "Well, she was no good for you, anyway."

It had been yet another of the many bones of contention between them. Still, despite all of those bones, he loved his mother. And he'd never been so foolish as to ignore the many qualities she'd helped to instill in him from childhood.

So he had always known that, if he were to find a woman to be his wife, it would have to be a woman who could interact with his mother on an equal footing. He'd avoided thinking too much about a future with Serena, for that reason as much as any other.

Yes, her life and her work were here in Florida. But he suspected that distance was a problem which could easily be resolved. Florida was as good a home base for his work as an art dealer as anywhere else in the world. Yes, he'd be traveling a lot, but he traveled a lot regardless. It was the nature of his profession. He had to go where the art was, whether it was in Europe, South Africa, America, or, increasingly, Japan and Hong Kong. So yes, he could see himself settling in Florida.

If he weren't the Prince of Masolimia, that is. He supposed he wouldn't have to be there *all* the time. After all, didn't the Prince of Monaco globe-trot on a regular basis? Sure, he would have to spend considerable time in his homeland. There would be administrative duties and the other trappings of the position. But he wasn't about to give up his career.

And he wasn't about to give up Serena. Assuming she wouldn't give up on him, knowing how much he'd be away. Somehow, though, she seemed like the kind of woman for whom love transcended difficulty, not because it was easy, but because it was worth the effort. He hoped so.

He watched silently as she completed tracing the lines from painting to page, then sat back to double-check her work. Even his mother had fallen silent, which he deemed something of a minor miracle. Serena's eyes darted back and forth, comparing, taking in details even his practiced eye had missed, adding here, erasing there, touching up, until she was satisfied.

"I think I've got it," she said.

"Looks good to me," Darius agreed.

"It had better be," Maria Teresa said. "There's only the future of a people hanging in the balance."

Serena merely fixed her with an icy stare and returned to her work. Yes, she definitely had his mother's number. His mother's nature was to push only until a person pushed back. Provided they pushed back in the right way, she would relent. Not because she was cowed—he doubted anyone could cow his mother—but because she respected strength.

And apparently she'd found something to respect in

Serena, for when she met Darius's eyes, she gave another approving nod. It might as well have been a papal blessing. It was certainly equally difficult to acquire.

"Interesting," Serena said, after a long moment.

"What?" Darius asked, leaning forward.

Nine other heads leaned in also. Darius thought it looked rather like the start of a rugby scrum. At that moment Mas let out a belch smelling of pizza and cola, and the huddle parted like a flower opening its petals.

"Perdón," Mas said.

"De nada," Darius answered.

"Well, not exactly *nothing*," Maria Teresa said.

"Fascinating," Serena mused aloud, still studying the page intently.

"What?" Maria Teresa asked, this time leading the charge as everyone hunched forward again.

"Hmmm?" Serena said.

"¿Qué?" Mas and Menos asked.

The huddle grew closer, Darius jockeying for position and wondering if Serena could even breathe in the middle of such a crush. Then, from the corner of his eye, he saw a look of concern. Whether she was indeed feeling crowded, or had the first glimmer of an idea, he couldn't be sure. "Amazing," she said.

"What?" everyone said in unison.

"Apparently," she said, "our painter was something of a Renaissance man. He was not only a talented artist, but an expert in human anatomy. And well ahead of his time, in fact. I'd love to look at his notes sometime. Absolutely…fascinating."

This time no one asked. Instead Ariel spoke softly.

"I think they're getting impatient."

"Well," Serena said, "at the time of this work, which I believe dates to the late-fifteenth century, science had only just begun to understand the structure and function of the human body. Western science, that is. We knew the skeleton, of course, and the locations of the major organs. And we had a pretty fair understanding of the circulatory system. But nothing like this. Not at this time."

"Perhaps you could explain further?" Darius suggested.

"It's quite simple, actually," she said. "I knew the lines on her face were symbolic because they don't follow the circulatory system. Not exactly. They do in places, and in other places they don't."

"Right," Darius said. "It's a map of the catacombs."

"And a fascinating map at that," Serena said. "Because, where the lines don't follow the arteries, veins, and capillaries of the face, they follow something else. Something no one at that time could have known."

She was obviously drawing out the conclusion for some reason. Darius decided to play the straight man.

"Okay, I'll bite. What do the other lines follow?"

"The facial nerves," Serena said.

"Why is that so amazing?" Maria Teresa asked. "If they knew where the veins and arteries were, they should have known where the nerves were, too. Shouldn't they?"

Serena smiled. "Well, no. The veins and arteries are comparatively large. You can see them with the naked eye. Many of the nerves, though, are tiny. You can't see them without a magnifying glass. That's why neurosurgery is such a demanding discipline. We didn't map the human nervous system for another three or four centuries. And he had it right. In this painting."

"Wow," Darius said.

"Wow, indeed," Serena replied.

"Okay, wow," Maria Teresa said. "That's a fascinating piece of trivia. But how does it help us?"

"Oh, it's a huge help," Serena said, one corner of her mouth turned down in a slight frown. "Because the various family trees of Masolimia are mapped along anatomical lines. Your family, Mrs. Maxwell, starts here, on the chin, at this mole."

"Yes," Maria Teresa said. "So?"

"So we follow the mental nerve back to the inferior alveolar, along the line of the lower teeth, here." She traced over the line she'd copied from the painting, highlighting it as it ran up the princess's chin. "There are other offshoots, but the primary line runs through. And if we compare that with the initial survey map that was done earlier this year, that nerve ganglion is the line of primogeniture for your family.

"Meanwhile," she said, "the current royal line, at the time of this painting, begins on the princess's nose, at this pimple. The primogeniture line follows the facial artery, which branches off from the common carotid in the throat, curls up under the chin, across the cheek, where it meets the infraorbital artery beneath the eye, and on up to the eyebrow where it joins with the supraorbital artery. In between, right alongside the nose, smaller arteries run out to the tip of the nose, and to this pimple."

She pointed.

"This is all very interesting, Doctor," Gina said. "But does it really solve anything?"

"Yes, it does," Serena said. "Because as the facial artery crosses through the cheek, there is a network of capillaries, here."

She pointed to what seemed like a splotch.

"That goes into the deep facial vein, which passes alongside the mental artery up the jaw."

"Mental?" Darius asked.

"Yes," Serena said. "The mental artery, which runs right alongside..."

"The mental nerve?" Darius said, as she traced the two parallel lines.

"Exactly. For at least five generations, the primogeniture line of your family ran parallel to the secondary line of the royal family."

"Meaning?" Gina asked.

"Meaning," Serena said, "somewhere along the way, probably under a molar somewhere..."

"Yes?" Maria Teresa asked, expectantly.

Serena looked up at Darius, took a deep breath and continued. "...I would guess beneath the wisdom tooth, right about *there*," she pointed again, "you became…a prince."

"Oh, no!" Mas said, eyeing Darius fearfully.

"Oh, yes!" Maria Teresa cried. Then she turned to Darius. "And to think, all those years I said you were getting on my nerves."

CHAPTER TWENTY-SEVEN

"WELL, HELL," Darius said. It would have been fair to say that he didn't look happy, unlike his mother, who was clearly ecstatic. Gina looked smug, Lead Legs looked as if he couldn't care less…and so for that matter did Sparks. Ariel looked as if she had known all along.

And Mas and Menos were slinking toward the nearest exit.

"Come back here, you two," Darius barked. Immediately they began to slink back in his direction.

He sounded like a prince, Serena thought. Sounded like one born to command. And frankly he looked the part. But her amusement at the map had died a quick and sudden death as reality struck home: Darius was the prince. The ruler of a country.

And she was nothing but a dermatologist whose entire life was centered on the far side of the Atlantic Ocean.

More than the gulf of distance divided them. Everything else did, too. Her stomach was plunging faster than an express elevator from the hundredth story. Barely born dreams, just barely flickering to life, were doused. It was over.

Darius looked at her. "I'm sorry..." His voice trailed off.

"Me, too," she said. She felt as if she had driven a stake through the very heart of their budding relationship. She had been the one who had given him the news he had not wanted to hear. She had consigned him to a life he dreaded.

Maybe she should have lied. But lying had never been her style. Except, perhaps, to lie to herself. How could she for one moment have thought this urbane, worldly man could maintain an interest in her?

"You'll come back with me," Maria Teresa announced. "We have arrangements to make."

"And a contract to be signed," Gina reminded them.

"Yes..." Darius might as well have just received a life sentence. Well, he *had* just received one. In the midst of her pain, Serena felt pain for him.

Maria Teresa clasped her hands. "Oh, the plans I have for your coronation!"

Darius grimaced, but offered no protest. He clearly had no way of avoiding this one.

Then he turned to Mas and Menos. "So," he said, "are you two going to get yourselves into a mess like this again?"

Both of them promptly shook their heads.

Then he turned to Gina. "I'm trusting you to make sure they walk the straight and narrow. You, too, for that matter. I'm promoting you, and giving you a raise, but I expect you to work for it."

She nodded. "Yes, Your Highness."

Again Darius grimaced. He plainly didn't like the sound of that.

A freight train chose that moment to approach. The deep thrumming of its engines grew louder and began to shake the walls.

"And," Darius announced, raising his voice, "we're moving this damn consulate!"

MARCO DROVE SERENA and Ariel home. She hadn't wanted to leave, because, after all, these were the last moments she would ever have to spend with Darius. But he had sent her away. Gently and kindly, but he had sent her away.

"I'm sorry," he'd said, drawing her aside.

"I'm sorry, too."

He sighed and drew her close, hugging her, not caring who might see. "I have to go."

"Of course." She was proud that there was only a little break in her voice, barely audible. The pain in her chest, the weight of sorrow, threatened to suffocate her, but she didn't want him to know that. He had enough burdens now. She could go home and weep to her heart's content, but not here. Not now. Not where Darius could see.

"Go home," he told her gently. "Get some sleep. I have to leave, but I'll be in touch."

"Sure." She managed to give him a smile. She was sure it wasn't much of a smile, when the corners of her mouth felt like lead, and her cheeks felt frozen, and her heart felt ready to burst from unendurable pain.

"Soon," he promised, then let go of her.

Unable to look at him again, she left with Marco and Ariel.

Ariel sat in the back of Darius's Ferrari, and Marco and Serena sat up front. No one spoke, and Marco drove slowly through darkened streets toward the expressways that would take them back to the barrier islands. It was as if he sensed that now there was no rush, that only emptiness awaited Serena at home.

But he said nothing, nor did Ariel, and Serena was so lost in grief that she hardly noticed the drive. Each breath she drew was so painful she doubted she could draw another one. Her life, which such a short time ago had been on such an even keel that she sought any means of tipping the boat, had now tipped so far it was in danger of sinking.

"He'll be back," Ariel said suddenly.

For the first time, Serena didn't believe her friend.

DARIUS WAS IN THE PROCESS of straightening out his mother on the way to the airport, while Tom Kelly drove and occasionally chimed in with a comment.

"So, Mother, you finally get your wish. I am the prince."

"Yes!" Maria Teresa looked rapturous, clasping her hands and telling all the saints above that it was about time they heeded her. After all, *she* knew best.

"And now that I am the prince," he continued firmly, "some things are going to change."

"Yess!" said Tom from the front seat. "You tell her, man." Beside him, Maria Teresa's maid nodded furiously.

Darius looked at them. "I take it you have a problem with my mother."

"Sure do, Your Honor," Tom replied. "She's got a mouth on her."

"Indeed." Darius looked at his mother. "So, I am not alone in this. I'm sure all the saints in heaven are sick of hearing from you."

"Darius!"

"Now we'll get a few things straight, once and for all."

"Really!"

"Really. If you ever so much as *think* about interfering in my life again, I'll banish you."

Maria Teresa squawked. "You can't do that! I'm your mother!"

"Damn," said Tom, "I wish I could do that to *my* mother-in-law."

"Sorry, dear fellow," Darius said, "you have to be a prince first."

"I don't suppose there's some country out there looking for one?"

"I doubt it. I think I just took the last one."

"You two are *abominable!*" Maria Teresa said.

"No more so than you," Darius told her sternly. "Now, I'm not kidding. I'm deadly serious here. I have had enough of your manipulations, petty dramas and underhanded attempts to change the course of my life. I am who I am, and you will learn to respect that, or you won't be allowed across the borders of Masolimia even for my coronation."

Maria Teresa gasped, her mouth opening and closing as if she were a fish out of water.

"Get used to it, Mother," Darius said firmly. "I'm royalty now."

CHAPTER TWENTY-EIGHT

AFTER TWO MONTHS of arguing with herself, and one phone call from Darius personally asking her to come, Serena sat in the second row of pews in the Cathedral of San Gabriel, surrounded by hundreds of gorgeously gowned women and formally attired men. The cathedral itself was a work of Templar beauty, one of their awe-inspiring constructions along with most of Europe's greatest churches.

A huge choir of a hundred voices sang out in praise, words that Serena couldn't understand. The moving melody echoed beautifully within the cathedral.

On the dais before the altar stood a bishop dressed all in white, his crosier in hand, his mitre on his head. Beside him was a gilded, ornate chair, upholstered in royal blue.

And from the rear of the church came the stately procession.

First there were boys carrying candles. Some of them were altar boys, but most were youths clad in cute little blue uniforms with gold sashes. They marched stiffly and nervously, and Serena guessed they were sons of important families who were being included for political reasons.

Then came the standard bearers, men uniformed in red, with golden breastplates gleaming in the light of thousands of candles. She supposed each banner carried a particular significance. Most of them looked like coats of arms. Some seemed more like regimental flags. She wished someone had written a guidebook for her.

Then came older men, clad in dark blue uniforms and capes lined in gold. On their heads were bicorn hats covered in gold braid and insignia. As they reached the head of the aisle they doffed their hats and bowed to the bishop before parting like a great wave and going to their reserved seats on either side of the altar.

Then came the crown and the scepter of Masolimia, carried on large royal-blue pillows by two very important-looking men in bright-green-and-gold uniforms. Behind them marched more red-clad soldiers with golden helmets, their swords held upright before their faces.

The crown itself was a simple gold circlet bearing a large sapphire in its front peak. The scepter was made of gold, shaped like a mace and crowned with a glittering array of jewels. These were borne up the steps, their guardians standing beside the bishop.

And last, but not least, was Darius. He strode alone, his gaze fixed firmly forward. He, too, wore a uniform, his of deep blue, heavily braided with gold. Around his waist he wore a sword belt, the silver scabbard ornate with carving, the hilt shaped like a cross and studded with a ruby at its heel.

Reaching the dais, he bowed to the bishop, then ascended the stairs and stood before the throne. There he turned and faced the pews.

The bishop spoke at some length in rapid Spanish. Then Darius spoke for a while. Finally it seemed the Bishop began asking him questions, and Darius answered each of them.

Then Darius sat on the throne. The bishop intoned as he took a cruet from one of the altar boys and anointed Darius's head. Then he intoned some more, obviously praying, as he set the crown on Darius's head and placed the scepter in his hands.

Darius Jacobus Maxwell III was now Prince Darius I of Masolimia, Defender of the Realm, Keeper of the Faith, Heart of the Lion, Protector of the Weak and a million other titles Serena couldn't keep straight.

As one the crowd rose to its feet and cheered.

IT WAS OVER. Serena considered escaping her palace room, where she had been stashed the day before by a page, and heading home. She had been invited to the private ball downstairs for family and the closest friends only, which she supposed for a prince meant nearly everyone who had been at the cathedral. She didn't know if she could stand it, not with her heart breaking.

But it would be so rude to leave without at least thanking him and wishing him well. And saying goodbye.

Steeling herself, she stepped out of her room. Immediately a page or a footman, or whatever he was, signaled her to follow him.

Night was falling over Masolimia. The palace ballroom was huge, big enough to hold a football game in, Serena thought. She had believed Masolimia a poor country, but once upon a time, it seemed, its rulers had been men of vast wealth.

The room was awash in people, women garbed in jewel-toned ball gowns, men in tailcoats. She thought she spotted a British prince, a Danish monarch and possibly even the King of Spain. She didn't belong among these people at all.

She finally spotted Darius at the far end of the ballroom. He was caught in a crush of adoring young women and important-looking people, and the likelihood of reaching him was slim indeed.

Feeling worn, sad and irritable, she slipped out through the open doors into the formal gardens. They were lit with lanterns. From various directions she could hear girlish laughter and male murmurs. The mountain air was cool, almost enough to make her shiver, but fresh, so fresh. Leaning against a terrace railing, she looked up at the stars and filled her lungs with the pine- and rose-scented purity of it.

Later, she told herself. The crowd would thin. And then she would say goodbye.

AN HOUR MIGHT HAVE PASSED, no more. The night air had grown chillier, and the sounds from the garden paths had grown fewer. The ball hadn't wound down at all, and Serena, growing chilled, began to think of seeking her room.

Then, causing goose bumps to rise on her flesh, a deep male voice said, "I thought I'd never find you."

Whirling, she found Darius standing just two steps behind her. He didn't much look like Darius anymore, in his fancy uniform, the crown of his country still riding his brow.

"I was…waiting for the crowd to thin."

He shook his head. "I doubt it will thin before dawn. But I've done my duty."

Stepping forward, he wrapped his arm around her shoulders. "Come with me."

It was like a dream, skimming down garden paths into the darkness with his arm around her, her slippers barely seeming to touch the ground. Finally they were around the far side of the castle and facing a stone wall in which stood a high wooden gate.

"My private garden," he said, with something like dry amusement. Pulling a huge key from his pocket, he unlocked it and drew her inside. Then he closed the door and locked it again.

"Now," he said, facing her, "we are truly alone."

Her heart fluttered with sudden fright and fearful hope. Maybe this was to be the coup de grâce. Or maybe not. She had no way of knowing.

"You're cold," he said. "Come."

Along another path, to a gazebo. There, under the roof that concealed the stars, he lifted the seat of a bench and pulled out a blanket, which he draped around her shoulders. The blanket was as soft as cashmere against her skin, and she felt incredibly treasured as he tucked it around her.

"Serena," he said, then with a groan he pulled her against him, wrapping her in the warm steel of his arms, seeking her mouth with a hunger that matched her own.

The world whirled away, forgotten.

"WE CAN MAKE IT WORK," he said.

They sat together on a bench, his arms around her, her lips still deliciously bruised from his kisses.

Her heart stopped. "Make what work?"

"A marriage."

"Darius…"

"We can," he said. Taking her by the shoulders, he turned her gently so that she was looking straight at him. "I've got it all planned. My base of operations will be Florida. I can still do that, you know. I don't have to be here every blessed minute. And I'm still going to be an art dealer. That means a lot of traveling regardless."

"But…"

"Shh," he said, laying a finger over her mouth. "I'm going to set up a constitutional monarchy. I'm going to set up a parliament. I'm going to give the people a vote. Initially it will keep me very busy, but later…later they will need me less and less. Serena, I love you. We *can* make it work."

She believed him. She believed him with her whole heart and soul. "I've missed you so much! I love you so much!"

He bent as if to kiss her again, but an all-too-familiar voice interrupted them.

"It's about time," said Maria Teresa. "If you hadn't dallied so long, Darius, I could have planned the wedding at the same time…."

"No!" said Serena, rising to her feet. "Don't even go there."

"But…"

"No! I'll plan my own wedding and if you try to get involved, I'll make you wish you'd said nothing at all."

Maria Teresa stood still a moment, then nodded approvingly. "Good girl. We'll get along fine."

Darius spoke. "And what the devil are you doing in my private garden, Mother?"

"Well, I'm the prince's mother, you know…"

"I don't want to hear it. Go. Go!"

"You'd be warmer in your chambers, Darius. Don't freeze the poor girl to death!"

Then with a sniff, Maria Teresa turned and marched away.

Darius looked at Serena. "Are you sure you want to put up with her forever?"

She smiled. "She's right about one thing."

"What's that?"

"It would be an awful lot *warmer* in your chambers."

A smile split his face, and he scooped her up into his arms, carrying her away with him.

* * * * *

Look for Sue Civil-Brown's
next romantic comedy
HURRICANE HANNAH
coming from HQN Books
Spring 2006

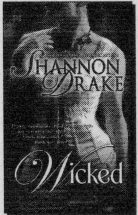

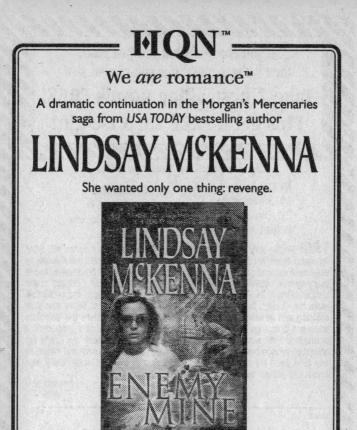

If you enjoyed what you just read,
then we've got an offer you can't resist!

Take 2 bestselling novels FREE!
Plus get a FREE surprise gift!